AL

Space War

By CW Lamb

I would like to thank my wife for patiently waiting while I finished this book. Sometimes living with a writer (even a part-time one) can be challenging.

Contents

Character page

Sector Nu Tau Beta

AL:ICE – Artificial Life: Intelligent Computing Environment

Jake Thomas– USMC Capt. Divorced orphan, wise ass. Sarcastic.

Sara Sullivan– Oldest of 3 sisters. Jake's second in command.

Bonnie Sullivan– Middle sis to Sara, quiet reserved, mother to Julie

Becky Sullivan– Little sis to Sara

Linda Jones– Commander in Nevada, mother to Tracy

Kathy Jones– Linda's sister, mother to Timothy

Sandy- Adopted mother to Padma and Jon

Abby – 10th cavalry Team leader

Brian – ALICE-3 Captain

Joseph – (just Joe) 10th Team leader

Jessie –Alaska Commander, mother to Ryan

James- Kola temp commander

Robert Jacobson – Bonnie's husband, Jake's Logistics Officer

Patti – Jake's gggdaughter

Jacob – Jake's gggson

ALICE1 Nevada medical labs - Alice

ALICE2 Texas ground vehicles - Dallas

ALICE3 Georgia (ALICE9)

ALICE4 Washington helo-rotary

ALICE5 Maine medical Research - Five

ALICE6 South Dakota weapons research –was Kola (now Dakota)

ALICE7 Alaska aviation research - Seven

ALICE8 Hawaii Marine – the bay is 2000 feet long and 600 feet wide.-Lanai

Kola- Now the ALICE controlling the space carrier

ALICE-3- Now ALICE in the Battleship

VF-84 Jolly Roger - Washington

VMFA -314 Black Knights - Texas

VMFA-112 Cowboys - Texas

VMFA-232 Red Devils - Nevada

VMFA-323 Death Rattlers - Alaska

1st Air Cavalry- South Dakota

BOOK 2--
Hector -ALICE-4 second in command
Chris Wade – LA compound leader.
10th Cavalry – A and B troops, Special Forces on hovercycles
Wawobash – 6 legged canine, shipyard
Kortisht – 3 legged humanoids repulser and faster than light
Crustacea – lobster people specialize in communications
Lanai Patrol/Transports – Steel hulled 500 feet long, 250 feet wide – 8 to 40 man crew
Cruiser - 384 feet in length and 284 feet in width- 30 man crew
Destroyer –200 feet long 75-80 feet wide, 20 man crew.
HeBak – NeHaw communications supervisor.
MeHak – head of the high council
Klinan – fourth treaty partner- artists – long angular people yellow with a .85 G planet
Netite – mercenary force for NeHaw – blue ape-like
NeHaw – light atmosphere – short stocky gray. 1.2 G planet

BOOK 3--
Chilterns AONB – between Oxford and London
Ju Huang – Chinese general
Ivan – Cossack
Nigel – London, Helen
Colonel Edwin Banks – SAS
Major Bo Chao – replaces Ju
Lance corporal Alicia Ramirez – died protecting Sandy
Gemma – brit engineer – Nigel's daughter
Jerrold – brit engineer
Lieutenant Daniel Atkins
Jon and Padma – Las Vegas kids 7 & 5

BOOK 4--
General KaLob – leader of the NeHaw coup
Hannah – SAS trooper on Phantom
Phantom – spy ship with cloaking unit
Samantha Watts – Marine/Analyst (Sam)
Private Grace Middleton – Southern girl
Isabella Connor – Kola captain

Chapter 1

Colonel Jake Thomas stood in full combat gear, hidden behind a ridge on an alien planet while peering over the edge to see a scraggly looking crater below. Above the crater and in all directions, there was desolate landscape, with no movement to be seen, and that was just the way he liked it. There was some form of plant life sporadically sprouting here and there, hardly more than grass and small bushes. The rest of the landscape was mostly dirt and rock.

With him were two fire teams from Alpha Company, Second Platoon, First Squad, of his 1st Space Marine Expeditionary Force. In addition to those eight Marines, there was an equal number of SAS troopers, a mix of British, Canadian, and Australian volunteers, giving him a total of 16 combat shooters.

Unlike previous operations, where the SAS troopers had the option of wearing whatever combat gear they desired, the current mission required them all to adopt the standard Marine off-planet kit. Although the alien world they stood on was almost Earth-like, the atmosphere wouldn't support humans without a little assistance from technology. Both the air and the temperature were outside the normal human standards.

As expected, their battle suits had changed patterns and colors to mask their presence in this world. With gravity at 1.15 times Earth normal, the available powered battle suits were a nice assist for those who chose that option, though certainly not required. However, with this group, none would even consider using them, instead, choosing the less cumbersome standard issue.

The suits were self-contained, with the EVA pack added to allow for extended use of the alien world. Jake had no desire to remain here any longer than the mission required, but they were prepared for an extended exposure should it be necessary. All of them were carrying an assortment of weapons drawn from the arsenal in the South Dakota Alice, newly named Dakota.

As this was their first mission against this unknown alien enemy, Jake was covering all his bases. Each shooter carried a primary weapon containing a combination of projectile and energy firepower. Secondary firepower was available in the form of sidearms, and several crew-served weapons Jake had specifically selected and assigned. These required more than one person to operate. Thus the term crew-served.

Trying to minimize his exposure to anyone below and using the magnification in his helmet like binoculars, Jake zoomed in on the activity in the crater. There, he could see about twenty small fighter-like spacecraft, each fitted with external weapons. Nearby were over one hundred aliens moving about, each in environmental suits of their own design. Many of them carried energy rifles identical to those previously captured from NeHaw warships.

"What do you think?" asked the SAS sergeant by his side, who had been receiving his helmet video feed. Jake had first met Sergeant Carson in London, during the first contact with the Brits there. The man had since volunteered for training in the US, which was how he ended up on this alien world with Jake.

"I think the Intel was good. These are definitely the guys."

After the failed armada attack on Earth, an effort that had been contrived by the previous head of the NeHaw High Council, a group of their military officers had successfully executed a power grab. They had managed to overthrow the High Council in a coup, and the outcome had left a splintered empire. Several worlds had thrown in with the Earth, while the remaining planets retreated to the relative safety of the known superpower.

Since then, a series of attacks and small skirmishes between the two sides resulted in chaos throughout the NeHaw Empire. For Jake, the escalation of hostilities was to be expected once it was confirmed the military now controlled NeHaw directly. Apparently, unlike their political predecessors, these leaders were creatures of direct action.

7

What most disturbed Jake most, however, was the new efficiency with which the NeHaw navy was operating. In several recent engagements, the Earth vessels, badly outnumbered, as usual, had been held to a stalemate forcing them to withdraw. Even with their superior shielding and firepower, they were unable to ravage the NeHaw as before, their numbers being just too great.

Someone at the top now understood what they were facing and was prepared to do what was necessary to confront and overcome. This is what brought Jake to his current location. A small group of NeHaw aligned ships had adopted the human concept of small attack fighters and was now harassing Earth aligned shipping with lightning raids.

The hit and run tactics of the raiders had Jake scrambling to counter the damage they were doing to the treaty planets. The urgency had been such that, when Jake got word of a possible hidden base from an allied informant, he scrambled to put a strike team together.

It wasn't just the aliens replicating Earth tactics that had proven so problematic. It was something else as well. In the few engagements between these fighters and the Earth aligned planets, reports of FTL drive failures were a constant. In every case, once the fighters appeared, the defenders needed to drive them off before FTL capabilities were restored. Jake was sure it wasn't a coincidence.

The Marines and SAS troopers now with him had been training together in Texas, where Jake had the stealth ship stored. Newly christened the Phantom, it was the same vessel used for a previous spying mission in NeHaw space. On that mission, Ivan, Edwin, and the NeHaw guest, HeBak, had discovered the alien armada that recently challenged Earth's defenses.

With a quick 24-hour turnaround, Dallas, the local ALICE system, had refitted the ship for this mission and had them on their way. It would not have been a problem for him to recruit a larger force for the mission; it was just that this ship couldn't support a larger number of troops for the journey.

The Phantom was considered a stealth ship because it had been fitted with a cloaking unit, replicated from the detained NeHaw ship, also currently stored in Texas. HeBak, a supposed NeHaw refugee, had been captured trying to flee Earth from a gold mining mission. Slipping onto the planet undetected, he had managed to accumulate enough wealth to secure a lofty retirement. However, his excitement overcame his caution, and he was discovered. While technically a guest and not a prisoner, he had elected to remain on Earth rather than face the new regime in power on the NeHaw homeworld.

The Phantom, then unnamed, had been ordered from the Wawobash with the specific intent of converting it into a spy ship. With minimal firepower on board, its intent was to slip in and out of hostile space, appearing as no more than a trading vessel should anyone come across them uncloaked. Its first mission had successfully proven the theory.

The four-day voyage to the edge of the solar system again reminded Jake of the need for a space station at the rim of the gravity well created by the sun. With the first station modules on order from the Wawobash- a race aligned with the Earth and the owners of a renowned shipyard- it was just a matter of time until one could be assembled. He had great hopes for its success as a base of operations. His design had taken into consideration not only the need for a supply and transfer base but also an armed fort at the edge of civilization.

The trip to the target world had taken several hours in FTL. With cloaking enabled, Jake was able to take the Phantom, with his combat team, and slip undetected into a canyon near the target location on the alien planet. They had been fortunate enough to follow several of the enemy ships down to the planet's surface, as they returned from some unknown mission. The cloaking unit continued to mask the ship's current resting location, while the humans moved cautiously closer to their target.

Backing away from the edge, while leaving a Marine to continue observations, he pulled the rest of the team together. He had everyone on point-to-point communications to keep their emissions signature as low as possible.

"Look, I don't want to get us too spread out. We may need to bug out as soon as we hit these guys. Intel says there isn't another base on the planet, but I don't want to push our luck."

With that, Jake sketched out a diagram in the dirt, positioning his people on three sides of the crater, not directly opposite each other. Splitting off part of the group into two teams of six, with the remainder staying with him, he sent each to work their way around the edges of the crater. While they moved into position, he and his men watched the activity below, looking for signs of discovery.

The lack of sentries bothered him. He worried about the omission, questioning if they were using some unknown technology for perimeter security. While he waited, the two-man team next to him prepared the recoilless rifle they were going to use against the aliens below. Known to Jake as a Carl Gustav, slang for a recoilless rifle from Earth's past, he taught the others the slang term when they were issued on Earth.

Each of the teams now moving into position carried two of these weapons as well, giving the entire force a significant amount of firepower. The goal was to take out the spacecraft and as much of their support infrastructure as possible. Should the aliens attempt to mount an offensive, each team had two shooters to defend the recoilless teams as they rained havoc on the aliens.

Within minutes, he received two clicks and then three clicks over his communications link. The clicks indicated both teams were in position and ready. Peering over the ridge again, he scanned the rim on each side of the crater, but couldn't see either team, which made him smile. All were in the prone position, and using bipods on the weapons, they would be invisible to those below until the last second.

With a thumbs up from his own team, the loader lying next to the gunner, Jake paused and then gave the attack order.

"GO!"

Almost in unison, Jake watched as five recoilless rounds streaked at blinding speeds toward the spacecraft parked below. The recoilless rounds of Jake's era traveled at close to 1,000 feet per second. These, however, sped from the launcher at over three times that rate. Rather than just firing rocket-powered rounds, these recoilless guns were a combination of rocket launcher and railgun.

They would fire each round as a railgun, with the rocket igniting once it was well clear of the shooter. The initial railgun launch produced a measurable recoil, which was absorbed by the inertial dampeners each rocket tube had incorporated in their construction. This gave it a manageable experience when standing, and barely noticeable with the bipod in a prone position.

The incorporated railgun, however, allowed the rocket to clear the area near the shooter before firing its motor. Traveling at a considerable rate of speed, it then ignited, adding additional speed to the projectile. This also prevented any telltale exhaust evidence, giving away the shooter's position.

With amazing speed, all five guns launched a second volley of rounds at the targets below, with each team concentrating on their priority targets. The aliens were attempting to return fire, with energy blasts fired wildly in all directions. Jake resisted the temptation to take up arms himself as he watched a group of suited figures gain refuge in a narrow space between buildings. Their return fire posed little threat, but it represented an attempt at organizing a defense.

Once all of the ships had been destroyed, Jake's orders were that they should remove as many of the support structures as possible before retreating. He watched as structure after structure exploded with rocket impacts. It was during this part of the operation that a blinding flash erupted in the crater below, engulfing the entire area and throwing Jake and his men back from the rim of the crater.

Scrambling to get back on his feet, his rifle ready, he rushed back to the crater's edge as his men rose around him. Scanning the area, with his rifle up and ready to fire, he noted that nothing in the area below was moving.

"Everyone, Sitrep!" he ordered on the open circuit, asking for their situation report.

"Team one, no casualties."

"Team two, no casualties, whisky tango foxtrot Colonel? What the hell was that?" He got from one of the Marines.

"Acknowledged. I have no idea, we must have hit their gas station," Jake replied as he verified his four men were standing nearby and unharmed. Lowering his rifle, he could see the troops now lining both rims of the crater, looking at the destruction before them. They had evidently hit some form of stored energy, as its release had obliterated everything in the crater below. All that remained was twisted wreckage and immobile bodies.

Checking the time, he set a timer and then passed out orders.

"Sergeant Carson, you four are with me. Teams one and two, drop the Carl's and cover us. Shoot anything that moves. We are going shopping for Intel."

----*----

General KaLob sat in his office at the Military High Command, reviewing the latest after-action reports. As the leader of the coup that had toppled the government of the NeHaw homeworld, he had no desire to occupy the seat, nor follow the examples of those he had deposed. He was a military man, made in the mold of those that had conquered the vast sectors of space they were now struggling to retain.

The NeHaw had not seen an enemy like this in many gigacycles. This adversary was cunning and ruthless in battle like the NeHaw once were. The NeHaw had become far too soft and decadent to deal with what lay before them. KaLob knew he needed to restore that heritage if they were to prevail.

His biggest challenge was in finding strong military leaders, uncorrupted by the ways of the politicians. He had found it necessary to execute the captains of more than half of his fleet and replace them with competent, capable combat oriented officers. Even now, some of those vessels still awaited their replacements.

His early appointments had already proven their value in several engagements with the enemy. While they had yet to see a total victory, any opportunity to drive the humans back was seen as a move in the right direction. The mystery of why the NeHaw firepower had such a minimal effect on their ships was yet to be discovered, but the combined attacks had proven effective at getting their attention.

That gave KaLob the hope that this enemy was not without limits. It was just that those limits had yet to be discovered. It was with that in mind that he had redeployed his ships, focusing more on combat and confrontation, and less on tribute collection. There would be plenty of time for that once the current crisis was resolved.

At present, he had every compliant race working on new and innovative ways to overcome the human ships. Others were commanded to analyze and explain the technologies currently used by humans. They had retrieved the projectiles they peppered NeHaw ships with, creating breaches in the toughest of shield plating. He only wished they could uncover the secret of their shields.

----*----

Sara was in the command center of the Nevada ALICE facility, feeling anxious, extremely irritated, and very uncomfortable, all at the same time. Well into her pregnancy, her sister Becky had notified her that she was to be the proud mother of twins. Becky was the head of the medical facility in Texas, but had returned to Nevada temporarily and appeared delighted at her sister's situation.

Why, of all the women associated with Jake, Sara had the misfortune to bear twins, she had no idea. She felt she was being punished for her earlier insistence that Jake cut off his relationships with the others. While delighted that her wishes appeared to be coming true, as one woman at a time looked to be naturally distancing herself from him, it was offset by her current misery.

On top of her current personal physical discomfort, she was impatiently waiting on word from Jake. She was used to his running off at a moment's notice while dealing with things here on Earth, but this was something entirely different. This, though, was maddening as he had run off to an unknown planet deep in NeHaw space, based on intelligence from an untested alien informant. Why didn't he see this was incredibly dangerous?

As she watched those working around her, she wondered if anyone but her was fretting over his absence.

"He will be alright," Linda said as she approached Sara from behind. Her comment a clear indication that Sara must look as upset as she felt.

"Probably, which infuriates me more," Sara replied as she turned to face the Nevada facility's commander. Linda was one of the women distancing herself from Jake. While still the mother of his daughter, Tracy, she was not making any personal demands on Jake beyond that.

"Rough pregnancy?" Linda replied, acknowledging Sara's frustration and changing the subject.

"I now completely understand Jake's favorite term, be careful what you ask for," she replied with a sigh.

"Ma'am, we have a message from Colonel Thomas," one of the many analysts surrounding the two announced. Both Sara and Linda hurried over to see the console display.

"Mission Complete" was all that was displayed on the monitor.

"Well, that's good news," Linda said with a smile.

"They won't contact us again until they drop out of FTL at the edge of our solar system," the analyst added, referring to traveling in faster than light mode. The mission plan had outlined a strict communications blackout, intended to reduce risk to the strike team.

With a nod in reply, Sara turned and left the command center, hoping to get some much-needed rest now that she knew he was alive.

Chapter 2

Colonel Edwin Banks nodded at the brief message relayed to him in London. With half the strike team made up of his people, Jake had the good manners to ensure Banks was properly informed of the mission status. He had wanted to accompany Jake on the mission, but good sense prevailed. They acknowledged that considering their positions, both men could not be off-planet at the same time.

Since Banks had led the SAS team in Hong Kong and accompanied Ivan on the reconnaissance mission that uncovered the alien armada, Jake had won out for this trip. Although the true extent of the mission's success was yet to be understood, Edwin presumed that the pesky raids had been dealt a lethal blow.

As outlined in the mission plan, Jake would not be delaying their departure to transmit the entire after-action report. Rather they would vacate the area as soon as possible and then report in full once they returned to friendly space. In Jake's absence, and with a full-blown war erupting, Edwin had been studying up on everything he could find regarding naval strategies.

Although the materials were predominantly terrestrial and nautical in content, he was able to extract the occasional gem of information that applied to their space fleet. Besides just studying the somewhat modern-ish British and American naval strategies, he also went back in history, reviewing Greek, Roman, Chinese, Japanese, and Russian tactics.

As he studied the references to tactics and strategies around naval conflict, there was one subject that enticed him. The Privateers of the 17th and 18th centuries were able to operate freely in enemy waters, striking targets of opportunity under a letter of marque, empowering them to carry on all forms of hostility at sea. While he didn't envision attacking NeHaw vessels, there were other prizes of interest.

He was also able to review much of the NeHaw data, recently translated by the ALICE systems and made available to all. He was also surprised to discover the ALICE archives contained much speculative information on what war in space would consist of.

While he had no idea who Robert Heinlein and Orson Scott Card were, he noted they had contributed a substantial amount of thought on the subject.

----*----

Jake sat at the navigation station, working on his after-action report as they traveled in FTL. He had made several attempts at completing it earlier, but always found a good reason to do something else. He scanned the contents on display before him, reviewing the sequence of described events for its accuracy.

After they destroyed the outpost, taking the forces there by surprise, they scoured the valley looking for anything that might be of interest. Satisfied they had recovered what little remained of the command center systems and other loose items from the ships, they then returned to the Phantom and made a hasty retreat. Heading directly away from the planet, he paused only long enough to send the success message.

As the only experienced pilot in the group, Jake assumed the pilot's seat until they had jumped to FTL. Once he was satisfied, all was well. He had a Marine, fresh from flight training, take the chair and monitor things while he worked nearby.

Although not an astronavigator himself, Jake had asked Dallas, the Texas ALICE, to pre-program the ship's navigation system to guide them to and from the target area. There were also a few added alternate flight plans, should they find themselves needing to evade hostile vessels. In addition, there was a return home option that flew them straight to Earth.

While he worked, Jake could hear laughter from down the passageway, likely emanating from the galley. That compartment had become the impromptu gathering area for the team, Marine, and SAS alike. Even though their meals were all pre-prepared and stored in stasis boxes, the galley was still the center of public life.

He was extremely pleased with how well the two groups had blended, both on combat and social activities. Men and women, SAS and Marine, all were interacting on an equal basis, which he found gratifying. He had no idea what the shared joke was, but from the sound of things, it was popular.

Jake had left it to Sergeant Carson, who, as the senior NCO, was to organize the troops for duties aboard ship, as not all functions were automated on such a small vessel. When not on duty, the free time activity of choice had turned the galley into more of a pub. While beer and wine were available, its consumption was regulated by the ship's Biomonitoring systems, and intoxication was not tolerated.

He was debating once more on delaying the completion of his report and joining those in the galley when alerts sounded on the bridge around him.

"Colonel, I think we have a problem," the Marine next to him announced.

"Let me check," Jake replied as he scanned the panel before him and then rose to look over the man's shoulders.

"We dropped out of FTL," Jake commented absently as he verified all the settings were correct on the pilot's console. He did a quick scan of the area, looking for any signs of vessels in the area before continuing to diagnose the situation.

"Problem, sir?" Sergeant Carson asked as he appeared at the hatch to the bridge, apparently drawn by the Audio alert. Cutting the alert before answering, Jake continued to work while replying.

"We dropped out of FTL, and I have no idea why," he answered as he continued to review the displays around him.

"Any hostiles in the area?" Carson asked as he glanced out the bridge windows.

"Nothing on the scanners, but I think we might need everyone at their station until we get this worked out," Jake said as he worked. At that, Carson left to get the troops organized and then returned to wait and watch as Jake worked. After a good ten minutes, he huffed in exasperation.

"Well, I have no idea what's wrong. Everything is as it should be, all systems report green, but we aren't moving."

"Do we know where we are, Sir? Maybe we can call for assistance, or perhaps we should put down?" Carson asked after a moment's consideration.

Stopping what he was doing, Jake moved back to the navigation station and flipped through a few displays. Suddenly, he jumped back over to the command console and breathed a sigh of relief. He turned to Sergeant Carson with a less worried expression.

"We should definitely set the ship down, get everyone ready. Thank goodness the cloaking is working because we are still deep in NeHaw space. We need to find someplace safe to hide until I get this fixed."

----*----

Leftenant Daniel Atkins was at a crossroads in his life. Entirely bewitched by the granddaughter of Colonel Thomas, he found himself being drawn into the inner circle of those directing Earth's recoveries. At Patti's side, he had been privy to all the intimate details of the battle plans and strategies put forth. His opinions were considered in everything they attempted.

Now, with a full-on war on the horizon, he was presented with a dilemma. Tied to Patti as he was, he could continue to work by her side and act as a military planner, his experience a keen addition. His other option was to continue to pursue his life's goal of commanding in the field, leading troops on missions, and securing the safety of more than just the Earth.

They were currently back in London, where Patti had agreed to accompany him and work. He was researching, using the NeHaw data, trying to predict the future. His intent was to categorize all the possible environments ground troops would encounter and verify Earth had the means to operate there.

19

While the Americans seemed to have an abundance of resources, most of their tactics involved large scale operations. From his personal experience, he very much doubted what they had would accommodate the SAS approach to things. SAS preferred a more subtle hand, slipping in and out of enemy strongholds, planting the seeds of discontent. Or maybe just a lot of bloody explosive.

He was happy to find that a good number of potential battlegrounds could support human life with little or no additional equipment. For those that required more than just breathing assistance, his research suggested the American's complete battle suit, with optional power assist, addressed the challenges. As he logged and categorized each location, he could see the value in continuing his work. However, he could also envision himself leading the troops deployed to each potential confrontation he analyzed.

No closer to a decision on his future, he went back to his studies, relying on fate to help push him in the right direction.

----*----

Brian sat in the command chair of the battleship that was ALICE-3. As one of only two vessels possessed by an ALICE system, he liked to think he collaborated rather than commanded. With the escalation of hostilities, he had been ordered to take the ship and proceed to the Wawobash system. Once there, his instructions were to protect the shipyards at all costs.

Everyone expected the NeHaw to attempt to try and cut Earth's supply lines, and then through attrition, eventually deplete the fleet. As long as the humans had access to the Wawobash for ships and the Kortisht for drives, the Earth could continue to field far more ships than they had crews to operate them.

With all the ships the Wawobash currently had under construction, it was unlikely a Kortisht drive shortage would affect them anytime soon, so Wawobash was considered the top priority. Presently, the top Wawobash effort was the space station sections currently under construction. These sections, once assembled in place, would create the fortress intended for the edge of Earth's solar system. The need for resupply and rapid response location was now greater than ever.

To date, no other aligned world had offered ships and crews to help in the fight, but all were more than happy to supply the humans with anything they needed in that effort. To that end, Jake had allowed the ships that had surrendered after the last engagement, changing sides to align with Earth, to return to their homeworlds. It was his belief that sending them to defend their own people rather than trying to press them for direct support was of greater value. His argument is that people fought harder in defending their own homes.

Brian tended to agree with Jake's opinion, believing that they were better served to have the alien ships at their own home anyway. It was less work for Earth not having to directly protect those planets, and it avoided having halfhearted fighters in the fleet. By leaving them to defend their homeworlds, Earth could expect their absolute best effort, and it freed up other resources here.

Having stopped the ship in a stationary position just inside the edge of the Wawobash system, Brian asked ALICE-3 to deploy two of the four Lanai Combat Patrol Ships they had on board, crewed and ready for distributed firepower should the NeHaw come calling. Satisfied all was well, he then ordered the battleship closer to Wawobash, where they could intervene should it become necessary.

About two thirds the way there, he had ALICE-3 stop, establishing a stationary position. There, they were to wait for whatever the NeHaw dreamed up next. On a whim, he began an inventory of the ships under construction, as well as their readiness, just in case.

----*----

Jake had located a suitable planet, a moon actually, in a nearby system for them to put down. Its location permitted them to hide from any hostile space traffic, thus allowing

21

him to shut down the cloaking systems in an effort to determine the source of his FTL problem.

The star systems in this part of NeHaw space were densely packed, and the data in the ship's computers indicated a significant amount of non-FTL space travel here due to the closeness of the systems. Even so, it was a day's travel from their current location to the moon, which was orbiting a gas giant similar to Jupiter back home.

The moon had a gravity of .85 Earth normal and appeared to have a breathable atmosphere, with a slightly higher Oxygen content and a Helium/Nitrogen inert gas filler mix. The dense atmosphere was tolerable without environmental suits, and the moon's surface was uniformly flat, i.e., without mountains or valleys to hide in.

As he piloted the Phantom, he continued to run diagnostics on the ship's systems, looking for the cause of the FTL drive failure.

"Colonel, should we radio our status home?" the Marine sitting in the co-pilot's seat asked.

"No, I don't trust the NeHaw communications network not to betray our location. Even if they can't decrypt the message, they might be able to track the message back to our location."

"Sir, the scope is still clear of traffic, but that moon we are headed for is off the charts with plant life. I don't find anything resembling animal life, but that doesn't mean there isn't wildlife there," added the SAS female from the tactical station. She had stepped in to assist with the increased workload at tactical. With Sergeant Carson now occupying the navigation station, all four seats in the small cockpit were filled.

"The sensors are Wawobash standard, so we have to assume they would detect possible known lifeforms. Regardless, I don't plan on staying long enough to find out," Jake replied.

As the others watched, Jake piloted the Phantom, still cloaked, into the atmosphere. He worked cautiously as he tried his best to avoid cloudbanks that would betray their passing. To Jake, the ground below looked to be one continuous jungle, the dense growth covering all the dry portions of the planet's surface.

Rather than large oceans, the surface water appeared to be a patchwork of lakes and interconnecting rivers. Once below the clouds, Jake slowed the ship to a more reasonable speed, allowing them to cautiously survey the area below and search for a spot to put down.

"Still no signs of lifeforms beyond plant and insect. I have the sensors set to alert on those species dangerous to humans. No hits so far," the woman announced.

"What about there?" Sergeant Carson asked as he pointed over Jake's shoulder at a small clearing ahead. Jake nudged the ship to the right and slowed until they hovered right over the area Carson had indicated. In the display on the console, they could see directly below the ship, where they could make out what appeared to be several downed trees.

Well, Jake assumed they were trees, but their shape was not what he expected. The lower gravity and denser atmosphere allowed the plants to grow unusually thick and bushy. These must have fallen victim to an insect infestation, as there were no signs of fire or other destructive occurrences. The scanners did find an excessive number of minute critters about.

"Right, let's give it a try," Jake announced to the bridge crew, as he started to lower the ship into the clearing below. Still cloaked, he dropped the landing gear and placed the ship into an opening just large enough to accommodate the vessel with a minimal amount of disturbance to the surrounding vegetation. Although the ship was invisible, that didn't extend to the nearby plant life, so he wanted to prevent telltale indicators of their presence.

Once on the ground, Jake went through a series of checks to verify their stability on the surface of the moon. Satisfied that they were in no immediate danger, he turned to the others.

"Scanners still clear?" Jake asked the SAS woman.

"Yes sir, no traffic in orbit or local space," she replied confidently.

Looking at Carson, Jake directed, "OK, let's get a team together and scout the area, while I take a look at the ship and see if I can find the problem. I want to go topside and do an external survey. I'd like to see if maybe we picked up something in space that's disrupting the FTL field," he explained as he rose from his seat.

Turning, he flipped the switch that shuts down the ship's cloaking system. He then returned to addressing the SAS trooper and Marine, as Sergeant Carson had left to gather his scouting team.

"You two need to stay here and keep tabs on things. Shout if anything shows up on the scanner, and turn the cloaking back on whether I am back in or not. We don't want unexpected visitors spotting us here," Jake finished before leaving the bridge and heading for the ladder that would take him to the exit hatch on top of the hull.

----*----

Linda was becoming concerned. Jake and his team were starting to be noticeably past due. While she was well aware that unexpected things came up, this was now well outside the window of reasonable delays. Per her request, ALICE had reviewed all the recent intercepted NeHaw message traffic, and while she had found non-military references to the attack, there was nothing on the perpetrators.

The NeHaw military had begun protecting their transmissions in a fashion that the ALICE systems had yet to decipher. Once detected, Jake had them put a team of humans together to assist in the effort. So far, all attempts to break the encryption had left the group with gibberish.

Linda again flipped through the latest reports, looking for any positive data. Finishing, she was starting to leave the command center to go see Sara, when one of the staff called out to her.

"Ma'am, Colonel Banks is looking for you," the girl announced. Looking hardly older than 16, Linda could see

24

she was still in training with one of the senior command center staff nearby, coaching her. She sighed as she considered it wasn't so long ago that she had been learning here.

"Thanks, I'll take it over here," she replied as she moved to an open station.

"Colonel, what can I do for you?" she asked lightly just as Edwin's face appeared in the display.

"Major delighted to see you again. Have we heard from our wayward wanderers?" he asked, not entirely hiding his concern.

"Unfortunately, no. I was just about to call a meeting on the subject. As you know, they are traveling under a communications blackout, and any communications systems that might betray their location have been removed or disabled, lest they alert the enemy to their presence."

"More's the pity. Yes, I understand. Please feel free to include me at your convenience," Banks replied.

"I will notify you as soon as it's arranged," Linda replied and cut the connection. She understood that the Colonel was not implying his attendance was optional. Turning to the trainee that had put the call through, Linda waved at her and the trainer.

"Please call an emergency meeting of the Tactical Analysts. Include Colonel Banks, and I'll get Lt. Colonel Sullivan as well. Notify me as soon as it's set," Linda relayed as she left the command center in search of Sara. Some messages should be delivered personally.

Chapter 3

Patti and Daniel met Colonel Banks as they reached the conference room door, the two groups approaching from opposite directions. After a brief greeting, they entered the room, settling into three seats across from a wall monitor. Unlike the American facilities, the rooms in London still utilized flat panel displays instead of holographic projections for visual presentations.

The men waited for Patti to sit before selecting their own places. Almost as soon as they seated themselves, the display came to life. In the monitor, they could see several others in a room Patti recognized as her tactical center lovingly referred to as Patti's Pit, situated right off the command center in Nevada. Seated around an oval table were Linda, Sara, and Ivan. In a separate window on the monitor were Robert and Bonnie, presumably still in Texas.

"Thanks for getting together on such short notice," Linda began.

"What's wrong?" Patti asked almost immediately.

"Jake is missing," Sara blurted, before Linda could reply.

"The mission outline had them arriving at the edge of our system twenty four hours ago. Even allowing for delays in departing, the uninterrupted trip in faster than light should have them in friendly space by now," ALICE offered to the group.

"Can the NeHaw intercept a ship while traveling faster than light?" Colonel Banks asked.

"Not that we are aware of," ALICE replied, "and with the lack of other indicators, that probability rates low."

"Colonel Banks and I have spent considerable time on that vessel. It is difficult to imagine they had a failure of some kind?" Ivan offered from the Nevada location.

"There may have been fighting near the ship, damaging it?" Patti suggested.

"Such an occurrence might have damaged the faster than light drives, causing them to fail at any time during the voyage," ALICE proposed.

"And without a call home, we can't pinpoint their location?" Sara offered as more of a question than a statement.

"No. And there is a lot of space between where they were and home. Unfortunately, most of it belongs to the NeHaw," Linda solemnly supplied.

----*----

General KaLob had restored many of the ancient military traditions since taking power. One such activity was regular staff meetings with his sector commanders. At a pre-appointed time, all would halt whatever activities they had in progress, excluding battle, and connect into the network for a status briefing.

It was in just such a briefing that the devastation on planet S-12653 was uncovered. When the commander of the base there had failed to check in, a scout ship was dispatched to determine the reason. They arrived to find the entire facility leveled from a single catastrophic blast. Initial reports passed it off as an accident, the center of the blast obvious when viewed from above. They determined that the energy reservoir for the main power distribution system had exploded due to a failed power regulator.

However, further investigations, something the General had insisted upon, uncovered unexplained smaller blast points on the many spacecraft and buildings in the depression. It was one of those that had caused the power regulator to fail, providing the larger explosion. An expanded search beyond the crater found further evidence confirming the attack.

Prints in the dirt, both in the crater and above on the rim, told a tale of stealth and guile. KaLob had no idea how the humans had managed to land undetected, but their execution and efficiency in the attack was to be admired. The best information his analysts had provided stated that the humans had not developed or acquired any technology that rendered them undetectable, but that presumption was now in question.

He ordered an immediate search for the perpetrators but held little hope of their discovery with so much lost time. The loss of those forces would be felt, as they had experienced some success with their unorthodox approach in fighting the humans. Pushing that aside, KaLob focused on their next target, one selected to put a stranglehold on the human supply chain.

----*----

Jake had gone over every inch of both FTL drives as well as the entire upper surface of the ship, looking for any clues to the failure. While he had no idea what he was looking for, he was sure he could detect something out of order. So far, all was as it should be.

As he roved over the top of the ship, he caught occasional glimpses of Sergeant Carson and a mixed team of SAS troopers and Marines. They would disappear and reappear as they made their way through the dense growth surrounding the ship. Like him, he suspected they had no idea what they were looking for, but performed their duties diligently.

The dense atmosphere was breathable, if not somewhat overly warm and muggy. It reminded Jake of a trip to the Florida Keys he had made one August, long ago. There had been so much moisture in the air; you could almost swim from place to place.

Returning inside to the cool climate-controlled interior, Jake went back to the bridge where its two occupants fell silent, watching him as he began resetting the drive power systems. Even though the FTL drive wouldn't work inside the gravity well of the solar system they occupied, he knew what to look for on the control panel.

When the humans first recovered the initial NeHaw exploration craft, the FTL drives had been a mystery. Nothing the scientists did could get the engines to operate, and so they were ignored, presumed damaged in the crash.

Fast forward to today, and the humans had been educated on the drive functionality and limitations. While inoperable inside a star's gravitational influence, there were still indicators of proper installation and operation.

The Wawobash, with assistance from the Kortisht drive builders, had long ago developed monitors and instrumentation to validate the proper installation and operation before taking the ship to space. If Jake was reading the output from his displays correctly, all systems were green and ready for space.

With one indicator red, showing they were under the current's star's influence, the green light next to it declared the FTL drive operable. When both were green, they were ready and outside the star's effect on them. That was exactly the state they had found themselves in when they dropped from FTL the day before, green, green. Jake's frustration was starting to mount when the woman at the tactical station spoke up.

"Colonel, I am getting a reading from just outside this solar system. There are two NeHaw destroyers, and they appear to be headed this way," she announced.

"Pull everyone inside, I am going to engage the cloaking unit," Jake replied as he checked the console. He was happy to see the Marine jump out of his seat and go get Carson and the others, rather than risk transmitting the recall signal.

Once the console went green, indicating everyone was inside, Jake enabled the cloaking unit and stood next to the tactical station, watching the NeHaw ships approach.

----*----

Brian had caught more than a few of the transmissions regarding the unknown whereabouts of Jake and his strike team. He and ALICE-3 discussed the issue at length as they floated just outside the Wawobash shipyards.

"I have reached out to my sisters, and the consensus with the highest degree of probability indicates they have lost FTL capability. Without more data on their location, any rescue mission would be impossible."

"The fact that they were able to transmit the success message means they could call for help?" Brian asked more than stated.

"Yes, however, without FTL, they would be unable to escape the NeHaw if detected. Were they to do so, we are likely to be the closest available resource to respond to the call. Other ships have been ordered to the edges of their systems, but they are not currently positioned to go to FTL in less than 24 hours. This all presumes the Phantom is in a position to safely call for assistance, which is not presumed to be the case."

As they were talking, Brian noted on his navigation screen that ALICE-3 was nudging the ship farther out to be in a position just inside the Wawobash gravity well, ensuring the ability for an almost instant FTL, should the need arise.

----*----

Colonel Bo Chao sat in his Hong Kong headquarters, going over the mountain of paperwork before him. Assuming command after the death of General Ju Huang, something triggered by Huang's mishandling of the American's contact overtures, Bo had managed to salvage the situation.

Now a member of Earth's central command, representing the planet's single largest global force, he had the misfortune of commanding the most dysfunctional organizations of all. Still reeling over the loss of General Ju, the ancestral leader of the Chinese military after the fall, many units were struggling with the change.

It had taken a substantial amount of his time and effort to restructure the command into something stable and trustworthy. In so doing, Bo had been able to avoid the large-scale executions, historically necessary with this type of regime change.

Instead, he had chosen to transfer select officers and senior NCO's to America and England, where they were introduced to a new way of life. He had received word most had survived the transition.

----*----

Jake was watching the display where the SAS female was tracking the inbound NeHaw ships when Sergeant Carson stuck his head into the bridge.

"Colonel, we have a bit of an issue, I believe."

"Besides the inbound destroyers?" Jake asked dryly in reply.

"Yes, sir. I think you should come to take a look at this," Carson replied as he turned to lead Jake below. Winding through the passage and descending to the lower level of the ship, Jake could see Carson was heading to the exit ramp. Pausing long enough to drop the ramp, the sergeant stopped halfway down before pointing to one side.

Jake was aware that dropping the ramp while the cloaking was engaged would expose the underside of the ship. That, however, wasn't a concern as it wouldn't be visible from someone looking down from above. Following the sergeant's extended arm, Jake looked beneath the hull of the ship, finding one of the landing gear struts completely covered in insects. Turning, he found the other just as infested.

"What are they doing?" Jake asked as he stepped off the ramp and approached the strut extending from the bay above that housed it when retracted. Flicking a few of the insects off the strut, he could see where they had been chewing on the metal, marring the surface in the process.

The insects had only made it about halfway up the leg on this side and were almost as high on the others. Jake estimated that if they reached the ship, all hell would break loose as they chewed on the hull.

Turning quickly, Jake ascended the ramp until he found a communications station. Hitting the activate button, he queried the bridge. By using the internal communications system, he avoided any open broadcasts.

"Bridge," he shouted.

"Bridge here," he got in reply, the distinct English accent giving away the identity of the responder. Jake suddenly

31

realized he didn't know the SAS trooper's name. Turning to Carson, he motioned to the speaker, while covering the mike.

"Hannah, sir," Carson replied with a smile.

"Hannah, didn't you say you adjusted the sensors to alert on hazardous life forms?" Jake asked.

"Why, yes, sir. So far, we've had no indications of such," she replied, the confusion clear in her voice.

"Please remove the filter," Jake asked calmly. The sudden beeping in the speaker came as no surprise to Jake.

"Oh dear, it appears the ship itself is under attack. We are detecting multiple life forms attached to the landing gear, and they are consuming the metal alloy at an alarming rate," Hannah reported.

"Sir, if they reach the ship, we might not be able to leave. They seem particularly fond of the metal the ship's drives are made of."

"Send some people down to help us clear the landing gear," Jake replied.

"Sir, I am detecting other locations on the exterior of the ship where the insects have already taken hold. I am afraid if we don't leave soon, we shan't be leaving at all."

"Are the NeHaw still there?" Jake asked, the frustration evident in his voice.

"Yes sir, although they have stopped just outside the gravity well of this system. They appear to be, well, just sitting there, waiting."

----*----

Robert Jacobson had been acting as Jake's Logistics Officer for quite a while, tirelessly performing his duties in the background. He was responsible for tracking down and delivering all the materials necessary for the ALICEs' automated manufacturing facilities to maintain production.

Outside of the Wawobash ships, the ALICEs provided the necessary manufactured goods needed to keep the Earth ahead of the tech curve in their fight with the NeHaw. The fighters and patrol ships with stasis shields and railguns all came from ALICE factories.

And all those factories relied on his supply line. His scrounging activities had taken him from Canada to Mexico and across the oceans into Europe and Asia. He had encountered more people around the globe than any of the others in leadership roles and established relationships everywhere he went.

He commanded the largest single transport force the Earth possessed, with over twenty air transport craft of various types and other ground vehicles and hundreds of people. He had pilots, loaders, and security forces, all working together locating, collecting, and transporting whatever items the factories needed to continue their production. He had built much to be proud of.

Even so, Robert was extremely frustrated. Having lived as a man of action his entire life is a proud descendant of a Fort Hood soldier, he was tired of chasing down steel plate and copper wiring. He had recovered more platinum, gold, and silver than they could spend in several lifetimes, turning the precious metals storage hangar in Texas into Fort Knox on steroids.

His current activity was chasing down steel plates for the Lanai ALICE. He had found a massive steel mill in Chelyabinsk, Russia, and was in the process of taking several of the Lanai transports there to fill them. With all other stockpiles high, and inventory filling warehouses, Robert decided it was time to enhance his unit's capabilities.

As the husband of the commander of the Texas ALICE, he was well aware of the coming war. It was time to expand the abilities of his operation one more time.

----*----

Kola was on her way to the edge of the solar system. After the emergency meeting of the Tactical Analysts and other leaders, it was decided to position her at the edge of the gravity well. Without a specific search area to investigate, they could only place themselves in a position to act, should a call for help arrive.

33

Just over a day's travel from Earth, she still had several more to go before she could jump to FTL if asked. In the meantime, she had her human occupants training and learning all of her combat systems. With far less than a full complement on board, the opportunities for those crew members were limitless, and the possibility of combat was a reality.

Her hangars had both of the attack squadrons, VMFA-314 Black Knights and the VMFA-112 Cowboys, aboard as well as three of the Lanai combat patrol craft. All ships were currently available for training while in transit to the edge of the solar system. Once they were asked to go to FTL, all would need to be masked under stasis bubbles to prevent their ferrous hulls from interfering with the FTL drive.

Kola did find herself less than thrilled at the duo placed on board for this trip. Ivan and his Cossack followers had been selected as crew for the Lanai Patrol ships. The Russians had shown a particular fondness for the smaller ships and had a high degree of success in combat operations.

Two of the ships had been operating at the edge of the solar system when several NeHaw destroyers appeared in what was suspected to be a probing attack. It was suggested that the NeHaw were testing the Earth's defense network in the escalating war.

The aggressive response from the Russians operating the two vessels, and their methodical annihilation of a couple of the NeHaw ships, ensured no further probing would occur. The retreating ships were all savaged by the two Russian crews in some capacity. Video replay confirmed the Russian weapon's accuracy and tactical efficiency working in tandem had overwhelmed the enemy.

The other half of the duo was Colonel Edwin Banks. While not the ship's captain, as that position was assigned to one of Brian's protégé's, he was still the senior officer aboard. It was of no concern or slight to Banks as he admittedly did not have enough experience for such a position.

He had gathered a SAS ground team and rushed them on board in the hours after the decision to go to the edge of the system and wait. Should they need to hasten to Jake's aid on some distant planet, his team was ready to land and cover the retreat.

The unfortunate part of all this was, while it was well known that Edwin and Ivan were best of friends, it was also a fact that the two rarely saw eye to eye on anything. So it was now as the two stood on the bridge, discussing the possible location of Jake and his wayward vessel.

"I tell you, Edwin. Jake is on the alien planet. He destroyed the raiders, but was unable to leave afterward."

"Ivan, my friend, that is not possible. Think man! He wouldn't send the success code until he had departed the planet's surface. He must be dead in space, floating free, or on repulser drives with a damaged FTL drive."

"Nyet! You know that little ship as well as I. She is sturdy and would take considerable punishment."

"I must agree with you there; however, it is possible the ship was attacked as they departed, thus providing the instrument of failure," Banks countered.

"Possibly, however, I do not see Colonel Jake leaving anything behind that could do them harm. It would have to be a weapon in space, more likely something in orbit?" Ivan replied.

"Gentlemen, might I suggest you take this conversation elsewhere as I have a ship to run?" Kola supplied, generating a few snickers from the bridge crew and a smile from the captain standing nearby.

"As you wish," Bank responded as he led Ivan out the main door and into the passageway beyond. The two could still be heard arguing in the distance.

"Thank you, Kola," came the comment from the captain.

"You are welcome."

Chapter 4

Sara was doing her absolute best to put a smile on her face as Sandy and the kids dropped by for a visit. Jake's idea of placing Sandy in charge, as guardian of Jon and Padma, had been brilliant in concept. In practice, Sandy ran with it much like everything else she did, and the results were over the top.

She decided to move from the Texas facility to the Nevada location because ALICE-1 had the best schools, in her opinion. Jon, who is about eight, was studying to be a doctor, and Padma wanted to be a facility commander. All according to Sandy, anyway.

To Sara, they looked like two happy kids, content with Sandy doting over them. In taking this role, Sandy had relinquished all of her former duties and obligations, including those intimately tied to Jake. Sara felt no guilt in her part of that. Especially since Sandy had made that decision on her own.

As Sara was seeing everyone at the door, with parting hugs and kisses for Auntie Sara from both kids, she wondered if the same thing would work with Becky.

----*----

Working with the rotation of the moon, they waited until they were visually hidden from the NeHaw ships and then dropped the cloaking so people could see what they were doing. Jake had several of the crew now scouring the outside of the ship, removing as many of the insects as they could find while he checked on the NeHaw destroyers. As he looked over Hannah's shoulder, he could see the two ships in a stationary location just outside the system, as the sensors didn't need line of sight to work.

"Colonel, sensors indicate we still have bugs on the hull. If we don't go to space soon, we are going to be in a spot of trouble," Hannah replied with a worried tone.

"Ok, get everyone inside, guess we need to make a run for it," Jake answered as he took the empty pilot's seat.

Checking that everything was still green for the FTL drive and cloaking was off, he waited for the all-clear before engaging it. He did one more check and then slowly powered up the drives. As the ship gently rose from the moon's surface, Jake left the landing gear extended.

As they passed through the clouds, still on the far side of the moon from the NeHaw, Jake moved particularly slowly to ensure he created as little a disturbance as possible. Soon, they cleared the last of the atmosphere and slowly reentered the blackness of space. Suddenly an alarm sounded on the bridge.

"Sir, we have several small hull breaches. Activating self-patching systems," Hannah announced.

Jake was aware that the ship had a hull patching capability, intended to address small meteorite strikes and other minor injuries to the pressure hull. He had just never had to use it.

"All signs of life are gone from the outside of the ship. I believe you may retract the landing gear if you like," Hannah announced finally.

"You might hold on that, sir. Both NeHaw ships are scanning the area, and the power surge might tip them off," the Marine in the copilot's seat declared as he worked the controls on the panel before him.

Checking his own displays, Jake could see both NeHaw destroyers floating ahead. His instruments indicated several sensor scans in progress, but not specifically directed at them. He dialed back the ship's power until he was only using enough to hold them clear of the moon's gravity.

With that, the three continued to wait and watch.

----*----

DeFor was staring at the sensor display, trying to make sense of the readings. Since General KaLob had taken power, it was not a smart thing to ignore unexplained phenomena. One of the few ship's commanders to still retain his position, he was constantly expecting to receive that order stating he had been replaced. That meant death.

Therefore, when the latest order came through telling him to take JeGot and search this sector for signs of saboteurs, he sped with all haste. He had seen the report of the attack on S-12653, describing the devastation there. He could only assume that those responsible were the focus of the search. It was with that in mind that he selected this interstellar crossroads to begin his search.

He was very aware of human guile and ruthlessness. He had lost several comrades to their attacks in the past. That was why he was currently so confused. Surely the attack on S-12653 had been executed by a superior force consisting of many ships. How else would they overcome and obliterate the entire base, exterminating every last being there?

However, instead of locating a massive energy signature hiding among the planets here, he was getting a transient energy reading. It was as if something were slipping in and out of reality, hovering at the edge of existence.

On a whim, DeFor ordered his tactical officer to link with his counterpart on JeGot's ship and see if they couldn't cross-reference the sensor shadow.

----*----

Jake had everyone turn off all nonessential power systems as he slowly nudged the Phantom out of orbit. His order had been if it's not essential to live, shut it down. Once free of the moon's gravity, he could kill everything but the cloaking unit. Moving in irregular bursts, he tried not to set any pattern that might be detectable to the NeHaw as artificial.

He would watch the displays as he maneuvered the ship, waiting for drops in the scanning intensity before executing his next move. Several times, he had to cut his move short, lest he prolongs the power surge in the drives.

Finally, they reached the point where, if they had working FTL drives, they could have burst away. Showing two green lights, the ship said it was good to go, but Jake had seen that on the way in. When they had originally dropped from FTL, they were well outside the star's effects, but the

FTL had still not worked. The trip to the moon had been lengthy because of where the FTL failed, not due to the star's influence.

"Now we wait," Jake announced as he killed everything but life support and cloaking.

----*----

DeFor was sure there was something out there. Even though it had not registered on any of his ship's sensors for more than a few microcycles, both his and JeGot's ships were seeing the same readings. Without more information, though, he felt it unwise to sound the alarm and call in more ships.

With the sensor reading fading, DeFor ordered JeGot to start moving away, while they headed in opposite directions. The hope was one of the two ships would pick up the readings again.

----*----

Jake could see the two destroyers were starting to drift apart. On the one hand, that was a good sign as it meant they had not locked onto the Phantom's location. The bad part was one of the two was heading in their direction.

Resisting the urge to move the ship, Jake had his hand hovering over the stasis shield button. Should the destroyer get too close, the shields would prevent the ships from making contact and possibly damaging the Phantom. Unfortunately, it would absolutely give their position away.

Jake did a mental inventory of the guns on board and dismissed the thought of fighting his way out. While the shields were as good as any in the Earth's fleet, the guns were NeHaw standard for a small ship like this and would do little against the combined assault from the two destroyers.

Returning his attention back to the encroaching vessel, Jake's hand floated over to the stasis shields switch again. In a few more minutes, the destroyer would be blocking their access to open space. If they didn't move soon, they were going to be in a tight situation.

Almost as a distraction, Jake checked the navigation settings for the FTL and hit the button one last time. There was a sudden sensation as the inertial dampeners reacted to the leap into faster than light, leaving the bridge crew in stunned silence.

----*----

JeGot had called asking if he had seen the energy spike. DeFor acknowledged the call and confirmed both the spike and the total loss of signal. Whatever they had been chasing, it had departed the area without a trace.

DeFor debated his next move, taking great care in considering his options. In the past, they would have ignored the incident and moved on to their next tribute collection point. Those ways, and the commanders who excelled in them, were gone.

Taking a deep breath, DeFor composed a report, and once he was satisfied with its accuracy, he transmitted a copy to the High Command and one for JeGot. Once complete, he ordered JeGot to follow as they continued their search of the sector.

----*----

Jake had everyone on the bridge do complete systems checks before allowing anything else on the ship to be reactivated. One by one, they reanimated the various systems they had shut down, waiting to see which may have been the culprit in killing the FTL drive earlier.

They were a good two hours into the flight when they turned the last of the systems back on.

"Well, that's it, then? No other systems are still offline?" Jake asked the assembled bridge crew.

"That is it, sir. Everything is up and running. Maybe the insect damage fixed the driving issue?" Hannah replied, with the Marine nodding in agreement.

"Well, I guess we will never know? Let's go get something to drink," Jake replied. No sooner had everyone started to rise from their seats when the Phantom dropped out of FTL once again.

"No, no, no!" Jake shouted as he once more went over all the settings on the pilot's console.

"Sir, we are still in NeHaw space but have dropped out of FTL in a very remote area. The scope is clear, and I see no other ships in the vicinity," Hannah reported, anticipating the request.

"Closest planet of any kind?" Jake asked, thinking about a place to hide.

"Not within days, sir," Hannah replied somberly.

For the next hour, the bridge crew went back over all the ship's systems, resetting the various power and drive systems without success. Finally, Jake stood up in exasperation.

"I'm taking a break. Keep us cloaked and powered down until I get back," he said as he walked out of the bridge without looking back.

----*----

Brian was conferring with his analytics team off to one side of the massive bridge that ALICE-3 called her human brain trust. Even though ALICE-3 could fly the ship she called home all by herself, the ALICE/Human combination had shown time and again that the union proved far greater than the parts.

The focus of their attention was the data they were receiving from the drones they had been asked to dispatch in the search for Jake and the Phantom. As the closest ship to open space, they were able to send automated pilotless FTL capable drones to various possible locations, searching for signs of the lost ship and crew.

Each drone was programmed to fly in FTL to a predetermined location. Once there, they would attach to the nearest NeHaw network node and relay their findings upon arrival. Once connected to the network, they could be remotely directed in a detailed search, based on the initial readings.

The drone assigned to the original target was able to confirm the destruction of the alien base as well as record several NeHaw destroyers in the area before it was discovered and attacked. Its destruction was confirmed as the live feed transmitted the convergence of two NeHaw ships firing before the signal was lost. The last message from the drone was the self-destruct confirmation.

"So, other than the drone we lost, still no signs of the Phantom?" Brian asked the analysts pouring over the inbound data.

"No, sir, not the Phantom. We have, however, noted an exceedingly high number of NeHaw military vessels everywhere we looked. We have been able to keep the drones hidden from them, but we suspect they are looking for something as well."

"That's good then. It probably means they are searching for Jake. However, that also suggests they might have damaged the Phantom as they retreated from the fight?" Brian said thoughtfully.

"Yes sir, or possibly an encounter after the attack, we can't be sure," the lead analyst replied.

"Be sure to forward this all to Earth," Brian said as he turned away to deal with other less interesting but more pressing matters.

----*----

Linda was reviewing the information ALICE-3 was forwarding to them from the drones. Her current obsession was the data from the original target, the base they had attacked. They had captured quite a bit of data and imagery before the drone was destroyed, and she wanted to complete a breakdown of that engagement as possible.

Her hope was they could find any indication of a definitive reason for the Phantom's disappearance. The lack of wreckage in space or on the surface of the planet gave them hope that the issue lay elsewhere and was not critical.

The fact that the planet seemed to be getting the once over from the NeHaw as well gave support to the theory that the Phantom had escaped and was held up elsewhere. Scanning the room, she could see a dozen analysts all doing the same as she.

----*----

In his own world, Jake had left the bridge and headed straight to the galley, where he grabbed himself a beer from the ship's stores. After taking a sip, he took stock of his surroundings for the first time as his head had been elsewhere as he entered the room. The galley had fallen silent, and everyone was watching his every move.

"As you were," Jake said while raising his bottle to the assembled crew, and then turned to leave them to their own devices. Proceeding down the passageway, he descended down into the cargo hold. Here, ALICE had converted the open area to half barracks and half general use area.

Jake could see Marines and SAS troopers intermingled throughout the open space. As he wandered, his head was not on his location but was tracing all the systems and circuits that he knew made up the ship's drive systems.

Having performed the same exercise multiple times already on the bridge, he hoped a change in scenery would jolt his memory. He stopped and scanned the room, noting that most of its occupants were paying him little attention. Some were on their bunks reading or talking to one another.

Others were exercising or servicing their gear in the large open space beyond the bunks. Jake noticed one lone female Marine sitting at the far end of the bay with a large stack of recovered alien hardware spread across a workbench. Crossing the room, his curiosity getting the better of him, Jake approached the woman. Waving her back into her seat as she started to rise from the stool she was using, he pointed at the stacks of equipment on the bench.

"What's going on here?' Jake asked after taking another sip of his beer. He used the bottle as a pointer, directing it toward the various piles spread around her.

"Since we have been delayed in returning home, I decided to use my free time to identify and catalog as much of the equipment we recovered as possible," the Marine replied.

"Those over there are pieces of the communications gear we pulled from the wreckage of the ships and the command hooch. That bunch there is weapons control and navigation. Most of the rest is memory cores and data storage that we will need to get back to Earth if we want them to read," she replied with a tone of frustration.

Jake laughed to himself at the reference of the "hooch." The term was familiar to him as slang from the Viet Nam war. He had encouraged all his Marines to study military history, as it helped gain perspective on the challenges they had yet to face.

"Are you qualified to be doing this?" Jake asked, trying not to insult the woman, but concerned that misidentifying some of these items might delay much-needed Intel.

"Oh, yes, sir. Before boot camp, I was trained as an analyst. I also spent some time in Patti's Pit, doing military intelligence work."

"Well, I would say that qualifies you as well as anyone on board. What is that you are playing with," Jake asked, indicating the small piece of hardware she had hooked up to a power source. It looked like a small cube, several inches square. He could see an indicator light showing it was active, but no other controls or displays were present.

"I have no idea, I've been playing with this thing off and on since we left the planet, and I can't seem to find its purpose. We pulled a couple off the wrecked ships, but as best we could tell, not all the ships had one. I thought it was some kind of communicator or even an IFF unit, but the analyzer there doesn't show any known communication transmissions," she explained.

Jake knew that the IFF reference meant Identification Friend or Foe. On Earth, it was used to help prevent friendly fire incidents. By transmitting known identifiers, combatants could distinguish those on their side by the signals received.

"Well, good luck," Jake replied and started to turn when he stopped in his tracks.

"When did you first power that thing up?" he asked, returning to the bench.

"Oh, I don't know for sure, Sir, maybe an hour or two after we bugged out," she replied.

"And has that thing been powered up the whole time since?" Jake asked pointedly.

"No, Sir, I pulled it off the power supply when we landed on that moon. I just repowered it up a little while ago," the Marine replied, growing concerned at Jake's intensity.

"Shut it down," Jake ordered without explanation.

"Yes, Sir," she replied without hesitation and pulled the leads connected to the cube.

"Bridge, do you hear me?" Jake asked over his communications link.

"Yes, Sir," the Marine in the co-pilot's chair replied.

"Go to FTL," Jake ordered. He swore he could feel the ship lurch as the FTL drive was activated.

"We are a go on FTL Colonel. What did you do?" Hannah asked from the bridge.

"I'll explain later, just take us home," Jake replied, cutting the link to the bridge.

"What's your name, Marine?" Jake asked with a smile as he took the cube from her hands.

"Watts, Sir. Samantha Watts, but most just call me Sam," she replied hesitantly.

"Well, Sam, I know what that is," Jake said as he looked at the woman while tossing the cube in the air. He then handed her the cube back, still grinning.

"Good work, but don't power up anything more until we get home," Jake told the Marine as he slapped her hard on the back in congratulations, his excitement and relief overcoming his normally calm demeanor. The poor woman almost lost her seat as she grabbed the bench to steady herself.

Turning with a smile, Jake left the cargo hold to update what he was sure was a confused bridge crew.

Chapter 5

The Phantom's sudden appearance at the edge of the solar system took everyone by surprise. Kola was still just short of 2 days from the edge of the solar system and was the first to spot the missing ship and crew.

"Where the bloody hell have you been?" Banks asked after the initial announcement of arrival from the crewman monitoring the space around them, his normal composure abandoned. He happened to be on the bridge reviewing training results with the ship's captain at the time.

"We had some challenges," Jake replied with a smile that lit up the bridge display.

"I am directly transmitting our report now, not via the NeHaw link. I also have need of a special mission," Jake added as others joined in on the conversation.

"What's up, Jake?" Linda asked as her image appeared. Next to her, Sara and Becky stood impatiently nearby.

"We need to run some tech to the Kortisht for analysis. I think we have found out how the NeHaw raiders have been interrupting the FTL of our ships," he said as he waved a cube for all to see.

"You will need to hold our position, then, until we can provide an FTL capable ship for the transport," Linda replied as she motioned to someone off-screen.

"Jake, what happened to you guys?' Sara asked finally, unable to contain herself any longer.

"Well, let's just say we discovered these things by accident," he replied while tossing the cube from one hand to another, a broad smile crossing his face.

----*----

It would be several hours before a destroyer finally arrived to assume the responsibility of transporting the FTL blocking device to the Kortisht. While they waited, Jake held an impromptu conference call, being less concerned about using the NeHaw network for verbal communications versus transmitting the raid report data.

"So, the raid was a complete success?" Linda asked after listening to Jake's synopsis of the activities there.

"Combat operations were 100%. The Intel losses, though, were significant. Whatever that was that we hit, it destroyed a lot of the equipment and all of the alien staff members," he replied.

"We grabbed anything we could scrounge from the wreckage, hoping it might contain data, but the analysts are going to have to figure out how to access the contents," he finished.

"And FTL failure?" Sara asked, her voice betraying her emotions.

"Yeah, that was interesting," Jake replied with a grin.

"That's not the word I would use," Sara replied with a frown.

"Trust me, no one was more frustrated than I was," Jake replied with a sigh.

"Ahem," Jake heard from the SAS trooper sitting in the cockpit nearby.

"Oh, and Hannah," Jake added with a smile.

As they talked, the two ships docked, and the cube was transported to the ship ferrying it to Kortisht for analysis. It took no more than a few minutes, and then the destroyer disappeared. Jake was relieved to see it on its way and happy to be beyond its influence and free of its effects, once and for all.

With the mystery device handed off for transport to the Kortisht, Jake ordered the Phantom home. At some point, early in the trip, they understood they would be passing Kola, thus giving them an opportunity to transfer any passengers on either ship.

With the increase in hostile activity, it was decided that Kola would take up station at the edge of the solar system, acting as a temporary space station until the modules arrived from the Wawobash. Her additional patrol ships would act as a small border protection fleet. While incapable of FTL, the sturdy ships had proven tough adversaries in battle.

Fortunately, Brian had reported that the first of seven separate sections would soon be ready for delivery. Jake had designed the space station to be made up of several smaller modules, all connected together with tubes. While strong enough to hold the sections together under normal conditions, the tubes were really needed to allow movement from one module to another.

Each section was actually its own ship, capable of FTL spaceflight as well as maneuvering inside a gravity well. Once all the sections were linked together, they could act as one, giving the station a combined capability of movement and holding station.

Each section was a saucer, made up of five concentric rings. There was a large central ring with two smaller above and below. Each ring represented two levels within, giving each module ten levels in all, containing compartments for living quarters, command center, and all the other necessary spaces. Jake had emphasized the particular need for recreational facilities, as this was also intended as an R&R facility for the deep-space crews.

The horizontal tubes connecting the saucers had two levels of passageways, while the vertical tubes contained multiple elevators, required due to the artificial gravity. Once assembled, ships could dock with any of the sections, allowing for resupply or crew access. The sections were not large enough to take anything bigger than a fighter inside, but external docking ports permitted direct access to all but the largest ships. Those would require tenders to ferry crew and supplies.

In addition, Jake had ordered all modules to be equipped with a sizable number of energy cannons, all to be installed by the Wawobash on the top and bottom of each ring section. With guns on top and bottom, they had an incredible amount of overlapping firepower. Once in Earth space, these turrets would be augmented with railguns, while the modules themselves would be fitted with shield generators.

Jake's grand vision was a fortress at the edge of the solar system, capable of inflicting massive amounts of damage on any incoming NeHaw ships. It was intended to ravage an armada like they had seen in the last engagement. It was his hope to never again draw from the weapons store in Georgia, where he kept their darkest secrets hidden away.

In his opinion, it couldn't get here fast enough.

----*----

Brian was watching from the bridge of ALICE-3 as the Wawobash were preparing to release the first three space station modules. The Wawobash project manager had explained that these three would be assembled vertically once on-site, making the center hub of the station. There would be four more identical saucers that will be attached to the center saucer of the vertical hub later, spreading out horizontally. These would be connected at 90-degree intervals, balancing the configuration in three dimensions.

They had agreed that ALICE-3 would take control and guide the three pieces out to the edge of the system remotely, where their pre-programmed flight plan would send the unmanned sections to an anxious Kola. Once they arrived in near-Earth space, Kola could remotely maneuver the sections into a position where the waiting humans and bots could assemble the connecting tubes from materials stored inside the three saucers.

From everything he was reading in his display, the three sections were fully functional, though combat limited without their enhanced shields or railguns. Jake was adamant that these items were Earth only technologies, not to be shared. Brian understood the position, but it did make for a ton of work for their limited workforce. Thank goodness for the ALICEs and the bots.

"Brian, I have received word from the Wawobash that I can guide the sections out of space dock," he heard ALICE-3 announce.

"That's great news. Let's not tell Earth, yet, until they are safely out of here and on their way," Brian mentioned as an afterthought. This was new to everyone, the Wawobash included. He wanted to be sure they were actually on their way before getting everyone excited.

"Agreed," was the only reply from ALICE-3.

Looking around the bridge, he could see the entire bridge crew watching as the three saucers slowly pulled free of the skeletal structures surrounding each saucer. Apparently, the Wawobash had a modular system of manufacturing that expanded outward, as they assembled whatever they were contracted to build.

As each saucer emerged from the web like infrastructure, he watched the construction framework break apart, only to form up into smaller sections, ready to take on their next task. Soon, all three saucers were floating free and heading toward the battleship that hosted the human buyers.

Brian could see the bridge crew had suddenly become active, as ALICE-3 transferred tasks to each station. From his position in the command chair, he could tell that she was delegating system checks and other non-vital duties, while she maintained navigation and engineering functions.

Tracking their progress on his own display, he could see the three saucers pass below ALICE-3 on their way to the edge of the Wawobash system. From there, he knew they would perform a final safety check before engaging the pre-programmed flight plan, sending all three home to Earth via FTL.

With the wayward Phantom now home, ALICE-3 had resumed its position just off the shipyards and well inside the Wawobash system. When the three saucers reached the halfway point between ALICE-3 and the edge of the Wawobash system, the bridge suddenly came alive with alarms.

"We have incoming ships," the tactical officer announced from her station.

"Brian, I make five NeHaw cruisers and a number of unidentified vessels with each, heading inbound," ALICE-3 added.

Switching his display to a duplicate of the tactical station, he could see the ships ALICE-3 described. Slowly, several of the ships not initially tagged on display started showing type and origin. Brian frowned as he realized they were all warships from NeHaw aligned planets.

"Battle stations!" Brian announced as he started counting ships. While not as large as the armada that had attacked Earth, this was still a lot of firepower. From the approach vector, it was clear they were headed straight for the shipyards.

----*----

Ivan and Edwin had transferred to the Phantom as the two ships passed each other. Rather than attempting anything fancy, they had simply stopped Kola long enough to take the Phantom aboard and move the necessary personnel around. As it turned out, a majority of the Marines and SAS on board were scheduled for training on the combat patrol ships now housed in Kola's hangars.

With little more than a skeleton crew left on board, Jake had guided the Phantom out of Kola's hangar and watched in his display as the massive ship proceeded on its way.

"Steady as she goes, sir?" Hannah asked as Jake got up from the pilot's seat. She had requested to remain with the small ship, a request Jake was only too happy to grant. He gave her a crash course in the ship's operation, and he found her a quick study.

He was glad to have her stay, as it was always better to have someone he knew he could trust backing him up. The Marine analyst, Sam Watts, had also requested to stay aboard to oversee the intelligence materials delivery. Jake was appreciative of that request as well. Other than those two, it was just him, Ivan, and Edwin left to run things.

"Yes, thank you," he replied with a smile as he turned away from her. He had almost made it to the hatch leading out of the bridge when he heard the alarm.

"Sir, we are receiving an urgent message from the Wawobash," Hannah explained as she brought the text upon her monitor for both to read. Jake scanned the information

51

and then brought up several still images provided in the message. It was the incoming NeHaw force.

With Kola still over a day's travel from the edge of the system and no other available fighting ships in the area, he was afraid that Brian and ALICE-3 were on their own.

"Let me know if we get any more messages as soon as they come in," Jake said in frustration. He then turned to go find the others to brief them on the latest crisis.

----*----

GeSec sat in the command chair of his cruiser, assessing the situation before him. He had very specific instructions from General KaLob, ordering an attack on the Wawobash shipyards, destroying as much of the shipbuilding infrastructure as possible. These same orders specified he was not to attack the planet, just remove as much of the shipbuilding capability as possible, thus removing the human's source of combat vessels.

While they had expected some form of resistance to their efforts, what GeSec had before him was something else entirely. Since KaLob had taken power, the increase in available military intelligence had been overwhelming. GeSec now had access to all of the after-action reports and analysis of the human capabilities.

Because of that, he immediately recognized the battleship sitting between him and the shipyards as the one captured from the NeHaw and refitted for human use. Its presence alone gave him a reason to reconsider the pending attack. However, it was the addition of the three disk shapes between his ships and the battleship that created the greatest concern.

Although he had never seen such vessels before, he recognized the gun turrets flooding the superstructure. His tactical officer verified they were all powered up and appeared functional. To his relief, none sported the human projectile weapons the NeHaw had come to fear.

"Sir, we have more ships exiting the battleship," his tactical officer announced.

Checking his own display, he got the identity of the newcomers, as the tactical systems verified them against the database.

"This is unfortunate," GeSec said aloud as the system verified that several of the devil ships were exiting the hangar of the battleship. He had seen reports of these ships' capabilities. How the humans had been able to transport that much ferrous metal in FTL was still a mystery to the NeHaw.

Their crude iron hulls and advanced energy shields made these ships a contradiction in technology. Their firepower was capable of battering any vessel unlucky enough to encounter one, while the sturdy iron hulls absorbed a pounding, far better than the advanced composites of the FTL ships.

Although the NeHaw had held a few to a stalemate, driving them off in the end, they had yet to destroy a single ship of this type.

Fortunately, General KaLob did not expect his commanders to sacrifice themselves needlessly, as had the previous leadership. GeSec was just expected to challenge the humans, creating as much destruction as possible before retreating to fight another day.

The concept was a new one to GeSec and the other ship commanders, but it was one they all embraced with enthusiasm.

"Order all ships to execute formation Gama. Direct JaDos and RiFos to engage the disk ships while everyone else heads for the shipyards. We will distract the battleship," GeSec ordered, trying to sound more confident than he felt.

----*----

Brian watched as the NeHaw ships grew larger in the bridge display. He had moved from his command chair to stand next to the tactical officer as she tracked the incoming vessels. He could see the indicators applied to each ship as its type and planet of origin was identified by ALICE-3.

"Brian, it appears that the NeHaw are splitting up and leading five clusters of ships, each headed by a NeHaw cruiser. The other vessels are warships from subjugated NeHaw worlds," ALICE-3 explained.

"I think we can safely say they are more like allied planets now," Brian replied, not convinced that you could force someone to fight for you unwillingly.

"Semantics," ALICE-3 replied with a tinge of sarcasm, or so Brian interpreted.

"Sir, they are diverting course and breaking up their formations," the tactical officer announced.

Brian could see that each NeHaw cruiser was indeed leading its cluster of ships in differing directions. Some were still headed directly to the space station sections while others were swinging wide as if attempting to go around the blockade they presented.

"What weapons are aboard those space station sections?" Brian asked, indicating the three disks.

"Each section has twelve gun turret's top and bottom, providing for a total of twenty four batteries. Unfortunately, they are only equipped with energy cannons at the moment. They were slated for railgun installation when they arrived home," the tactical officer replied.

"Nothing else? No missile systems?" Brian asked.

"No, sir, additional weapons systems were to be delivered from the Klinan after the sections were assembled back home," she answered.

"The Klinan? Aren't they artists?" Brian asked, distracted from the moment by the comment.

"The Klinan are artists. However, after the attack on their homeworld, they have taken up trading with other races, collecting war materials in an effort to repay Earth for turning back the NeHaw attack," ALICE-3 replied.

"OK, well, I guess that leaves ALICE-3 fighting the three space station sections remotely while the patrol ships split up and challenge the groups doing the end run," Brian explained as he indicated each group of ships as he spoke. They had changed the display to a 3D hologram at the tactical station to get a better sense of the pending battle. In that view, it became quite obvious what each cluster was doing.

Each NeHaw cruiser had a cluster of anywhere from six to ten additional vessels, all warcraft and heavily armed. The four combat patrol ships ALICE-3 had in her hangars allowed for two each to break away and try and stop a superior number of alien vessels.

While the correlation of forces was undesirable, Brian had decided to sacrifice the three space station sections against the larger central force, rather than risking the possible loss of their creators, the Wawobash. As he watched the scene unfold before him, he couldn't help but note the improvement in the NeHaw battle tactics from previous encounters.

"Is the center force slowing?" Brian asked as he indicated the central group of three cruisers and about thirty support vessels.

"Yes sir, they are delaying to allow those outlying groups time to get into position for a coordinate strike," the tactical officer confirmed.

Brian gave out an audible sigh as he realized he was going to have a dog fight on his hands.

"ALICE, do the Wawobash have *any* other ships ready for battle?" Brian asked. He was hoping for additional firepower to confront the ships swinging wide.

"They have confirmed, there is no other battle ready vessels available at this time," ALICE-3 replied after a pause.

"OK, I guess we are on our own," Brian replied with another, deeper sigh.

----*----

HeBak was not feeling particularly good, having attempted to eat some of the human food supplied to him at his request. Boredom had inspired him to try something different, and so he had researched the available foodstuff. The automated systems they called ALICE provided a wide variety of things for the humans to eat.

His ship's system analysis had identified several dishes that were compatible with his physiology, in that they were not poisonous to his species. As to their appeal, that was left to him to decide.

His excitement as something new had him trying several different options, finding some to his liking while others were exceeding bland. Unfortunately, he may have sampled too many at once as his head was aching, and he was sure the food was the cause.

Reckoning that humans must experience similar effects to their consumption of these meals, he began searching for remedies from the same source. He quickly determined that humans preferred one medication over all others for this condition, and it was not toxic to the NeHaw.

With a simple request, one of the many robotic attendants, rampant in the facility, delivered the relief HeBak was craving. Opening the packet they arrived in, he dropped the wrapper on the floor while studying the contents in his hand.

Popping two of the tablets in his mouth, he swallowed the pair quickly and stood waiting for relief to come. The last thing he saw was the floor rushing up to meet him before he passed out.

Chapter 6

Jake was sitting in the lounge area of the Phantom, watching the feed from Wawobash with Ivan and Edwin. While there was an open channel to both Earth and ALICE-3, he had specifically ordered no interference with the on-site command there. There was nothing worse in his mind than those in the rear second-guessing the commander in the field. If Brian needed anything, he would ask.

That, however, didn't remove his own desire to intercede one little bit, and it was an urge he suppressed. As they watched the hologram depicting the 3D battlefield, there was a constant dialog between the three men aboard the Phantom and those watching from the various facilities on Earth. Jake knew the ALICEs would be exchanging updates and combat data in the background, and had to satisfy himself that they would supply all the help Brian needed. It wasn't like he had a fleet ready to pounce anyway.

"Jake, are you watching this?" he heard Linda ask from the command center in Nevada.

"You mean the new tactics?" Jake replied as he watched the NeHaw attack group split up into three pieces.

"It is a good move. It reduces the opportunity for concentrated fire from a smaller force," Ivan commented as they watched their own patrol ships break away from the battleship to intercept the new groups.

That comment from Ivan got Jake to thinking. Even with all their advanced technologies, the NeHaw had actually been at a disadvantage in the fight so far. It had been the discovery of the stasis shields and the birth of the ALICE systems that had given the Earth a fighting chance. The NeHaw had overwhelming numbers and a vast empire to draw from. It had only been their steadfast adherence to outdated tactics that had assisted in crippling their cause.

Now, Jake was seeing creative strategies emerging from their enemy that put the humans' chance of overall victory in jeopardy. The FTL jammers hit and run tactics, and now this attack on their supply line. These all added up to a military commander who had thrown out the rule book, and that was a concern for Jake.

He watched as the smaller clusters of NeHaw ships went wide, avoiding the picket line of space station modules and their gun batteries. He could see how Brian had placed them as the first line of defense, with ALICE-3 between the modules and the Wawobash shipyards. Besides the defense in layers, the enveloping maneuver the NeHaw had executed was being countered with the paired combat patrol ships.

He was amazed at how the combat patrol ships, originally intended for near-Earth activities like a coast guard, had developed into a fighting force of their own. While actually 40% larger than a NeHaw cruiser, they were considered a supplemental craft, designed to reinforce the smaller interstellar ships rather than usurp them. Jake thought of them as a World War 2 PT boat, but a really big one.

Here, he was watching as two pairs were on intercept courses, intending to block much larger forces, directed to attack the shipyard beyond. Leaning over to the console, mounted on the wall in the lounge, he tapped in some queries and nodded at the response. While the other two men watched him, neither broke the silence as they returned their attention to the holograph.

Suddenly, the display before them lit up, as the NeHaw launched their attack on the space station modules. The clustered ships attacking the modules had put some distance between themselves, giving the NeHaw an even great area to work with as the saucers returned fire.

Jake tried to stay dispassionate as he evaluated the exchange of fire. He noted that the space station batteries had an exceptional field of fire with the outer ring able to depress their guns for an overlap of coverage, top to bottom. Unfortunately, they had only been equipped with the NeHaw standard energy cannons, so the effects were less than desired.

Since the NeHaw ships had been designed to encounter this type of weapon, the attacking vessels were able to absorb a good deal of punishment and keep coming. The NeHaw cruisers acted as the center of each group and were uncharacteristically leading the charge and taking the greater pounding.

All at once, there was a blinding bright light as the central space station module, in the line of three, exploded from the concentrated NeHaw cruiser fire. A few smaller ships had gotten too close and were engulfed in the explosion, creating their own contribution to the sphere of light. Jake understood that without the additional shields, these modules were less prepared than their aggressors to engage in this fight.

"That's not good," Edwin commented in the otherwise silent room.

----*----

Remotely controlling both weapons and navigation, ALICE-3 returned fire from the three space station modules as soon as the NeHaw initiated the contact. While she was tracking everything moving in nearby space, her primary responsibility was the three modules and her own ship. The staffed combat patrol ships were on their own missions.

She was attempting to engage every ship in the NeHaw central clusters firing upon the modules, spreading her firepower across all antagonists. A minor number of ships immediately felt the effects of the energy cannon fire as their small size made them more vulnerable. Unfortunately, the bigger ships seemed to absorb the hits without effect. She could see the center saucer was taking a considerably larger amount of fire from the enemy when compared to the other two.

Before she could adjust things, the center saucer exploded in a bright ball of light, taking a few NeHaw ships with it.

"ALICE-3, concentrate your fire on the bigger ships," she heard Brian say. While he was the human commander of the ship, they had operated as more of a team, so she took the command more as advice than an order.

59

"Adjusting targeting to the larger ships," she replied, confirming the suggestion.

By now, the NeHaw ships had engulfed the two remaining saucers, surrounding them on all sides, but permitting ALICE-3 to bring her guns on the battleship into play for those closest to her. With the addition of her railguns and energy cannon batteries, there were several explosions, obliterating several ships as the NeHaw forces encountered the additional fire.

"What are those ships doing," she heard Brian ask. She could detect what he was referring to in the display and noted that one cluster of NeHaw vessels had separated from the others battling the two remaining saucers and was headed directly toward them.

"Why in the world would they do that?' she heard Brian comment quietly.

----*----

HeBak awoke to find several humans in their environmental gear crouching over his prone form.

"Are you ok?" one of them asked, as the ship's translation systems provided the question in NeHaw.

"Why are you here?" he asked, completely confused about what was happening. The last thing he remembered was considering human food as an alternative to his own to counter his boredom. As he attempted to rise, his head exploded in pain.

"Your ship alerted us to your condition, we hurried to assist," the human explained as it tried to prevent him from rising.

"Did I injure my head?" he asked as he lay back down while using both hands to explore for injuries.

"Nothing visible, but you might have impacted the deck when you fell?" the human replied as it examined his head as well.

"You may leave, I am unharmed," HeBak stated, waving them toward the airlock, dismissing them.

"What is the last thing you remember?' the human asked, ignoring the statement, not moving from its place next to him.

Pausing to consider the question, he decided to answer honestly.

"I was considering trying your planet's culinary options. As I am to be a resident for the foreseeable future, I thought it appropriate."

"And you don't remember eating that," the human said as it pointed to the partially consumed items on the nearby platform next to his seating arrangement.

From the number of items in a partial state of being, HeBak had to assume that something had occurred, but he had no recollection of consuming any of it. Nearby he could see another human examining a wad of paper before handing it to the human examining him.

"Did you take these?" it inquired as it presented the paper for his consideration.

"What is As pir in?" he asked, confused at what had happened to him.

----*----

Jake was now moving between the 3D holograph and the display panel on the wall as he monitored the battle. He noted the change in targeting as ALICE-3 stopped diluting her firepower by attempting to target every vessel and now concentrated on the larger ships. The two smaller clusters of ships had yet to engage the patrol craft, but they were still on an intercept course.

"Jake, look at this," Edwin commented, pulling Jake's attention away from the wall panel and back to the holograph.

The explosion of the center space station module had created a gap in their line of defense. While the ships clustered about each module continued to pound on them, a significant number of ships, led by a NeHaw cruiser, slipped through the gap and headed directly toward ALICE-3. He could see ALICE-3 was now using her ship's guns to assist the modules in the fight as well as to confront the new threat.

"That lead cruiser is taking a significant amount of fire, and is still coming on," Edwin said while pointing at the display.

Jake hit a few settings on the wall panel, and the holograph changed to highlight the gunfire hitting just the cruiser.

"That is railgun fire!" Ivan announced as he pointed to the streams coming from ALICE-3. Jake had separated the types of fire, red for railguns and green for energy cannons, allowing them to distinguish what guns were being used on the cruiser.

As the three men watched, an overwhelming number of direct hits were being absorbed by the cruiser. There were several flares of light, as smaller ships surrounding the cruiser went up in blinding flashes. The explosions came as they were raked with the same fire as the cruiser.

"We may be seeing something new here," Jake said absently as he continued to focus on the cruiser facing ALICE-3. They watched as the support ships attempted to fall in behind the cruiser, using it for cover.

It was then the cruiser stopped in space, apparently choosing not to close the distance any further, lest the concentrated fire from the battleship rips it to shreds. Even at that distance, Jake could see the vessel almost glow as the combined firepower of ALICE-3 raked its exposed hull.

----*----

Gregor was in command of the combat patrol ship P5, and as senior officer, he was leading its sister ship, P8, toward one of the two clusters of NeHaw vessels attempting to evade the battleship. The enemy attempted to circle around the defenses and attack the shipyards from an exposed angle. Like many of his fellow Russians, he found duty on the heavily armed vessels to his personal liking.

Designed to fight, the combat patrol craft were wondrous ships to the Russians. As a crew of 8 to 10 could fight the ship quite easily, only half that number were required for day to day operations. The roomy interior, intended as cargo areas on the transport version, permitted for individual quarters and lounging space. Duty aboard P5 had been a joy so far.

Gregor had been in command of P5, protecting the edge of the solar system, the last time the NeHaw had attacked Earth. There was a glorious battle, and the NeHaw had learned a lesson that day. So long as the enemy stayed in the envelope of the sun's gravity, the patrol ships were more than a match for anything the NeHaw had to throw at them.

He was watching his tactical display from the command chair as they closed on the seven ships that were to be their prey this day. P8 was on his right, mimicking their every move as they prepared their attack. Just as they closed within weapons range, his tactical officer gave a warning.

"Sir, all ships have just launched missiles," the man announced.

"Shields up," Gregor ordered.

"No, sir, they didn't launch at us. They are targeting the shipyard," the man corrected.

Checking his display, Gregor could see the projected trajectory of the forty-plus missiles heading into the heart of the construction area. Just as he was about to order their destruction, the ship shook from the impact of multiple hits. He could see the NeHaw vessels had now turned and were directly confronting the two patrol craft in an attempt to prevent them from intercepting the missiles.

"Return fire," Gregor announced as he checks his display. The NeHaw had planned this maneuver well. From the angle of attack and the distance to ALICE-3, there was no way to prevent the missiles from striking their targets without exposing their rear to the enemy.

"Order Alexi to take P8 and pursue the missiles, we will entertain our guests," Gregor ordered. He watched in his display as P8 diverted course in pursuit of the missile launch while he positioned P5 to protect P8's rear. He just hoped they could catch the bombs in time.

----*----

Linda had the battle projected in the command center of the Nevada ALICE facility. The room was packed with staff and observers, as everyone was interested in the latest NeHaw attack. So far, the loss of the space station module was offset by close to fifteen NeHaw vessels destroyed.

There were several disturbing elements of this attack that had her itching to get at the data. The central NeHaw cruiser was taking a considerable pounding from ALICE-3 but was still in play, returning fire and otherwise tying up the battleship from other issues.

The second thing that caught Linda's eye was the coordinated multipronged attack. In the past, the NeHaw had simply tried the brute force method of overwhelming their opponent. This attack was well thought out and properly timed to tie up all the Earth forces on site. The fact that the space station modules and ALICE-3, for that matter, were new additions meant that the NeHaw had likely needed to modify their attack plans to changing conditions.

Checking her IFF indicator display, she could see that P5 and P8 had done a good job of covering their area of responsibility. P8 had engaged and destroyed almost half of the missiles launched at the shipyard, while P5 had engaged the enemy directly. However, their counterparts P10 and P13 had been completely duped. As both vessels sat engaged with the enemy ships, and almost fifty missiles charged unchallenged toward the construction zone.

She only hoped that the damage about to be done to the shipyard was not debilitating.

----*----

"Sir, our hull is showing signs of weakness in several areas. We cannot safely continue this engagement," the tactical officer reported to GeSec. Just then, he noted several explosions in the shipyard as a host of missiles found their targets. As if to balance the victory, the cruiser engaging two of those devil ships exploded in a plume of white.

"Order a full retreat, all ships to return home," GeSec commanded as he watched several more detonations in the Wawobash shipyard. He verified that the damage was being recorded for High Command to analyze. He then ran over the data from the ship's engineer, estimating his own hull damage. As the first of its kind, this cruiser was designed specifically to battle the Earth's weapons that had been so devastatingly effective.

The NeHaw had been working with several races, scouring the empire for technology and materials capable of withstanding the impact of those projectiles. This ship had been the result of that research, and this was its trial by fire.

"All ships acknowledging, setting course for home," the navigation officer replied. As he continued to watch the ships around him explode, GeSec had a sense of accomplishment. His mission goals had been met, and while he hadn't inflicted the damage he had hoped on the Wawobash, they had made their presence known.

GeSec checked his display, confirming all surviving vessels had disengaged from the enemy and were heading to the edge of the system with all haste. He noted the loss of two cruisers and more than twenty assorted supporting craft. He suspected that the new High Commander would confirm this as a success.

More importantly, GeSec was pleased with their own survival. The improved shields and hull plating had increased their survivability in confronting human weapons. Now if they could just do the same for their offensive capabilities.

----*----

Brian double-checked his tactical display to confirm his estimation that the NeHaw were, in fact, retreating. While ALICE-3 had managed to intercept and destroy some of the incoming missiles, far too many had found a target in the shipyard. He could hear his communications officer in an exchange with the Wawobash as she worked getting a damage report. He feared it was not going to be good.

65

"Sir, the commander of P5, reports the NeHaw are retreating. He wants to know if they should pursue?" the tactical officer asked.

"Negative, have them hold their positions until we are sure the NeHaw are leaving the system. I don't want everyone drawn away from their positions, only to have to face the second wave of attacks," Brian replied as they watched the P5 patrol craft take a stationary position, while P8 rejoined its wingman after chasing down a number of the missiles fired at the shipyard.

That thought had Brian turning his attention to the damage caused by the NeHaw. Although the Wawobash had a vast area of space around their homeworld converted to ship construction, only specific parts were dedicated to military applications. From the initial reports, those were the areas targeted by the missile strikes.

He suspected it would be some time before the total damage assessment was completed, but he was positive the damage was extensive.

Chapter 7

The remaining two days the Phantom spent on its return to Earth found its occupants tied up in after-action reviews of the attack on the Wawobash shipyard. The loss of one of the three space station modules was the least of Jake's concerns from the early analysis. Since the remaining two were deemed space worthy, despite the pounding they took, they were released for delivery. The mystery NeHaw cruiser occupied most of their time and conversation.

By the time the Phantom had touched down on Earth, both surviving space station modules had arrived, with Kola acting as the assembly supervisor. She had taken up a position at the edge of the solar system, to act as a surrogate gate guard until the real space station could be made operational. The end goal was to create a fortress at the rim of the solar system, and this one had already shown its battle worth, hindered as it was without the human upgrades.

While the Phantom was normally housed in Texas, Jake had decided to set it down in Nevada first, allowing them to offload all the Intel they had gathered before having the ship returned to Texas for processing. In the care of Dallas, the ALICE system there, it would be repaired, refitted, and readied for the next possible mission.

The Nevada desert was sunny and warm as it was now midsummer. Jake could see the heat waves shimmering across the barren landscape from the bridge window as they descended. As he guided the ship down, the massive hangar doors retracted, providing a sizeable opening for him to drop the ship through.

Once inside, it took him a moment to adjust to the relative darkness of the hangar, in comparison to the bright daylight above. He paused in his descent until he could see properly, moving to the displays on his console to verify a clear landing space below and to his right. Sliding the Phantom right, he finished his descent, resting softly on the ships landing struts.

"Home, sweet home," he announced to the other occupants on the bridge.

Ivan and Edwin had joined him and Hannah on the bridge, as they prepared to land. Jake knew the two men had spent a considerable amount of time on the ship and were more than familiar with its operation. On more than one occasion, he caught the Russian checking his piloting from the navigation chair, as Hannah had taken the copilots seat, at Jake's request.

"Hannah, please go below and see to the transfer of the Intel take for analysis," Jake asked the SAS trooper.

"Yes, sir," she replied as she rose from the copilot's seat.

"And don't let them give you or Sam any flack. She is in charge of that material until I say otherwise," Jake said sternly.

He saw the smile cross Hannah's face as she nodded in reply. The two women had worked tirelessly for the last two days, and Jake intended to see that they were properly recognized. Turning back to the bridge windows, he could see the expected reception committee standing nearby.

"Glad to be home, old son?" Edwin asked as he started to rise.

"Maybe," Jake replied as he pointed to the crowd outside. Edwin granted him a smile and a nod of understanding. While he was glad to be home, he had enjoyed the relative quiet of the last few days. From the crowd gathered outside, he expected that would be a distant memory all too soon.

----*----

With the space station modules delivered to Earth, Brian and ALICE-3 were doing their own damage assessments and defensive planning. Although they had offered to assist the Wawobash in repairing the significant amount of destruction caused by the NeHaw attack, they were politely refused. Brian felt like it was the apprentice asking to fix things for the master builder.

As he reviewed the shipyard repairs currently underway, he was amazed at how the Wawobash had attacked the problem. Rather than repairing the damaged areas, they simply removed the infrastructure and reorganized. The shipyard was evidently built-in modular sections allowing the Wawobash to reconfigure their infrastructure based on the required workload.

Here the damaged modules were removed, and the voids were filled with modules from other parts of the shipyard. ALICE-3 estimated that the military construction would be back to full production in less than two months.

The other good news was the space station modules still under construction had survived the attack, mostly unscathed. Two had been lightly damaged, requiring delivery delays as they rebuilt portions of the saucer skin. The module destroyed in the fighting would have to be completely rebuilt, and so would be the last for delivery.

Brian had been instructed to inform the Wawobash no penalties would be incurred due to late delivery, and the replacement module would be paid for in full. While that seemed obvious to Brian, something hardly worth mentioning, the emissary he spoke with appeared visibly relieved to hear the news. It again reminded him why he was never going to be a diplomat.

"Brian, I have received word that all four patrol craft is in position," ALICE-3 announced.

"Thanks," Brian answered absently as he checked their own position just off the shipyards.

Once the NeHaw had retreated from the fight and eventually left the system, it had been suggested that they might have left some ships behind to harass shipping to and from Wawobash. Brian had ordered the four patrol craft to search the flight path common to normal space traffic, looking for any signs of ambush.

After a thorough sweep of the area and an all-clear declared, ALICE-3 had proposed placing the four ships at the midway point, replicating the position of the space station modules. While significantly smaller than the modules, their additional railgun firepower and stasis shields gave them similar abilities should another attack come.

Because the NeHaw were acting in an uncharacteristic manner, no one would dispute the possibility of a return visit so soon. As he scanned the status logs, Brian let out a sigh. He had the feeling they were going to be here for a very long time.

----*----

Jacob was standing above Assembly Bay Two, watching the latest batch of combat patrol craft being constructed. By now, they had released more than enough transport models to meet the needs here on Earth and had cut over to the combat model almost exclusively.

He was gratified with all the reports he was receiving of the successes of the ships they produced here. Even though they were not FTL capable, their firepower and toughness made them a hit with their crews. As he stood there, he referred to the touchpad he was carrying several times, comparing its status to what he was observing.

To any casual onlooker, it would be clear the man was agitated. Jacob was concerned that the materials he needed to complete these ships wouldn't arrive in time. Things were on such a tight schedule that any material shipment delays would halt the assembly process and tie up all the assembly bays.

"How is it looking, Luv?" Jacob heard in a British accent, as a redheaded woman took his arm and gave him a squeeze.

Gemma had become his right arm since first arriving from London. The daughter of the head of a British facility outside of London, she had chosen to come to Hawaii as part of an exchange program. She and Jacob had fallen for each other almost immediately, without the knowledge of who each was back home.

Their coming out had been a surprise to each other as much as their families. She had thought him nothing more than the head of manufacturing, and he thought she just

70

another engineer, escaping the English weather. While Jake was elated at the union, Gemma's mother had other opinions on the subject.

"I am afraid that our entire operation here might be brought to a standstill if Robert doesn't get that plate steel here in time," Jacob replied while returning the squeeze.

"Let me see that," she replied affectionately while taking the pad from Jacob's hands and scanning through the displays.

"How about we stop work in Bay Three and just concentrate on the builds in One and Two. That way, we can clear them and ensure we don't stall in all three?" Gemma asked as she continued to flip through the screens. Satisfied at her assessment, she offered the pad back to Jacob.

Taking the offered pad, Jacob moved through several screens until he found what he was looking for. Tapping out a few instructions, he handed Gemma the pad back for her review.

"Consider it done!" he said with a smile.

"Excellent, now come with me," she replied with a dazzling smile of her own.

Jacob found himself being led back into the facility and down into the family area of the crew's quarters. He was surprised to discover a number of children playing in one of the recreation rooms there. The entire area had been built with long term family occupancy in mind, and as such, it was well equipped with a number of entertainment and recreation zones.

Lanai itself was one of the lesser populated ALICE facilities, if, for no other reason than its primary function, shipbuilding didn't require a lot of on-hand personnel. It was, however, a very popular R&R destination, one of the few places that allowed staff to go outside, unencumbered with combat suits. Jacob assumed that many of these families were here just to enjoy time outside in safety.

As Gemma led him down the halls, his hand firmly in her grasp, he realized he had never even visited the recreational facilities here. With his constant workload and the ever-increasing demands, his life was one of continuous work. He was considering this as Gemma stopped in front of one of the personnel quarter's doors on this level. With a flourish, she waved it open and led him inside.

Standing in the main room, they had passed one bathroom located on their right as they entered. The main room itself consisted of a lounging area with a pair of couches and two overstuffed chairs on one side. The other side had a large dining room table with eight chairs, all of dark wood.

Farther back, behind the table and chairs, was a small kitchen. As he crossed the room, Jacob could see it had everything one would need to cook their own meals, should you choose that option over Lanai's automated kitchens. He could see that the automated option was available as well, with one of the walls holding the familiar door in the wall where the automated deliveries arrived.

"Come see," Gemma said as she led him further into the quarters. On the back wall was an opening to a hall that led into three bedrooms and a bathroom accessed from the hall. The master bedroom was at the end and included a spacious sitting area, king-size bed, and included an en suite bathroom. All in all, Jacob counted a 3 bedroom, 3 bath family unit.

"Now, I have saved the best for last," Gemma said with a smile as she led Jacob back into the hall and into one of the smaller bedrooms. Here, he found a completely furnished nursery, with everything one might need to care for a newborn.

"Gemma, what is all this?" Jacob asked, confused by the tour.

"I asked Lanai where the Commanding Officer's family lived. She said that this was one of several officer's quarters that served that purpose. She was able to send some bots out shopping for me on the other islands and gathered everything I needed to decorate it properly," she replied, obviously quite proud of her accomplishment.

"Well, it's beautiful, but the wedding isn't for a few months yet. You know how your mother has been procrastinating. Besides, my place is plenty big enough for the two of us," Jacob replied as he took her hands in his.

"Jacob, this room isn't for show," Gemma replied softly.

As it hit Jacob that they were standing in the nursery, his heart leaped, and he swept Gemma up. His kiss was gentle but firm. Suddenly, he stopped, and he held her out at arm's length.

"Your mom is going to shit."

----*----

Jake was sitting in his quarters, tablet in hand, as he scanned the backlog of reports that had stacked up in his absence. As he expected, everyone was more than holding up their areas of responsibility, so he was just trying to catch up. While he read, Sara sat on the couch, looking particularly miserable as she shifted around, trying to find a comfortable position.

"Can I get you anything?" he asked as she finally settled in place.

"A new body!" she replied before yielding him a weak smile.

Jake wisely chose not to remind her that this was something she had wanted. Granted, the twins were not in the equation at the time, but he firmly believed you had to be careful what you wished for. He provided the most sympathetic smile he could and went back to his reading.

The Phantom had set down midday local time, and from the moment he exited the ship until now, he had been in continuous debriefings. Between providing all the intimate details of their own mission to reviewing the events at Wawobash, Jake and the others had attempted to cover weeks of activity in seven hours.

During that time, he had both Hannah and Sam come in and report their own observations. He would have liked to have Sergeant Carson there as well, but the sergeant was

73

currently working with Kola, who was getting the space station sections assembled.

The sergeant and the men and women with him were training in the combat patrol ships at the edge of the solar system. As fighting vessels, the Lanai built craft had proven the most popular with the troops. Jake suspected it had something to do with the overabundance of weaponry, a compensation for their lack of FTL capabilities. If they couldn't run, they needed to fight like hell.

While the Earth had a significant number of ships, mostly destroyers, acting as convoy protection for the allied planets, the Lanai ships were 100% combat vessels, made to engage and destroy enemy ships, period. Their success in that capacity had freed up the rest of the fleet for interstellar use, while they remained behind to protect Earth.

"Oh god, I need to pee again," Sara suddenly announced. Jake quickly rose to help her up and then watched as she headed into the bedroom.

"I think I am going to lay down after," she added, giving him the briefest smile and a quick kiss before she disappeared.

"I'll be there shortly," Jake answered sympathetically as he returned to his seat. He had noticed that since his return, Sara had not left his side. She had attended every debrief of the day, sitting quietly at his side. While he wasn't tired, he knew better than to leave her alone just yet, and so intended to go join her soon.

With a nod of understanding, he went back to his reports, just happy to be home.

----*----

Colonel Bo Chao was not quite sure what to make of the American sitting across from him. While he had never met the man before, he was well aware of his reputation as Colonel Thomas's logistics officer. Technically a Major, the Americans didn't stand on ceremony when it came to non-combat assignments.

"As you can see, I have a significant number of moderately armed transport ships at my disposal," Robert Jacobson stated as he indicated the paperwork in front of Bo.

"And you wish to train with my men for combat?" Bo asked skeptically.

"Yes. I have the prime resource for moving large quantities anywhere on the planet. You have the largest concentrated force on the planet. It seems logical that we should plan for such a need?' Robert replied.

"Does Colonel Thomas know of this?" Bo asked.

"No, he has been unavailable, as you may have heard. However, I have discussed the subject with my wife, and she thinks it's a great idea," Robert answered with a smile.

"Your wife?" Bo asked flatly, his composure slipping for a second.

"Yes. We talked it over, and she sees great value in the idea. By the way, I should mention she is the commander of the ALICE facility in Texas and Lt Colonel Sullivan's sister," Robert replied with a broad smile.

Bo realized he had been played by underestimating the connections Robert had, then answered with a smile of his own. Americans had very strange ideas of humor.

"So, where exactly were you thinking we would be practicing these assault landings?" Bo asked after a moment.

"The moon," Robert replied, turning quite serious.

After a moment, Bo nodded with a much more genuine smile.

"Your wife was right, that is an excellent idea."

Chapter 8

Jake awoke in the stillness of his personal quarters deep in the Alice-1 facility. He was immediately aware of the warmth of his beloved Sara, still snuggled up close to his bareback. A smile crossed his face as he also felt her a rather large baby bump against his spine. More than anything, he wanted to gently wake her, embrace her tenderly, and spend the day with her.

The time away from her, the difficulties in returning home, and the fighting yet to come, all had him basking in the moment. Her slow, steady breathing was like a siren's call, beckoning him to stay in bed with her.

More than anything, he wanted to live what most would consider a normal life with her. However, Jake's life would never be normal, and before that thought was through his mind, he questioned if that was ok with Sara. The other women in his life would always be a source of chaos and confusion, but excluding them was not an option.

His life was one of turmoil, and he desperately did not want that to be the case for his children and his grandchildren. That thought filled him with an unshakable resolve to secure a future for more than just him and Sara. Carefully, he slipped from the bed, leaving Sara asleep. Turning as he rose, he looked down at her and smiled again, but as he headed to the other room to change, he set his jaw for the tough road ahead.

Dressed in his usual workout clothing, Jake had left a slumbering Sara to get a workout in before starting his day. The time aboard the Phantom had left him little opportunity to exercise as he liked, so he was motivated. Sometimes, he just needed to break a sweat to get his thoughts in order.

He grabbed one of the elevators, dropping to the level that contained the gym as well as other recreational distractions for the staff. Entering the gym, he was greeted by a sea of unfamiliar faces, none who gave him more than a passing glance as he moved to the open mat to begin stretching.

It was times like this that Jake appreciated the anonymity he enjoyed. As their operation had grown, he had felt no need to ensure everyone knew who he was. It was quite the opposite, in fact, as he deemed the facility commanders should be the face of their authority. That was why he could enter the gym without throwing the place into disarray, appearing no more than any other staff member.

While he stretched, he subtly observed those working out around him. He could see a good mix of men and women, and he detected several nationalities. He was happy to see there were as many mixed groups as there were clusters of like individuals. He could identify the combination of Chinese, Russian, American, Brits, and Aussie's, although, with the last, he was not sophisticated enough to pick the accents apart. They were just different.

By now, he had warmed up and was ready to begin his cardio. Using the Exercycle before going on the treadmill, he utilized both devices extensively. Both devices had changed little in the eighty-plus years between when he went into stasis and the bombing by the NeHaw. Both did now have a hologram mode where one could choose to be anywhere in the world while doing their workout. Jake, however, chose not to activate that option.

It was as he started the strength training that he was approached.

"Colonel, might I have a word? You are Colonel Thomas, right?" a young woman asked with a slight accent as she stepped up to the exercise machine Jake was using.

"Yeah, that's me, how can I help you," Jake replied with a smile. While he hated interruptions when working out, he had a firm open door policy when it came to anyone who reported to him, and these days that was just about everyone. He continued to work the exercise machine as he waited for the young woman to reply.

"Sir, my name is Private Grace Middleton, and I am from Georgia," she replied. Jake could now detect the distinct southern accent the young woman sported.

"I have been told that anyone wishing to transfer to ALICE-9 in Georgia must have your specific approval to do so?" she added.

The mention of ALICE-9 made Jake stop what he was doing and give Grace his undivided attention. Most had known that before the first NeHaw attack, ALICE-9, then ALICE -3, had been a weapons research facility. It had been chartered with trying to replicate advanced alien weapons, things translated from the crashed NeHaw exploration ship's data stores.

What only Jake and the ALICEs were aware of was, they had successfully replicated several weapons from the NeHaw forbidden weapons reference, due to a mistake in translation. There were things stored in the security vaults in Georgia that could obliterate the sun, thus destroying the entire solar system.

With the scare over the system crash and the eventual emergence of ALICE-9, Jake had taken personal control over anything involving ALICE-9 or her occupants.

"Why are you interested in ALICE-9?" Jake asked calmly, his demeanor trying to hide his anxiety.

"As I said, I am from that area. It is my impression that we are not doing much to improve the circumstances of the people there. Now don't get me wrong, I am not complaining, as I was recruited from there. It's just that I have been told that we are not looking to sponsor any nearby communities, nor are we increasing our presence there," Grace replied.

The last time Jake had been to Georgia, it was to secure one of the doomsday devices he had planned to use as a last resort in the attack of the alien armada. Thankfully, it had proved to be unnecessary, and he quickly locked the weapon safely away. Since then, he had limited the staff to those ALICE-9 required to operate, plus a substantial security team made up of his most trusted personnel. There were a small number of people restoring damaged art as well, but they were restricted to the upper levels.

It was for all these reasons that Jake had not promoted the idea of sponsoring or expanding into the local communities, to minimize the damage there. In part, he knew it was irrational, as any accidental discharge would destroy the entire planet, not just Georgia. However, he was not at all interested in increasing the number of people occupying the location. Just one mistake from a well-meaning staff member and all was lost.

"I completely understand your interest in helping your friends and family. However, it is well known that the facility there was used in weapons research, and we have not been able to ensure everyone's safety as of yet," Jake replied, drawing upon the cover story he had created early on.

"I am prepared to dedicate my life to making it a safe place to be. Since arriving here, I have been studying hard to learn what is necessary to repair what was damaged. I must say, however, getting information on that has proven challenging," she said with a shrug.

"I have also worked for Miss Patti as an analyst, before transferring to go to boot camp," she added, in an apparent hope to get on Jake's good side.

Jake knew a fanatic when he saw one, or to be fair, a woman passionate about helping her family. It would not be an easy thing to sway her focus. After a few minutes, he nodded.

"Let me think about it. I will contact you by tomorrow, and we can talk more," he replied, and then went back to exercising. As Grace walked away, he stared at her back without really seeing her. ALICE-9 did deserve better than she had been getting as well as the people in the southeast. Jake just needed to find a safe way to do it.

----*----

Patti was sitting in her office in the London facility, going over all the activity reports for the last few months. It was clear from all the engagements that they were now in a real space war with the NeHaw. All indications were that the

NeHaw General, who had seized power, was rooting out the political commanders and replacing them with actual fighting men. Well, rather, fighting NeHaw.

While neither side had scored a decisive victory against the other since the destruction of the armada that had attacked Earth, the number of overall actions of a serious nature was way up. Before, Patti could count on convoy harassment or the occasional planetary raid on an aligned world. These were usually short fought, and the NeHaw would run at the first sign of reinforcements.

Now they were seeing concentrated attacks, like the one on Wawobash, as well as devices designed to trap the Earth ship, blocking FTL capabilities. This prevented small groups of Earth aligned ships from running when ambushed by superior numbers.

Also, in the past, the unexpected discovery of a capital ship like battleship ALICE-3 would have aborted an attack, sending the NeHaw home to regroup. Now they pressed on, adapting to the circumstances. Everything she had seen so far gave the NeHaw a plus one on that effort, as they had inflicted a measurable amount of damage and lived to fight another day.

The problem was in all these activities, Patti was not seeing a clear objective giving Earth a path to victory. It was possible that destroying the NeHaw homeworld would so devastate and demoralize them that they would give up. However, like the nuclear strategies of Earth's 20th and 21st centuries, the ships at sea had the ability to retaliate. Destroying their homeworld might only give them a greater reason to fight.

Another option was to destabilize the NeHaw aligned worlds, creating internal discord and forcing the NeHaw to focus inward. This was something they had already achieved, to a small extent, but it was far from enough to get them to leave Earth alone. If Earth chose to increase the internal disruptions, they would need to start considering attacks on the supporting planets, something they had hoped to avoid preferring to draw on them as allies.

There had been a hope that in freeing the oppressed planets, they would take up arms and work to overthrow the NeHaw. Some had done just that, like the five treaty planets that had come to Earth and established relations. They came in hopes of deposing the NeHaw once and for all. Otherworlds, however, had chosen to stay and support the NeHaw, whether out of fear or better the devil you know, Patti wasn't exactly sure.

Jake's latest attack on a military installation on an abandoned world was how she hoped to see things continue. She felt they needed to keep the fighting away from the civilized worlds for fear of ostracizing Earth. Nothing in her research had led her to believe creating hardships on civilian populations, as the NeHaw had attempted to do on Klinan, would help in their efforts.

Putting her thoughts in a memo, she shot the missive off to her team in Nevada, for more consideration. She knew the gang in "Patti's Pit" would attack the problem with enthusiasm.

----*----

Bonnie was used to Robert bringing back all kinds of odd things in his travels around the world. She had seen him arrive with everything from fine art to piles of gold, silver, and other precious metals and even cattle and other livestock. So it was with this in mind that she stood watching the line of Chinese combat vehicles being offloaded in the main hangar.

"Hi, honey. You know Colonel Bo don't you?" Robert asked as he led the Chinese Colonel from the transport and over to where Bonnie was standing.

The roof hangar doors in the Texas, Nevada, and Alaska ALICE facilities had been modified to more easily accept the oversized Lanai transport ships. It had taken over a year to enlarge the openings sufficiently to accept the ships. Not originally designed for use inside the hangars, the ships had become invaluable in moving vast amounts of cargo and people around the world in record time.

"Colonel, it is a pleasure," Bonnie replied as she took the offered hand. As she was a Major to his superior rank, she should have displayed more deference, but neither seemed interested in standing on ceremony.

"Major, the pleasure is mine," Colonel Bo replied, accepting the offered hand and adding a slight bow of respect, one Bonnie returned.

"Dear, why are you bringing me armor?" Bonnie asked while waving at the rows of existing American armor already lining the back walls of the hangar.

"This is not for you. Colonel Bo and I are working on a project, and we need the use of your facility in upgrading his equipment," Robert replied with a smile, recognizing the trigger word every husband understood. When your wife uses "Dear," it's not in affection.

"Your husband has proposed a solution to several of my problems, and I am very thankful for your support in this," Colonel Bo offered.

"We need to make his armor space worthy. Remember our conversation?" Robert added.

Bonnie recalled a discussion she had with her husband regarding using the transport ships as landing craft. Considering that was in part why Jake had ordered the ships built in the first place, it was an easy thing to agree to. However, she was now beginning to see her husband had taken the concept and ran with it.

"My equipment is already quite airtight, well mostly. It was designed to withstand chemical attacks and temperature variances of great magnitude. We feel conversion to alien environments won't require a great deal of modification," Chao explained as they continued to watch the tracked and wheeled vehicles roll out of the transport.

Bonnie just nodded as she looked at the two men, both appearing anxious to hear her response.

"I would upgrade the weapons systems as well. Not all planets will support your current firepower," she said with a sigh. With that, she turned and headed back inside, leaving the two men smiling broadly.

----*----

James had been doing his best to quietly keep the South Dakota ALICE facility on track and continuing to meet the manufacturing needs of the Earth's armed forces while Dakota, the new ALICE system, matured. Early on, he had the help of several of the other ALICEs as Dakota was gently educated on who and what she was. Now, they would occasionally check in on the newborn's progress.

Unlike poor ALICE-9, who came to life after an unexpected reboot of the core computer systems that made them who they were, Dakota was a result of a brain transfer of sorts. Kola, the Artificial Life that controlled the massive space carrier currently at the edge of the solar system, was methodically transferred from her South Dakota home and into the ship.

Once she was safely resurrected, Dakota was brought to life in her place. Since then, she had been groomed to become an independent member of the ALICE community. Where Kola had been anxious to escape her terrestrial confinement, Dakota was anxious to assume her role as master of the South Dakota location.

So, it was with some concern that James began the conversation with Dakota regarding their latest request. Her enthusiasm had possibly allowed her to bite off more than she could chew.

"I see you have accepted the order from Dallas," he began as he seated himself at his desk in his quarters.

"I assume you are referring to the combat suit request for the Chinese, the ones capable of extended use in space," Dakota replied.

James noted she still had an overly formal tone to her speech as they talked. Jake had promoted the concept of individuality for the ALICEs, but at heart, they were computers first. He wondered how much of the personality has been just for show.

"Eighteen thousand five hundred units to start?" he asked.

"I believe the five hundred are intended as spares," Dakota answered, causing James to laugh aloud.

"Regardless, you are not concerned about meeting their delivery requests?" James asked as he double-checked the timeline.

"My sisters have assured me that the materials required are in the existing inventory. The deliveries will be in lots of 3,000, so I should become faster as I progress. In addition, the necessary sizes only fall into three standard categories," Dakota theorized.

"And the weapons?" James asked, changing the subject.

"We have a significant number of those on hand already. The larger weapons for the vehicles will be more challenging, but I have secured assistance from ALICE-4 in Washington State."

"And Dallas will handle the installation in Texas?" James asked, seeing the notation in the documentation.

"Yes, she is better equipped to perform the installation than I. Besides, all the vehicles are currently under refit there as it is. While they are making them airtight, they can exchange the weapons systems," Dakota replied confidently.

As she was speaking, James brought up the plans for the armor refit on his display. While the alterations to each type of vehicle were extensive, the use of alien technology made the additions less intrusive. There were two large changes in the works. The first was the addition of environmental controls, providing a breathable atmosphere, even in the vacuum of space.

The second was swapping out the power plant, removing the diesel engines, and replacing them with the same electric powered systems that the US equipment used. Like the others, they could be operated for extended periods between charges and had hot-swappable power packs for quick turnaround.

The recovered space, where the large diesel engine once lived, plus the exchange of human electronics for alien controls, gave the vehicles a much roomier interior. Even so, the thought of cramming four or five people into the small compartment of those vehicles for possibly days was not something James found enticing.

Like everyone else, he was well acquainted with the Battle of Klinan. There the humans had defeated an alien force in an environment unwelcoming to humans. That engagement was over quickly and did not require days in the field for the troops. These, however, were being prepared to fight in locations unfit for any life forms at all, and for days at a time.

"I'm glad I'm not going," was all James could say before shutting his display off for the night.

Chapter 9

Jake had been buried in work all day, but the question of ALICE-9 had never left the back of his mind. Grace had forced him to acknowledge his neglect of that region of the US, solely because of the contents of that facility. While the secure weapons store, buried deep in the Earth, was inaccessible to anyone but Jake, he still had nightmares of someone accidentally wandering into the vaults.

He had allowed Jessie and Helen to leverage the capabilities of ALICE-9 in their art recovery and restoration work, but that staff was limited to a select few, and they were not permitted in the lower levels. His motivations for that concession had nothing to do with a love of Art.

ALICE-9 desperately needed the human interactions, and Jake was doing everything he could to swing Helen over to his side regarding Gemma and Jacob. The announcement of the engagement of his grandson to Helen and Nigel's daughter had not gone well with Helen.

While Nigel was ecstatic, Helen's more traditional attitudes had questioned if Jacob was of proper heritage. It was ALICE's discovery of a forgotten knighthood, presented to Jake for services to the crown while he was in the Middle East, which had softened her opinion. Even so, she was still not overjoyed at the pending nuptials.

Presently, Jake was enjoying a moment of solitude as he sat in his office just off the command center in Nevada. He had a map of the US up on his display as he considered the question Grace has posed to him.

She was accurate in describing the situation. Most of what he would call the Deep South was completely ignored. While all the other locations had sponsored at least one local community, some several, Florida, Georgia, Alabama, Mississippi, Tennessee, and the Carolinas were a dead zone for them.

"ALICE, am I being paranoid about the ALICE-9 situation?" Jake finally asked, desperate for counsel on the subject.

"Your concerns over the lethality of the contents there are justified. Compounded by the natural curiosity of humans, limiting access, there is a valid precaution," ALICE replied.

"What do you mean, human curiosity?" Jake asked.

"There have been several attempts to access information relating to the nature of that facility and its contents. Private Middleton is not the only one attempting to discover its secrets," ALICE replied.

Jake had instituted a total blackout on information related to the work in Georgia prior to the attack by the NeHaw, so long ago. Besides burying the research, he had the source material used by the scientists segmented and move to computers only accessible in the vaults. Even the ALICEs couldn't get to the data.

"Who?" Jake asked, curious at the reference.

"Mostly, analysts challenged with finding ways of defeating the NeHaw, nothing unusual. Private Middleton, however, has been most persistent in her attempts to discover the issues preventing its use. In addition, she is quite intelligent and has been absorbing knowledge at a voracious rate. Her math, physics, chemistry, and biology scores are top of her class," ALICE answered.

Jake was always pleased to see recruits excelling at their chosen path. In this case, however, it indicated he was not likely to divert her attention.

"Recommendations?" he asked after a moment.

"Let her," ALICE replied lightly.

"I beg your pardon?" Jake answered quickly, not expecting the response.

"She is not yet ready to take on the tasks required of her, and she has already been working with ALICE-9 in her research. The two have developed a rapport that has supplemented your unavailability during your absence. Let her continue her studies and research of the southern states with ALICE-9. It will serve both her desire to do right by her family and friends while giving ALICE-9 much needed human interaction."

87

Jake understood he was being chastised for his neglect of ALICE-9. Early on, he had done all he could to work with the newborn, helping with her transition from feral to an integrated family member. His workload of late had been such that his once daily conversations with her had all but ceased.

"And when Grace finishes school?" Jake asked, pushing his own guilt aside.

"Then we will make her a facility's commander, or at least the second in command. Put her in a position of authority where she will need to consider the ramifications of her decisions. Possibly she will want a role in contracting and negotiating with local communities as Sandy does.

The responsibilities of such positions will have her occupied for years to come. In the meantime, I have ALICE-9 and others, adding additional security to the vaults. Currently, only your DNA will allow passage into the chamber housing the weapons."

"I hope you are right about this," Jake said with a shudder.

----*----

Leftanant Daniel Atkins was up late, reviewing the latest equipment order placed by the Chinese. Jake had insisted all such information was to be freely distributed, a policy Daniel appreciated very much. As he had been working on similar issues for the SAS teams, Daniel noted the differences between this list and his own. His was an outline for subtle, surgical strikes while the Chinese were preparing to batter the enemy into submission.

Earlier, he had been reading the reports filed by Sergeant Carson and the other SAS troopers from covering the action with Colonel Thomas. He wanted to see if they had experienced any issues with their gear in the last action. None had complained about the equipment beyond its uniformity.

In his earlier research, Daniel had identified possible targets of interest in NeHaw held space. He identified several planets that held targets of military importance, where a small insertion team could affect a lot of damage. He also acknowledged the challenges of inserting undetected into alien environments, where blending in with the locals was an impossibility.

The combination of the two had Daniel thinking about placing his own order with the Yanks. He just needed to find someone willing to help him design the special equipment they needed.

----*----

HeBak had been hiding out on Earth for many cycles now, no closer to his end goal than the day he was discovered hiding at the bottom of a lake in a place the humans called Russia. Many things had occurred since then that had found him trading small pieces of technology and information for payment the humans considered minor.

The creatures had been true to their word, though, and his hold was filled with more wealth than he would ever spend in his lifetime. The sums paid represented a fortune to the NeHaw.

That was of little value to him at the moment. Unfortunately, as the closest planet, he could spend it on was considered a war zone, and he was on the wrong side of that zone. He knew all this because the humans had allowed him to continue monitoring the communications network. While he was free to receive any communications that sparked interest, his outbound transmissions were heavily censored.

Who or whatever was monitoring his communications seemed to have a sophisticated understanding of the NeHaw language. Even the slightest use of a word or phrase referencing Earth, the humans, or his location was blocked. Unfortunately for HeBak, he, like most others of his kind, cared little for the languages of the subservient races. So rather than risk being labeled a spy, he was quite careful to keep his queries simple and without content concerning the humans.

He was permitted to leave his ship when he chose, which had been moved to a small hangar off to one side of the main area. On occasion, he would don his breathing equipment and wander the open spaces, watching the humans go about their business. It seemed to him they were always in a hurry. Then again, with such a short life span, he presumed he would have been rushed as well.

His one annoyance was the unmanaged constant racket the various radio waves caused around him. Since humans used primitive sound waves to communicate, they paid little attention to the constant barrage of radio transmissions they had rattling around them. Several times, HeBak had to wear headgear the NeHaw had designed specifically to deal with such places. He didn't even attempt to understand the unstructured content. He just did his best to block it out.

Presently, HeBak was scanning the unclassified reports coming from the NeHaw homeworld, describing the new leadership there. As he was used to processing all military reports for the High Command, he could tell even the public information was being managed more closely. Historically, NeHaw had little concern about secret classifications, beyond controlling material considered embarrassing or politically damaging to those in power.

Now he could find very little on ship movements or even boasts of glorious victories. What he did uncover spoke of human atrocities and loss of valuable NeHaw life and wealth. If he didn't know better, HeBak would have guessed that they were lies created to influence the subjugated planets.

The problem this created for HeBak was he could not be sure what planet he could seek refuge on, should he escape the human area of influence. Until then, he would do what NeHaw did best, he would wait.

----*----

Jake contacted Private Middleton and informed her of his decision. At first, the young woman was confused at his explanation but soon became excited at the ramifications. He

90

left her with instructions to continue working with ALICE-9 while she completed her education. Once the ALICEs found her ready, she was to contact him.

Jake had previously talked to ALICE-9, with ALICE included, to outline the restrictions he was placing on Grace. ALICE-9 well understood the critical nature of her weapons store but was excited at the planned growth of her area of responsibility. By the time the conversations were completed, Jake had only a slightly better feeling about things.

By the end of the day, he was ready for a quiet evening alone, but alas, that was not to be. While being uncharacteristically patient since his return, Becky had finally been able to insert herself into Jake's schedule. Having spent the day with him, Sara had left him with a kiss at the door of his quarters before making her way to her own room.

"There you are," Becky announced as Jake entered. From her outfit, Jake assumed she had been waiting for some time, as she had swapped out the medical scrubs she wore at work for a more comfortable option

"I'm sorry, I am late. It's been a crazy day," he replied as he accepted the welcoming kiss.

"Do you want to reschedule?" she asked as she paused mid-kiss, the question more mature than expected

"No," he replied firmly, drawing her to him to finish the motion. He had to admit she felt good as she pressed up against him.

"Now go get cleaned up while I order dinner," she replied while releasing him and pointing to the other room. He did as instructed with little concern for what she would order. By now, they were all familiar with his tastes.

He was surprised to find her attire more conservative than in the past. That didn't mean she was modestly dressed. Rather it meant she was dressed at all. She had chosen a thin-strapped black silk tank top that left her midriff bare. It was paired with a set of small shorts of the same material. On her figure, it made for an appealing combination, which he suspected was the idea.

He found a T-shirt and shorts laid out for him as he passed the bed and entered the bathroom. He quickly undressed, and with a quick shower and grooming completed, he dressed in the clothes provided and arrived in time to see the last of their meal laid out on the small table.

"Just in time," Becky said with a beaming smile. As she motioned for him to join her, he stopped only long enough to pull a drink from the bar near the wall. He could see her wine glass, already half empty, and a small half-filled bottle nearby.

"I wasn't sure..." she started as she motioned at the wine.

"I'm not really in a wine mood," he replied while holding up the beer bottle. While not much of a drinker at all, he did prefer beer to wine when he did drink.

As the two sat chatting all through dinner, Jake found Becky to be more, well, less like a teenager. They discussed Sara and the babies she carried. She updated him on Sandy and the emotional progress she had made since taking on Jon and Padma. The responsibility for the kids had done wonders for her trauma at the hands of General Huang and the loss of Lance Corporal Ramirez.

By the time they had finished dinner, Jake was feeling considerably better and much more relaxed. As they moved to the couch, Jake noted that Becky had poured the last of her wine into the glass she carried before snuggling up next to him while they continued to talk. He was sure she wasn't drunk by any means, but her demeanor was very relaxed.

She fed him all the latest gossip involving Bonnie, Patti, and the rumors of a pregnant Gemma. Jake was excited at the news but suspected Helen would not be so gratified.

"Come with me," Becky suddenly declared as she got up and drained the last of her glass. Taking the offered hand in his, she led him into the bedroom. There she turned in place and lifted his shirt over his head before motioning for him to lay face down on the bed.

After he had done so, he could feel her climb up onto the bed until she straddled him, sitting on his behind. On the table next to the bed, he saw a small bottle labeled oil. He then felt the warm oil on his back as she dripped it across him before beginning a gentle massage. He dropped into a trance as her fingers worked their way into the knotted muscles that lined his spine.

She continued to work her magic, helping him release the tension that had been building since his return. It wasn't until her warm breath on his ear brought him back to reality that he felt her bare skin on his. In one smooth motion, he spun in place, leaving them face to face as he kissed her passionately.

"Just what the doctor ordered," he heard her whisper as they discarded what little clothing remained.

----*----

Even with the negativity of the NeHaw attack on the Wawobash shipyard still fresh in his mind, Brian was happy to watch the next two space station modules make their way to the edge of the system. Considering the last time these modules were attacked when they went out of the shipyards, everyone was on alert. As he sat in his chair on the bridge, he watched the two saucers heading to the edge of the Wawobash system, where four Combat Patrol ships stood waiting.

"I won't notify Earth until the modules are on their way," ALICE-3 commented to Brian in advance of any instructions.

"Good plan," he said with a laugh in his tone. The last time gave them a good reason to wait.

"The Wawobash emissary has included the expected delivery date for the remaining three modules with their release. Everything should be in place in the next few months," ALICE-3 added.

With that comment, Brian pulled up the status report on the two modules already assembled back home. He could see from the images included in the report that a significant amount of work was still being done after the two were stacked, one atop the other with a tube connecting them. Turned on their side, they would appear to be wheels and an axle.

He knew the design called for one of the two currently being shipped to be placed atop the existing two to form a three-layered hub for the station. The remaining four saucers would spoke out from the central module in a ninety-degree radius, allowing for a central hub in 3 dimensions.

Ships could then dock at any of the modules, even in the open areas in the central module, space permitting, although Brian expected that to be an unnecessary risk. There would be plenty of places to dock on the other saucers.

Though the original motivation was to have a fortress at the edge of the solar system, a place for ships to stage for defense or run to the aid of others, Brian was well aware that there was another desire. Earth intended to make the space station a trading center for the many planets they did business with.

The modular design allowed the station to be expanded into three dimensions, growing up and out as needed. With each new section, the added capacity for cargo, servicing and even recreation were to be added. In addition, the firepower and shielding of each saucer gave the station greater protection.

By this time, both modules had reached their departure point, and ALICE-3 did one last check before sending both to meet her sister. Traveling unmanned, they would arrive to find a waiting Kola, prepared to put them in place for attachment to the core structure.

"You know, we are going to be here for a while," Brian said absently, the relief of seeing the space station sections depart unmolested apparent.

"You have a suggestion?" ALICE-3 asked.

"Well, I just thought that this shipyard is the equivalent of a spa to you, perhaps we should get you a manicure?" Brian said with a smile.

"Perhaps!" ALICE-3 replied excitedly

Chapter 10

The following morning Jake woke to find himself alone, Becky having slipped out earlier without disturbing him. Checking the time, he was surprised to see it was well past 10 am, and he should have been up hours ago. Getting up and heading to the shower, he shook his head as the memories of last night replayed.

Becky seemed to have a way of resetting his stress levels like no one else. He felt a twinge of guilt as he recalled Sara's insistence that he cut that tie. While the subject had been dropped well before his departure on the Phantom, he doubted it was forgotten.

Pushing it from his mind, he jumped into the shower, letting the warm water finish the job on his muscles that Becky had started. Rinsing, he turned the shower off and quickly dried, then he dressed for what he expected to be a busy day. Emerging from his bedroom, he was surprised to find breakfast waiting and Patti sitting nearby on the couch.

"Well, what brings you here so early? Aren't you eating?" he asked as he sat at the table and began eating. With all the people making themselves at home in his quarters, he wondered if he shouldn't just have the door removed.

"My day started a while ago, time differences and all, so I just hopped a flight to see my grandpa," she replied as she sipped her coffee.

"How's Daniel?" Jake asked, positive this wasn't a social visit.

"Conflicted. He can't decide if he wants to stay and work with me or go fight aliens. He doesn't know I'm aware of this, so don't say anything to him," she added.

"Not my place," Jake replied and then continued.

"You know what he's going to choose, don't you? Love of a good woman notwithstanding, he will choose to defend you and all this rather than let others do it for him," Jake replied in a conversational tone as if it were not in question.

"Yes, it appears I have chosen a man very much like my grandfather," Patti said in frustration.

"Apparently," Jake replied with a smile.

"With that in mind, I do have a question?" Patti asked.

Here it comes, Jake thought to himself.

"How do you intend to win this thing?" she asked openly.

"I'm not sure," Jake replied after a moment's consideration, not entirely surprised at the question.

"What?" Patti replied, showing surprise at the response.

"By now, I am sure you have realized that simply destroying the NeHaw homeworld won't get it done. They are too spread out over a vast empire, and should we destroy their home planet, we will give them greater motivation to see us wiped out as well. We would be creating an intergalactic blood feud," Jake replied.

"Doesn't it make this fight rather one-sided then? I mean, they can do everything they can to blow us to pieces while we restrict ourselves to lesser means?" Patti replied in frustration.

"I have it on good authority that the NeHaw do have limits to their brutality, and planet busters is one of those boundaries not to be crossed."

"How can you be so sure? I have my people researching every possible solution to this, and so far, no one has found any such weapons in their inventory, much less a restriction on using one," Patti asked, the suspicion clear in her voice.

"Even when we had no idea of their existence, they limited themselves when attacking a defenseless Earth," Jake responded.

"And that's your proof?" she said incredulously.

"Trust me," Jake replied with a smile.

"Great grandma was known to say that those are the words of philanderers and salesmen," Patti replied with a frown.

----*----

96

Jake finished breakfast and led Patti up to the command center. Passing through all the activity inside, the pair went straight into his office, only to find it was already occupied.

"I'm terribly sorry, we were told you were out. We had need of a private place, and Linda escorted us in here," Nigel announced as he stood next to his wife, Helen. The two looked as if they had been in a heated exchange, as Helen's face was quite red.

"No, I'm sorry, I had no idea you were in here. In fact, I was completely unaware you were even in town," Jake replied as he looked at Patti for an explanation.

"I do apologize for not reaching out sooner. Patti and I enjoyed the same flight here, and then I had intended to go north to meet with my wife. In an unexpected turn of events, she chose to come to meet me here," Nigel replied while motioning to Helen.

"Perhaps it is better that you are here," Helen started.

"How so?" Jake replied, without thinking.

"How do you intend on addressing the completely inappropriate behavior of your, your......grandson with our daughter? This situation is completely unacceptable!" she blurted in response.

"I'm afraid you have me at a disadvantage," Jake replied as he realized he had stepped right in the middle of a family argument. The problem was they were about to become his family too.

"Our Gemma has just informed me that she is, well, in a family way," Helen started.

"That's fabulous!" Jake responded before Helen could reply.

Jake quickly swept her up in a hug, his actions taking her completely by surprise. Just as quickly, he set her down and turned away, taking Nigel's hand in his, while passing him a wink of knowing.

Thankfully, Nigel was paying attention enough to catch Jake's attempt to defuse his wife's outrage.

"My thoughts, as well!" Nigel replied as he embraced Jake.

"Yes, well, I…." Helen started before Jake cut her off again.

"Oh my, where are my manners. ALICE, can you send someone to escort Helen to her room so she can freshen up and get settled. We have much to do," Jake declared. Before he had even finished, there was a knock on the door, and two of the command center staff entered.

"Can we help with anything," one of the young women asked.

"Well, I hadn't really intended…" Helen started before Jake cut her off.

"Nonsense, we have some celebrating to do, and plans to make for a London wedding!" Jake replied as he motioned the two forward to escort Helen to her quarters.

"Yes, well, perhaps I should change then," she replied as she let the two young women lead her away. Clearly, a bit confused at the change of direction Jake had introduced.

"Thanks, lad," Nigel offered as he watched his wife being led away.

"Yes, I could see she was building up a head of steam," Jake replied as he motioned Nigel and Patti to open chairs. Taking the seat behind his desk, he let out a sigh.

"Something to drink. Coffee, tea?" he offered.

"Scotch!" Nigel replied as he stood again and headed to the small bar to one side of the room.

"Can I pour for you?" he asked as he raised the bottle.

"A small one for me," Jake replied, not really interested in one at all, but he felt the need to set his guest at ease.

"Me as well, please," Patti added, giving Jake a knowing glance as she did so. Everyone waited until Nigel returned with the three glasses before they spoke again.

"To the kids," Jake said as he raised his glass in a toast after thanking the man.

"So, how do we fix this?" Jake asked.

"You were right on target. Helen will want to see them married quickly, and a London wedding is a must. Westminster Cathedral or even St Paul's Cathedral might do the trick," he replied after a sip from his glass.

"Not to be rude, but is it safe?" Jake asked as he set his glass to one side and switched his attention to the display on his desk. Hitting a few keys on his keyboard, he soon had a holograph visual, depicting the map of London for all three to see.

"As a rule, yes, however, I expect Helen to make an event of this. As such, a large crowd will be in attendance, and it might draw unwanted attention," Nigel replied after some thought.

Once Jake had located the two venues, he switched over to a real-time video feed. All locations deemed strategically important had stationary overhead monitoring satellites.

"We can up the troop count in the area and start regular patrols. That will drive out any troublemakers," Patti offered.

"Shouldn't we be talking to Jacob and Gemma right about now?" Jake asked as he realized they were planning for others.

"Gemma knew bloody well how her mother would take this news. She can just deal with the consequences," Nigel replied with a smile as he held his glass up as if to toast again.

----*----

Kola was nudging the latest arrivals into position, the space station saucers having arrived as expected. ALICE-3 had notified her of their departure and warned her the remaining modules would be later than desired. It was not an issue for her as she enjoyed her position as guardian of the gate at the edge of the solar system.

As if to show off, she was moving both sections into place at the same time. This seemed to put her human occupants at a disadvantage since they couldn't track the movements of both as easily as she could. It was no surprise to her when the Captain split her crew into two, each group responsible for monitoring one of the two modules.

Once she had them both where she wanted them, she would lock the positioning motors in place, syncing them to the other modules. With all modules linked as one, the entire station could be positioned and moved as a single entity. In this configuration, the station could even be flown in FTL from place to place, should the need ever arise.

Once she was satisfied that all was as it should be, she notified her humans.

"Captain, you may begin your work," Kola announced.

"Thank you, Kola," the captain replied.

While Kola missed Brian, as he had transferred to ALICE-3 for the Wawobash guard duty, her new Captain was one of his protégée's. In her early 30's Captain Isabella Connor was a recruit from London. One of the first volunteers, she had risen quickly in the space training program, frequently finishing top of her class.

She had studied in London before the Americans came, working on using the limited technology on hand to watch for aliens. With the windfall of technology and opportunity the Americans had provided, she had flourished.

Kola could tell that life here at the edge of the solar system was thrilling for Isabella, but she was more of a scientist and less a warrior. Apparently, Brian had detected that as well as he had recommended that the combat operations officer, a senior officer formerly under him, also be assigned here. The pair worked well together and seemed to have formed mutual respect.

"Launching construction shuttles," someone on the bridge announced as several small shuttles left one of Kola's hangars and headed to the space station.

The humans on board the shuttles would work both in space and aboard the modules moving the materials stored inside into positions where they could be joined to other modules. Once in the various airlocks, the materials would be moved into a position where the bots, controlled by Kola, would assemble them. These would be the tunnels and elevators that connected the modules with airtight passages, forming a single station.

Once things were stable, Kola had been stocked with provisions and other items destined for use on the station. Besides food and water, the additional armaments and shield generators were hers to install here in space. As it was, the first two modules were well on their way to becoming fully functional and ready for battle.

"Kola, you may now begin as well," she heard Captain Connor announce once the shuttles reached their destinations.

"As you wish," Kola replied, disappointed she couldn't smirk as she replied.

----*----

ALICE was reviewing all the latest status reports from her sisters. With ALICE-3 light-years away and Kola at the edge of the solar system, she was now truly a member of an interstellar race. The newborns, ALICE-9, and Dakota were stable and progressing well. It had been some time since a new ALICE system had been brought online, so the addition of two so close together had been exciting.

Since reawakening Jake, the entire ALICE community had gone from stagnant and bored to active to the point of almost reaching maximum capacity at times. Production facilities in Hawaii, South Dakota, Texas, and Alaska were all producing war materials as quickly as they could. Only ALICE-4 in Washington State was underused, performing supplemental work as she assisted the others.

Nevada, her home, Maine, and Georgia were technically not manufacturing locations. Nevada and Maine now acted more like personnel centers, Georgia not included in that for a good reason. In that, ALICE was gratified to see that the intervention of Private Middleton had opened the door for ALICE-9 to become more active.

Jake's concerns there were valid, as humans did have a tendency to get into trouble when unsupervised. However, the additional security barriers placed there should put his mind at ease. As it was, the work being performed there with the art restoration was giving ALICE-9 enough to do for the moment.

With regards to the art recovery, Jessie and Helen were hosting out of Seven in Alaska. She noted that they had reached the city of New York. Her data store suggested that there were quite a number of museums in the area, and the work there could be substantial.

Unfortunately, it was also an area known to be rife with gangs and other such troublemakers. In her estimation, the area was worse than Los Angeles with regards to outlaws. It was for that reason she could see that Jessie had commandeered the 10th Cavalry once more to work as her security force.

----*----

Joe and Abby were parked on the edge of a rooftop, their hovercycles sitting side by side as they watched the activities below. As the senior members of the 10th, it was their responsibility to oversee its day to day operations and protect the teams working in the transports recovering art.

The 10th Cavalry had been created by Jake as a sort of Special Forces unit, its mission to handle the more unorthodox challenges. As those challenges increased in numbers, the 10th had been required to grow with them. Their ranks had swollen to twice their original numbers with four troops, A, B, C, and D, now included.

Originally Troop Leaders had been reorganized so that Joe oversaw Troops A and B while Abby ran C and D, giving the 10th 18 active participants, themselves included. That was great because the New York effort required every one of them to act in coordination to secure the area for the art recovery teams.

With all the buildings so close together in this area, they had set the transport down in Central Park and were using armored transport vehicles to ferry the ground teams and the recovered items back and forth. In addition, there were a few Marines on the ground embedded with the teams to act as additional security once inside the buildings.

Of everything they had done to date, this operation gave Joe the most concern. With the number of structures and the inability to track movement in the mass of underground tunnels, they were flying blind. He could just imagine roving gangs sneaking in on them unobserved from above.

As it was, the recovery teams below had split up into three groups, each with a 10th Cavalry troop overhead shadowing their movements. The free troop, D Troop, was being held in reserve, in the park below, near the transports, ready to fly at a moment's notice.

"C Troop, spread out a little more, will you? If anyone slips past you and attacks that recovery team, I will have your asses!" Joe heard Abby shout over the open net.

"Acknowledged," was the only reply, although Joe swore he heard a few snickers mixed in.

Chapter 11

Sara was feeling a bit better as she wandered down the hallway, headed to Jake's office. As she did so, she passed Helen being led in the opposite direction with two staff members attending to her. From the small exchange she heard as they passed, she was happy just to smile and wave.

As she entered the command center, she was greeted by several of the staff, all wanting to know how she was. It took her several minutes to cross the open space and finally enter Jake's office. As she crossed the room, Sara wasn't sure what bothered her more. The sympathetic looks from those women who had been where she is now or the looks of horror from those still undecided on ever becoming a mother.

With a quick knock, she slipped inside Jake's office, only to find him deep in conversation with Patti and Nigel.

"Oh, hi, sweetie!" Jake declared as she entered the room. Raising from his desk, he was quickly at her side, helping her to one of the more comfortable chairs near his desk. Sara was more appreciative of the effort while not actually needing the assistance.

"Have you heard the news? Gemma is going to have a baby," Patti offered with Jake and Nigel nodding in agreement.

"The poor girl," was the first words that slipped out of her mouth before she realized it.

"I'm sorry, I didn't mean that," she followed up with, though she very much did mean it.

"I understand. Helen had a difficult pregnancy with Gemma. She got quite ill actually," Nigel said in sympathy.

"Morning sickness," Sara replied with a sigh, trying hard not to snap at the man. She had recently developed a lack of tolerance for any man attempting to empathize with her condition. By definition, it meant putting yourself in the other position, something no man could ever do.

"Something to drink?" Jake asked, waiting for an answer before attempting to return to his chair?

"No, thank you. It will just make me need to pee again," she replied miserably.

"We were just discussing Jacob and Gemma's wedding date. With the latest announcement, we will need to push it up," Patti said as Jake returned to his chair.

"Ah, that explains Helen. I saw her in the hallway on the way here. She looked a bit distracted," Sara replied with a nod.

"Jake, we have a problem in New York," ALICE suddenly interrupted.

With that, a holograph appeared with images of a Lanai transport in a wooded area, tall buildings acting as a backdrop. As they watched and listened, he could hear the distinct sounds of battle and his people giving orders to the forces there.

"ALICE, is that Joe and the 10th I hear?" Jake asked.

"Yes, the 10th is acting as security for the art recovery teams there. I believe they were working around the Metropolitan Museum of Art when a sizeable force emerged from a nearby building to challenge them," ALICE replied.

"Are those armored vehicles?" Nigel asked as they watched the hologram projected over Jake's desk.

"Yes, apparently they were acquired from one of the many military arsenals or armories in the area just outside the city. Their weapons appear to be of the same military-grade," ALICE added.

As the four watched, they could see the recovery teams pulling back to the transport, settled in a large open area nearby, just opposite the museum. To Sara's eye, the 10th was not attempting to destroy the attackers. Rather they were simply providing cover fire for the retreating recovery teams. She was sure all would have been required to wear protective uniforms as part of this effort.

"Has anyone been hurt?" she asked as she watched the last of several vehicles run up the loading ramp and into the transport.

"No, the overhead security forces identified the threat before they could reach the recovery teams. It is fortunate that this happened now as the next targets for recovery are located across the street and mixed in the buildings there. They would have been surrounded."

The group continued to watch as the transport began to rise, the 10th hovercycles standing off in all directions, watching for threats. Hovering just a few hundred feet off the ground, Sara could see they were still taking small arms fire from those on the ground.

She gave them credit, showing restraint in not returning fire on those below. She was well aware of the offensive firepower each of the eighteen hovercycles contained.

"Why aren't they shooting back?" Nigel finally asked as the transport cleared the area, leaving a clustered group of hostiles in the open grassy area below.

"Rules of engagement. These are not combat missions, and as such, any hostiles encountered are assumed to be protecting themselves. At no point in what we observed was any of our people in any real danger. Now, had they been able to field, say a tank or antiaircraft gun that could take out a hovercycle, then they would have been free to remove that threat," Patti explained.

"Our next step will be to try and establish contact with this group and evaluate their intentions. Should they prove belligerent, like the LA gangs, then they will be dealt with in a similar fashion," Patti added.

At the mention of LA, Sara felt a twinge of panic. Her experiences at the hands of the gangs there had left with a lingering paranoia when out in the field. A movement inside her reminded her that those days were behind her and her future lay along a far different path.

"I can see you are about to have your hands full again," Sara stated as she struggled up out of her chair. By the time she was up, Jake was at her side again. Giving him a quick kiss, she excused herself and headed out to try and find her sister Becky. There had to be a way to make this delivery come sooner!

----*----

General KaLob was pleased with the reports covering the attack on the Wawobash shipyards. While he had hoped for greater damage to the production facilities there, the positive results of the prototype cruiser were more than compensation.

Due to the scarcity of the required materials and the special processes required in construction, it would be some time before the NeHaw had a sufficient number of vessels equal to this one cruiser. Still, it was a step in the right direction, and the rumors of the ship's survivability were already making their way throughout the fleet.

He had ordered Commander GeSec back to the upgrade facility for a complete damage assessment and repairs. His hope was that they found it to be adequate for combat or possibly even overbuilt. If they could reduce the amount of materials in its construction, that limited supply could be spread further. This was precisely a case of less is more.

----*----

Jake was back to juggling priorities as he sat in his office, flipping through screen after screen of updates. With the departure of his earlier guests, he had the office all to himself, just the way he liked it. Between Jacob's accelerated nuptials and the outbreak of violence in New York, he had almost missed the latest intel from the allied planets.

Before Sandy had nearly lost her mind after the Hong Kong incident, she had begun negotiations with the treaty planets and other alien races to funnel relevant information of a military nature back to Earth. Jake laughed as it was just a politically correct way of saying spying.

After Sandy checked out, Patti had picked up the baton and run with things. The attack on the field base he led had been the result of information garnered from this network. What bothered Jake, though, was the inability of the Earth to gather their own information.

After much consideration, he resurrected a combination of two concepts from his past. The first was the US Marine's

Scout/Sniper teams, and the second was the Long Range Reconnaissance Patrols or lurps.

By virtue of the interstellar distances involved, every action these units attempted was to be extremely long range, and as such, they needed to be self-sufficient to a greater extent than ever experienced on Earth. In addition, the likelihood that they could survive detection was extremely low, so it was a high-risk unit.

For these reasons, Jake made the force 100% volunteer, and the training curriculum primarily survival training combined with extreme escape and evade. You couldn't even apply unless you were a top marksman to start.

To date, Jake was only aware of a dozen graduates, giving him three teams of four. All members had risen to at least lance corporal before acceptance, and most were veterans of earlier engagements.

It was one of these teams that Jake was focusing on at the moment. A lead had come in on an advanced weapons facility in NeHaw held space. The team had been sent to recon and report, not to engage.

As the first attempt at this type of insertion, Jake was anxious to see that his people were able to get in, gather data, and return safely. So far, their reports only confirmed the presence of facilities with alien activity, but no confirmation of their intent. He flagged the source as a priority one. Should anything more come from the team, he would be notified directly.

----*----

Sergeant Jason Hillestad was the leader of a four-person Marine Scout/Sniper team currently deployed on a hostile alien planet, noted in the NeHaw galactic maps as G-43578. He assumed what they were currently hunkered down in were bushes, but they were nothing like he had ever seen before on Earth.

His team was a split group of men and women, his spotter, and the second shooter, a female corporal. The two would trade off duties depending on the shot and the circumstances, or both act as active shooters if the opportunity allowed. Both veterans of the Battle of Klinan, they had served together a long time. He considered her a hell of a Marine and an excellent shooter, almost as good as himself. Almost.

The other half of his team were newer additions to the Corps, recruited in the buildup after the losses on Klinan. Jason considered them good additions, a brother and sister raised in the woods of Maine, and comfortable living off the land.

Not that it was an option here. While this planet had breathable air and the water could be safely filtered, most of the plant life was either poisonous to eat or had zero nutritional value. The water they could scrounge, but their concentrated foodstuff had been humped in with them.

Earth had started using unmanned drones to scout the NeHaw held worlds suspected of supporting their cause. As intel came available, leading them to target locations, drones would be sent to scout the planets in question. Unfortunately, they were not able to linger, as most were routinely discovered in orbit and destroyed.

Those efforts were not in vain, however as it became clear that the NeHaw monitoring and alerting technology was not immediately identifying the drones as a threat, nor was it effective in dealing with them once discovered. It was not unusual to achieve several orbits of the target planet, transmitting information the entire time, before they would be blasted by the nearest combat vessel.

These successes led to a theory that they could place recon teams on planets undetected if they stayed powered down. Once in place, they would burst transmit their findings at irregularly scheduled intervals, using links to the NeHaw network. The hope was they would not be detected as the network traffic would appear as just another of many sources on the planet. Jason's team was the first attempt at such an incursion.

Graduates of the Scout/Sniper school, they had been pulled from additional training, and the four had been placed on the Lanai Combat Patrol craft, P7, and shipped off to the new space station. Still, under construction at the edge of the solar system, it had already begun operational activities. While in transit, they were briefed on the mission as well as provided two hovercycles for the insertion. Fortunately, they had four days to become familiar with their rides before they used them.

Once they had reached the space station, the team and their equipment had been transferred to a waiting destroyer, D23, where they were whisked in FTL to the drop point at the edge of this system. As the hovercycles had to stay in a stasis bubble while in FTL, they had little time to ready themselves before being pushed out of the destroyer hangar. Jason had a clear memory of watching the destroyer disappear as they sat floating in space before heading to the target world.

He shivered as he recalled the trip in from the edge of this solar system. They had to travel for 23 hours, 17 minutes in open space from the drop point to the edge of the planet's atmosphere, and he remembered every minute of it. Their only means of survival had been their combat suits, sealed and enhanced for the trip. The hovercycles held the EVA packs necessary for each to endure the extended exposure to open space.

The trip inbound had been both terrifying and tedious, as all they could do was wait as they traveled. The entire time, the four watched for any indication they had been discovered and were about to die. Fortunately, the analysts had been correct, and the two hovercycles had reached the LZ undetected, where they sat hidden, waiting for the recall order.

They had landed three days ago, Earth time, as this planet was on a roughly 20-hour cycle of day and night. Those three days had been occupied with trekking from point to point, watching and recording all they saw.

One of the cautions in the mission brief was to minimize their power signature by using as little powered equipment as possible. It was theorized that the alien monitoring systems used equipment that detected the telltale signs of those emissions. As such, they had been provided things like film cameras, pads with pencils for longhand notes, and optical binoculars with no digital enhancements.

When taking digital images for transmission, they were done quickly, with the images embedded in the report at transmission time. The associated reports were recorded in a version of verbal shorthand that provided for the smallest possible file size.

With breathable air, they had shut down most of their suits powered functions, using hand signals when necessary and filtering water at intervals. Only one person would perform the data upload, and the duty was rotated in case the aliens detected the transmission. The signature would then change for the next broadcast, confusing the issue.

From their current location, they were overlooking a vast complex, its purpose completely indiscernible to the team. The mission brief had suggested that there might be manufacturing plants in several locations near the LZ. Their objective was to locate each undetected and to collect as much information about each as possible.

"Sarge," Jason heard softly as he felt a touch on his shoulder. Glancing to his left side, he could see his spotter pointing up in the opposite direction he had been looking. There, he could see a NeHaw cruiser approaching from high orbit and heading in their general direction.

Using the binoculars, he located the ship on approach just before it disappeared behind a hill covered in heavy vegetation. Pulling out the map they had with the target locations indicated, he found their hide and the manufacturing plant to his right. From all indications, the cruiser had landed at their second objective.

Glancing back to his right and seeing no interesting activity, he signaled for his team to gather their equipment and move out to Target 2.

Chapter 12

Daniel had been closely following the American Scout/Sniper reports as he worked on his own plans. While he admired the bravery and contribution the teams were providing, he envisioned his SAS to be more interactive in destroying the enemy rather than just observing. The joint strike force Colonel Thomas had led was a model for his thinking.

In his research, he had identified several such targets, places where a small group of determined men and women could strike a blow for the war effort. His biggest challenge was locating the right type of equipment to support his people in the alien world's environment.

It was with this in mind that he was talking with the woman who had captured his heart. Patti had just returned from a quick trip to America, where he knew she had met with her great grandfather.

"Are you happy to be back, Luv?" Daniel asked as he and Patti settled down to a quiet dinner together.

"You have no idea. Things are really getting crazy, what with the disaster in New York during the art recovery, and now it looks like we will be hosting a hasty wedding as Jacob and Gemma are expecting," she replied in exasperation before taking a bite.

"Gemma is pregnant?" he replied, surprised at the news.

"Yes, and her mom is pissed!" Patti replied with a mischievous laugh.

"Just so," Daniel replied as he imagined the wrath of Nigel's wife. It was well known that she was a woman of tradition. A child out of wedlock was not something she would likely entertain. After taking a few bites of his own meal, he decided to broach the subject on his mind.

"Speaking of Jacob and Gemma, have you had the opportunity to chat with either recently?" Daniel asked lightly.

"Not directly, Jacob and I have exchanged a few messages, but nothing personal, just business. Why?" she asked before taking another bite of her dinner.

"I was wondering if they might be persuaded to accept a little side endeavor. Just some tidbits for my mates in the troops," he asked lightly.

"Daniel, what are you up to?" Patti asked directly as she stopped eating to stare at him.

"I've been doing a little research and find that the American off-planet gear is not quite right for a proper SAS mission. I was wondering if your delightful engineer brother, and his brilliant soon to be engineer wife, could whip up some goodies for us," he replied, applying all the charm he could muster.

Patti just stared at him for a moment, before she finally took another bite.

"OK, I need to hit the office early tomorrow. I will reach out to him right after and see if they have some bandwidth," she said with a smile.

"Splendid!" Daniel replied as he attacked his plate.

----*----

After an unusually quiet night alone, Jake found himself the following morning in his small workshop, wrenching on the 1965 Ferrari 275 GTB/C he had rescued with a 1966 Cobra Super Snake from Los Angeles. As the cars had been recovered from a museum, this one wasn't in horrible shape. It was just losing all of the degradable parts that allowed it to run. It was Jake's intention to see the thing completely restored.

That, however, was not why he came to work on it whenever he had a free moment. Jake found that the time he spent on the car gave him the ability to think. As he removed rotted hoses and belts, replaced the bushings, and removed the shocks to be rebuilt later, his mind was elsewhere. It also helped that he had his music blasting in the tiny space drowning out any outside noises.

Currently, he was dwelling on the conversation he had with Patti on the war objectives. In the beginning, it had been simply a matter of survival. It had been inevitable that the NeHaw would return as the Earth scratched its way back from oblivion.

With every effort he made in restoring the planet to its former glory, he was risking detection, and he knew it. With the NeHaw return, it had been a mix of cleverness and sheer luck that had overcome the initial challenges. Compounded with the inherent corruption of the NeHaw leadership, Jake had succeeded in leading a revolution that had spread throughout the NeHaw Empire.

Now he was expected to come up with some grand vision for defeating the NeHaw and bringing peace to Earth. Compared to this, the Middle East conflict of his time was simple. As he ran option after option through his head, he continued to work on the Ferrari, occasionally noting on a pad the various parts he would need to make.

There was a budding idea at the back of his head that wasn't quite formed. He recalled such issues in Earth's past, where the planet was faced with devastating wars and challenges that had humans on the brink of total annihilation. There was something there that he couldn't put his finger on.

He was just in the middle of removing one of the front tires to gain access to the rotted brake line when ALICE chimed in, muting the music to allow herself to be heard.

"Jake, I believe Patti is trying to find you. She said it was important," ALICE announced.

"Crap, I lost it," Jake said to himself as the thought dissipated.

"OK, tell her I'm on my way to my office now," he added as he set his tools aside and went to wash up.

Not bothering to change his clothes, Jake cleaned his hands and then brushed off the flakes of decayed rubber as he crossed the open hangar. Moving briskly, he made his way into the facility and on to his private office off the command center.

By now, his reputation for unconventional attire had everyone simply shaking their heads as he passed by.

"OK, what's up? Jake asked aloud as he entered his office and pulled a cold drink from the refrigerator by the small bar. Actually a stasis locker, it allowed for both hot and cold items to be placed together while retaining their state.

"Check this out," Jake heard Patti say, as a video clip appeared in the open area over his desk. In the image was a NeHaw cruiser, setting down in an open area surrounded by buildings Jake had never seen before. As he analyzed the image, he confirmed that the background wasn't like anything on Earth.

"OK, so why am I looking at this?" Jake asked Patti, whom he assumed was still in London.

"Now check this out," Patti replied. As he watched the image split, the one on the left showing the cruiser he had been watching and the one on the right displaying a cruiser in space. Next, both images zoomed until only the cruiser was in the window, each filling the display.

"This cruiser is the one that attacked ALICE-3 in orbit around Wawobash," Patti explained as the image of the ship in space highlighted momentarily. Next, he saw several red circles appear depicting areas on the ship's hull.

"Here, you can see where the ship was damaged in the engagement," she explained.

Sure enough, Jake could see the discolorations where the ship's plating had been compromised. In some areas, the breach was evident as the exposed internal structures were visible.

"Now look here," Patti directed as she circled the same spots on the other ship.

"They are the same, that is the ship that attacked Wawobash," Jake confirmed.

"This image was sent a few minutes ago from the Scout/Sniper team we sent to investigate a lead on a secret NeHaw weapons facility. We think this is where they are reinforcing their ships to withstand the railguns," she finished.

Jake had her back the image out, removing the one used for comparison, and surveyed the area around the ship. He could see the skeletal structures being moved into place as the workers began repairing the damaged sections of the ship. The clip was of short duration, as he knew the team was under strict communications protocols.

"Pull a meeting together ASAP. I want to see our options on setting this place on fire," Jake finally announced before he turned to his display to see what else his insertion team had provided.

----*----

Robert was working with Dallas on the Chinese heavy equipment upgrades. He and Colonel Bo had several ideas beyond swapping out the firepower and making them survivable in hostile environments. By replacing the traditional propellant driven munitions with railgun and charged particle weapons, they changed the entire dynamics of the vehicles.

Taking a page out of the hovercycle design book, they had proposed swapping out the treads and drive wheels on several of the vehicles and replacing them with repulser motors. They did not intend to make the tanks and fighting vehicles fly. They just needed to hover a respectable distance above the terrain.

This allowed them to move faster and even hover over water obstacles, negating the need for bridges. With the addition of inertial dampeners and the reduced recoil weaponry, they were still a stable platform to fire from. Early tests on a prototype, taken above ground in Nevada, showed great promise. While the design was more than capable of handling the energy cannon, more work was needed to address the railgun forces in rapid-fire mode. The engineers were confident it was a tuning issue.

Besides their work on the armor, the first delivery of the combat suits had come in from South Dakota. Robert could see the effect they had on Colonel Bo's men as they worked through the evaluation tests designed to validate their use in the armored vehicles. Even the Colonel couldn't resist testing the tankers suits, as they had been nicknamed.

It was during one of these tests that Dallas pulled the two men away from their work.

"Robert, you and Colonel Bo are requested to attend a meeting," Dallas announced.

"Is it important?" he asked as he hated meetings in general, and this one was interfering with his current priority.

"Jake called it," was her only reply.

"We will be right there," Robert answered as he caught the nod of agreement from Chao.

----*----

Entering the conference room, Jake noted that the number of faces he couldn't place names to was significant. He did recognize Grace Middleton in a group he pegged as Patti's analysts. He assumed that as they were the ones preparing the briefing materials as he walked over to his chair.

Nearby was Colonel Banks, but Nigel was not in the room, so he suspected he may have returned to London to begin preparations for Jacob and Gemma's wedding. Truth be told, that was part of the reason Jake went to hide in his workshop, as Helen could be exhausting. Jake had nothing but respect for Nigel when it came to handling his wife's demands.

On that note, Jake did not see Sara anywhere, although Linda was seated where she might normally be, next to Jake.

"Sara wasn't feeling well, so she asked me to be sure you had everything you needed," she offered as Jake sat. Jake made a mental note to go to her after the meeting and then motioned for the analysts to begin.

"For those of you that may not be aware, we have successfully inserted a team onto a planet of interest. There, they have located what we believe to be the manufacturing facility that upgrades NeHaw ships to better withstand railgun projectiles," Jake heard Patti say.

Rather than displaying her own image as she talked, she was presenting the visuals he had seen earlier from the insertion team.

"This was the ship that attacked ALICE-3 just off the Wawobash shipyards. Here you can see it as it both deflects and absorbs significant hits from her guns before finally withdrawing."

Jake continued to watch and listen as Patti walked everyone through the same information they had discussed earlier. Eventually, they got to some new data that drew Jake back into the conversation.

"Here we can see some of the indigenous life forms, installing replacement plating on the damaged areas of the ship," she explained as the short video clip played for all to see.

In it, Jake watched aliens with three arms and three legs moving about the ship, placing squares of some kind of sheeting over the damaged parts of the cruiser. The aliens looked like two tetrahedrons placed point to point, vertically. The head was like a ball with multiple eyes.

The top tetrahedron had flexible spindly arms like octopus tentacle arms, one at each point, while the bottom tetrahedron had stiff articulated legs, allowing for a change of direction without turning. The top and the bottom tetrahedrons were offset, so the arms didn't interfere with the legs when hanging down.

"All around the perimeter of the facility is an energy barrier that vaporizes anything that touches it," Patti explained as the next clip demonstrated the statement. Someone out of camera tossed a piece of a plant at a hazy red glow before them. As the object touched the red, it turned to black smoke and ash.

"And then there are these," Patti added as the image changed to towers throughout the facility grounds. Each tower held a gun turret, with a pair of energy cannons.

118

"So, the point of this meeting is to discuss options for destroying the facility and preventing the NeHaw from reinforcing more of their ships," Jake announced once Patti had finished.

"Do we know what they are doing there that makes the ships better?" someone in the room asked.

"No, unfortunately, our team hasn't been able to enter the area without risk of detection. All we have been able to record is workers attaching exterior plating to the ship's hull. The plating comes from inside the facility with no clues as to what is it or how it's made," Patti replied.

"Why don't we just take it, then?" Jake heard from a familiar voice.

"You have a suggestion, Robert?" Jake asked the faceless voice.

"Colonel Bo and I have been working on converting his armor for just such an attack. I propose we set an assault force on the ground and take possession of the place. Once we have it, we can see how they make those plates," he replied.

With that statement, the images in the room changed to the design drawings and 3D models Dallas had for the work they were doing in Texas.

"How many of these do you have?" Jake asked after the images were complete.

"We have one functional prototype each of the tanks and the fighting vehicles," Robert replied firmly.

"And how soon can you have a fighting force capable of taking this facility?" Jake asked slowly.

"We have two tank platoons and six fighting vehicles currently under modifications, say eighteen days?" Robert replied hesitantly.

"So, you will have eight tanks and six fighting vehicles, what about ground troops? Are you planning on using Marines?" Jake asked, still not committing one way or another.

"No, Jake, my men are being equipped with off-planet capabilities as well. We will be able to field two platoons of infantry as well as the armor," Colonel Bo replied.

"Help me understand this? You are proposing to use untested equipment and men in a hostile, alien environment. You intend to confront an entrenched enemy and take possession of their location for as long as necessary to understand what they are doing and how they do it?"

"Yes," both men replied in unison.

"Outstanding. Have a mission plan on my desk in three days. Oh, and gentlemen, I suggest you talk to Kola about transportation plans. Meeting dismissed," Jake finished as he rose and left the room, leaving several mouths agape.

----*----

"Are you insane?' Sara asked Jake as he sat with her in her quarters. Apparently, he had no sooner exited the briefing room than Bonnie had been on a call with Sara asking how Jake could allow Robert to run with such a hair-brained scheme.

"They have a great idea. If we could take the facility and hold it long enough to discern what the NeHaw are making there, it would be a huge coup," he replied as the two sat on her bed together.

Sara was reclining with a pile of pillows behind her. As the two sat talking, Sara would grab Jake's hand and place it where one of the twins was actively moving inside her.

"I swear they are going to be tap dancers!" she exclaimed as they both started moving, one inciting the other.

Jake smiled as he felt the twins moving inside.

"If they are anything like their mother, they are going to be hell on wheels," Jake replied with a laugh.

"Or maybe just crazy like their father," Sara replied, getting back on topic.

"Sara. That force will have at least three combat patrol craft and a dozen fighters providing air cover. Our biggest worry is whether or not we can discern how the NeHaw is

120

reinforcing their ships before we have to pull out," he replied with a sigh.

"I hope you are right," she replied with a sigh of her own.

Chapter 13

The next day, Jake was surprised to get a special invitation from both Kathy and Linda for an evening together with his children. As mothers to his son Timothy and daughter Tracy, they were members of the initial group Jake had rescued so long ago. If Sara had any comments on the event, she gave no outward indications she objected.

The sisters had been some of the first, in Jake's opinion, to fall victim to the ALICEs plot to ensure everyone's future. As altruistic as their motivations might have been, Jake was of the opinion that all held special feelings for one another.

Call it love, respect, or just affection, their relationship was based on more than just shared parental responsibilities. So, after a day of plotting and planning, it was with some hesitation that Jake presented himself at the door of Linda's quarters as requested.

"Come in, Jake," Kathy said warmly as she met him at the door. She greeted him with a hug followed by a lingering kiss, one they had not shared in quite a while.

Behind her, he could see the two toddlers playing on the floor together in the living room space. The table there had been moved aside, providing open space between the seating for the two. At the sight of their father, both began to move toward him as he approached.

While close in age, Tracy had managed an unsteady walk while Timothy slipped past her at a faster crawl. Dropping down to their level, Jake scooped up both kids and, with one in each arm, turned to find Linda right behind him.

"Hi," she said as she kissed his cheek and then repeated the process for both kids. The kiss from Linda was another familiarity he had not experienced in some time.

The next half hour or so was spent focusing on the two children, doing the things Jake remembered people did before the fall of civilization. As the only one in the room who had experienced that life, a part of him was sad his children would never know the world he had come from.

Once the kids were fed, Linda had the nanny both she and Kathy used together, take the pair into the other room so the three adults could dine in a more relaxed manner. From that point on, they stopped being mom and dad and were just grownups enjoying each other's company.

"Jake, did Sara ask you not to see us intimately anymore?" Linda finally asked after they had finished eating.

"No, not at all. Why do you ask?" he lied in reply. If he was going to cut it off officially with the others, he wasn't going to make Sara the fall guy.

"That's great news. We were afraid her hormones had gotten the best of her, and she had lowered the boom," Kathy replied with a laugh.

"No boom, but the hormones are definitely there," Jake replied, receiving knowing looks from the sisters.

"Well, with that not an issue, we wanted to talk to you about something," Linda started.

"We thought that, after the twins come and things are calmer, we would like to start the rotation again."

----*----

A few days later, Jake and Sara had snagged one of the corporate type jets converted to repulser for the trip to London. The aircraft was considerably slower than a fighter, but given Sara's condition, it was a far more comfortable trip for her. Becky had joined the pair, her concern for her sister putting her normally exuberant behavior on hold.

Jake had run to Alaska, in part to retrieve the aircraft, but also to visit Jessie and his son. After the dinner with Linda and Kathy, he was both feeling guilty about his other son, but also concerned about the latest turn of events.

He tried to balance his time with his kids, an effort that seemed to always be lacking. Jessie had been particularly attentive this time around, more affectionate than any time he could remember since Ryan's birth. If he hadn't known better, he would have thought she missed him or was in league with the sisters down south. Either way, Jake was worried he was headed for disaster in his personal life.

As the three arrived in Oxford, at one of the two entrances to the facility built by the British under the Chilterns AONB, they exited the craft to a waiting reception party. As there was no hangar available, the craft simply lifted off, returning to Nevada unmanned, courtesy of ALICE.

"How was the trip?" Patti asked Sara as they came to meet the three.

"Not terrible, they gave me the couch," she replied with a smile as she hugged the younger woman. Jake remembered Patti and Sara had bonded very early on, well before he knew she was his great granddaughter.

"Gemma and Jacob arrived earlier," Daniel offered as he took Jake's offered hand.

"Helen is a mess. She greeted them stiffly, burst out crying, and then ushered Gemma off somewhere to discuss the wedding. Jacob has been in hiding ever since," Patti added with a laugh. With that, she turned and, with Becky's help, assisted Sara to the tunnel leading to the underground train.

"Actually, he has been at the pub with my mates, getting pissed," Daniel confessed privately to Jake.

"Maybe we should join them!" Jake replied with a nod as he watched the women head inside. After the last few days, a good stiff drink sounded great.

----*----

Sergeant Hillestad was not particularly happy with his leadership at the moment. The team had moved off, away from the facility they had been monitoring, to hunker down and wait. They had been ordered to risk a rare, extended transmission that could potentially expose them to the enemy.

"How much longer," one of the shooters asked.

Jason replied by holding up his gloved hand and showing five fingers, indicating five more minutes. Everyone had their helmets on and were all ready to link together, point to point, to receive the transmission all at once.

124

"This is Charlie Oscar actual, acknowledge," came the message.

"Charlie Oscar actual, Alpha Team Lead here, over," Jason replied, acknowledging he understood he was talking to their commanding officer.

"Request authentication code Delta, over," came the response.

"Authentication code Delta, roger," Jason replied as he began transmitting one of the preassigned security codes that would confirm he was who he claimed to be.

"Code accepted. Transmitting orders, acknowledge receipt, over" came the reply.

Jason and his team watched their helmet display as a large data dump arrived for their review. When the indicator went green in his helmet display, Jason replied to the sender.

"Receipt confirmed."

"Will contact again as instructed, transmission complete."

With that, they dropped their communications link and began moving to another location before reviewing the data dump. Once they had settled in once more, positive no one had come looking for them, Jason began to review the information while the rest of his team took up security positions.

"They have got to be kidding," was all he could say as he read through their instructions.

----*----

Although Jake wasn't much of a drinker, the same could not be said for his hosts. At some point after the NeHaw bombing, the men and women of the London facility had completely relocated a traditional English pub from the streets of London and installed it here.

Jake was at a loss for words, as Daniel led him into the room and up to the bar on the far wall of the space. As he looked around, he could see the wood-paneled walls with interlaced stained glass windows.

"They put lighting on the other side to simulate sunlight," Daniel explained as he had caught Jake examining them.

With that, the two men approached the group that appeared well ahead of them.

"Danny, me, boy! What took you so long?" one of the men at the bar shouted as he turned to greet the two.

"Right, and who might this be then?" another asked as he referred to Jake.

"This is…" Daniel started before Jake cut him off.

"No one of any importance, just call me Jake. I'm just happy to be invited to drink with you," Jake supplied.

"Another Yank, huh? Well, this one is quite all right," the first man answered while pointing to Jacob.

"OI! Gaffer, another round!" one of the men shouted at the old-timer behind the bar.

At that, Jake and Daniel worked their way among the men at the bar as he listened to the stories, only military men tell.

----*----

Robert was buried in work when his wife came in to check on him. In her role as facilities Commander, she was up on everything he was doing and wasn't happy about it one bit.

"You are not really going to go through with this?" Bonnie asked as she sat next to him while he worked. He pushed his papers aside as he turned to face her.

"Do you remember the day we met?" he asked, referring to the day she had shown up with a small army to chase down the raiders he had been forced to join.

"Yes, you were with that ragtag group in Texas. Because of you, they lived, well, most did," Bonnie replied after some reflection.

"And after," Robert asked.

"About wanting to make amends? Dear heart, you work so hard every day to make this all work," she replied as she waved all around her.

126

"If it wasn't for you, the ships and fighters and guns we need wouldn't get made. You have paid that debt in spades," she finished.

"Even so," he started to reply.

"Don't! Just admit you won't be satisfied until you get to shoot something down or blow some shit up?" she snapped back at him.

The statement brought a smile to his face. Not so much because of the contents as to the attitude Bonnie projected.

"Then come do it with me," Robert replied softly.

"You know I can't," Bonnie replied, the softness of his reply disarming the rage she had been building inside. With that, she kissed him firmly on the mouth and left the room without saying another word.

----*----

Linda had taken on the responsibility of resupplying the Scout/Sniper team they had in place on G-43578. They had decided long ago to continue using the NeHaw references to planets and other places in the many sectors of space they traveled to but called them something else in communications to prevent accidentally exposing operations.

This planet was now codenamed Rest-Stop, and the team there were referred to as Tourists. She had no idea who made this crap up, but she was sure the Marines were likely not happy being called tourists.

Her current dilemma was how she was going to get enough supplies delivered to the team under the noses of the local defense network. She needed to get them enough food to last several more weeks until they had the attack forces there and in position. Thankfully, they only required a food resupply, as their orders were not to engage. That left ammo and other depletable items still at capacity from their landing. Usable power they could regenerate via solar, but that usage was to be kept at a minimum to avoid detection.

The solution was to take several surveillance drones and strip them of their instrument packages. The vacated pockets were then packed with as much foodstuff as they would hold.

Jake had insisted that they find some special items to include in the delivery, but nothing could be in stasis boxes as the power signature could betray the delivery to the NeHaw sensors. He insisted that being stuck in the field under such circumstances, in his words, sucked.

As it was, the drones would be dropped at the edge of the system in one of the touch and go maneuvers the NeHaw had grown to expect from the human ships. The drones would launch and fly to a pre-programmed intercept point with the planet, traveling unpowered. At the very last minute, as they entered the atmosphere, they would power up and then brake, slowing their descent, and land in one of the selected drop points where their team could retrieve them as necessary.

Linda had queried the unit commander to get suggestions on what they might consider "special" meals or other items. The woman had been most helpful, although Linda suspected the team might have other opinions about her recommendations.

Satisfied with the decision, she shot a message to the space station to prepare the drones and coordinated a destroyer for the drop. The necessary foodstuff was already in the ship's stores on Kola, intended for transfer to the space station. Additional materials were also on route, currently halfway between Earth and the edge of the solar system where the station was under assembly.

----*----

Jake had done his best not to offend the group in the pub, with regards to their drink choices. Avoiding anything remotely hardcore, he had stuck with the beer on tap. In that way, he had managed to nurse his beers between rounds to put him several behind the others. He had also been in this position many times before and had learned how to pace himself. Poor Jacob, on the other hand, was well into his cups.

At some point during the afternoon, Nigel and come to join the festivities. Jake envied the way the man was greeted as one of their own, no pretense on standing or authority issues. While he worked hard to maintain that with his own people, it wasn't always achievable.

He chalked it up to the more intimate settings of the London facility in comparison to the nationwide network of locations he had to manage. The sheer size and number of people involved made it really hard for him to spend quality time with anyone.

The group sat singing one of the numerous military drinking songs, this one involving running from the army, all over god's creation, getting someone pregnant, and then back into the army. Jake laughed as he thought this the most appropriate for Jacob's current situation. Only it was to be the Army coming to his aid in securing the venue for the pending nuptials for him and the pregnant Gemma.

As he scanned the group, he caught a glance from Daniel, not nearly as drunk as the others, and watching Jake with a keen eye. Jake knew the look of a man planning something, but he would have to wait until the lieutenant came to him with whatever concoction he had cooked up. Patti had warned him that Daniel was struggling with deciding his lot in life. It looked to Jake as if he had come to a decision.

----*----

Jessie was in the main hangar in Alaska, watching the transports unloading from New York. Although the mission had been cut short, they had recovered a substantial amount of art before the city erupted in gunfire. She watched as several pieces were transferred to another smaller craft, destined for Georgia and ALICE-9, where they provided restoration services. With Helen's rapid departure, Jessie had been left to fend for herself in running the organization's efforts.

Although Jessie was technically responsible for the entire Alaskan operation, she left Seven, the ALICE there, to run the fighter construction. The Flight Training facilities were managed by the various military commanders, so all in all, she was free to pursue her art recovery efforts in relative peace.

Jessie was more of a history nut than an art lover. However, she still valued each and every piece they recovered. She didn't feel the need to appreciate the esthetics of a particular work, as Helen did. She just valued the age of the item. A 2,000-year-old common bronze statue was every bit as valuable to her as a 17th century Rembrandt.

Even so, with all this running through her head, it was something else that was eating at her. She had told herself from the beginning that just being in charge, being one of the decision-makers, was enough to make her happy. Lately, though, she found herself looking forward to Jake's visits, intended for the benefit of his son, Ryan, but organized as family time for the three of them.

More and more, she dreaded his departure, making up excuses for why he had to spend one more day before returning south. After his last visit, as she had watched him climb aboard the transport that was to take him to London when she put her finger on what was troubling her. She was lonely.

The day before, she had convinced Jake to spend one more night, staying in the quarters she and Ryan called home. That night while they did not make love, they slept together, and she drifted off to sleep, content in his arms as they wrapped about her from behind. It was that moment that Jessie decided she needed to step up her game and get Jake back into her life more actively.

----*----

Sergeant Hillestad was told to get his team settled in for a long wait. If, by settling in, you meant to do a full reconnaissance of all three target sites, then they were settled in already. The orders that had been transmitted to the team meant only one thing, there was going to be an attack.

Once they had established a camp for the night, Jason began going through the entire feed, his corporal doing the same while the two shooters kept watch. By his estimation, the rest of the forces would be coming in just over three weeks, Earth time. Since they only had supplies for about a week, he certainly hoped there was a resupply.

In the meantime, they were to survey all three target locations, locate defensive positions, and estimate alien force types and sizes. They were also to track any ship movements in and out of the area as well as record ship type and any marking that might permit identification.

All totaled, they were being charged to do exactly what they had been trained for.

"You think three weeks, Sarge?" one of the shooters asked as they discussed the change in plan.

"We getting a drop? We've already cleaned out the sleds," his corporal asked, referring to the supplies they had recovered from the hovercycles.

"We better," Hillestad replied, as he waved the meal container he had just emptied at her.

Chapter 14

Jake and Daniel guided the wavering Jacob back to the quarter's level of the London facility. Although Jake had been to London before, he was grateful for Daniel's directions as they wandered the maze of halls.

"You're late," Gemma greeted the three after Daniel had knocked.

"Allow, Luv," Jacob blurted, a mimic he had picked up earlier, still being held upright between Jake and Daniel.

"Don't allow Luv, me! We are supposed to meet my parents for dinner tonight, and you can't show up pissed!" Gemma snapped.

Sitting on the overstuffed chairs behind the enraged redhead, Jake could see Sara, Becky, and Patti, doing their best to suppress their laughter.

"It's my fault, Gemma. My mates took it upon themselves to help celebrate you're up the, ah, pea in the pod," Daniel explained, catching himself before repeating the less polite term used earlier in the pub.

"She's really cheesed off," Jacob whispered to Jake.

"Just go drop him on the bed please," Gemma said as she waved them into a side room.

Following instructions, Jake and Daniel ushered the unsteady Jacob into the side room and dropped him unceremoniously face down on the bed. They then turned and exited the room, leaving Jacob and Gemma alone.

"You should have watched him better," Patti admonished Daniel as he went to sit next to her.

"He was already three sheets to the wind when we arrived," Jake offered as he sat on the arm of the chair Sara occupied.

"Well, he is right wankered," Gemma announced to the room as she closed the door behind her.

"Let him sleep it off, he should be ok by dinner," Patti offered as Gemma sat opposite her in another of the overstuffed chairs.

"All my mum needs is a notion Jacob is a tosspot," she said sadly.

"You know better, besides, your mother has a wedding to plan. She will be more than preoccupied with that," Sara offered.

"I hope so," Gemma replied with a weak smile.

----*----

Colonel Bo was out on the test track of the Texas facility, reviewing the latest upgrades to his armor. He and Robert had determined they could get just enough of his equipment converted in time to execute the plan they had contrived. As he watched, the first four heavy tanks were performing basic field maneuvers, allowing their crews a chance to familiarize themselves with the changes.

No longer tracked vehicles, all hovered a short distance above the ground. The recesses, once containing treads and road wheels, were now home to repulser motors and extra power cells. Their turrets had been removed to allow for a sealed crew space. In their place, the gun carriage had been modified for the external operation of both an energy cannon and an auto-feed railgun.

It operated in full 360-degree rotation as before but didn't require a loader to directly access either gun. The command hatch was replaced with a hardened point containing an instrument package that gathered both visual and tactical data, including infrared, radar, and more.

All units had two small drones, which, once deployed, could give them a bird's eye view of the battlefield as well as act as scouts. One drone could feed the entire tank platoon, four vehicles in all, with all the data and video.

Finally, all these changes meant that the inside of the tanks had become more spacious. This permitted for adding items necessary for prolonged occupancy, should the environment require it. A lockout chamber was added to each, allowing crew, one at a time, to exit the vehicle without evacuating the entire interior. In more habitable environments, there were additional escape hatches in the traditional locations.

Bo was amazed at how the heavy equipment floated gracefully over the rough terrain, hardly acknowledging the gaps and outcrops as they floated by. He was anxious to take them topside to allow for the live-fire testing that would prove if the repulsers could hold a position during railgun fire. While he knew these guns had operated in space just fine, he needed to see for himself that there would be no recoil issues with this new design.

----*----

Jake was very thankful that dinner wasn't an overly formal affair. While not the t-shirt and blue jeans attire he would have preferred, the event was described as family formal rather than a State Dinner. He had grown used to ALICE providing the necessary attire, so the scramble for proper clothing had been a novelty.

Nigel was as boisterous as ever at the head of the table with Helen on his left. Jake found himself across from her on Nigel's right, with Sara to his right and Becky beyond Sara. Sara had mentioned that Patti had helped in finding appropriate maternity wear from sources in London.

Scanning the table, he was happy to see Jacob had managed to partially recover from their earlier celebration at the pub. He still looked a little worse for wear and seem to be avoiding certain dishes as they were passed around. Parked between Gemma and Patti, the two women were doing their best to steer any potential triggers away from him.

As Gemma was next to Helen, she could also shield any scrutiny her mother might initiate toward her betrothed. That left Daniel next to Becky and across from Patti, to balance the seating and allow for more intimate conversations.

Jake would have been happy with a serve yourself arrangement, but Helen had stewards assisting the kitchen staff. He doubted they lived like this usually, and really wished she wouldn't make such a big deal about his visits.

"Helen, I can't tell you how much we appreciate you having us here," Sara commented as if reading Jake's mind.

"Yes, you really needn't make such a fuss. We are going to be just family soon," Jake added with a smile and a nod toward Gemma.

"No bother at all," she replied lightly, dismissing it with a wave of her hand.

Jake had to suppress a laugh as one of the stewards attempted to place a dish with some kind of sauce covered fish in front of Jacob. In a swift move, Gemma diverted it away, ushering the plate down the table.

"I do apologize, but lately my stomach has been sensitive to certain aromas," she said quietly to the steward.

"Oh, my dear, I am so sorry. Although I don't recall having morning sickness with you?" Helen commented, appearing slightly confused.

"It comes and goes," Gemma said dismissively.

"Ah, well, maybe a soup?" Helen offered as she waved to one of the stewards.

"Have we decided on a venue?" Jake asked, hoping to redirect the conversation.

"We had hoped for Westminster Cathedral, isn't that right, dear?" Nigel replied, starting to catch on as Becky passed Jacob some bread to help settle his stomach. Having participated in the earlier drinking binge, he was a seasoned drinker and no worse for wear.

"Oh, what? Yes, that's right. The Leftanant promises he could have the area secure in no time at all," Helen replied as she turned her attention away from the retreating steward.

All eyes turned to Daniel, who simply nodded in acknowledgment of the statement.

"I am told that part of London is really quite civilized as it is," Nigel added.

"I wish I could say that about New York," Jake replied as he sipped from his drink.

"Troubles?" Nigel asked as they all started in on the meal.

"Helen missed all the excitement. One of the art recovery teams was set upon as they tried to clear out the Metropolitan Museum of Art," Sara offered.

"Oh, dear," Helen commented.

"No one was hurt, but they had to pull back for fear of damaging the artwork," Patti added.

"Might they need some assistance on the ground?" Daniel asked earnestly.

"Maybe. I had intended to visit New York after the incident, but my schedule has been usurped by other events," Jake replied with a grin. Though he received several questioning looks in reply, he was not prepared to delve into those subjects at the moment. His personal issues would stay off-limits.

"If you like, I can take a SAS troop and reinforce the 10th?" Daniel added.

"We may have to discuss that possibility. Right now, I just asked them to pull back until we can focus our attention on things there. The last thing I want is for a fight to break out where it's not necessary," Jake answered.

"I completely agree. By the way, Gemma, I was wondering if I might have a word with you and Jacob later," Daniel asked nonchalantly.

"Here it comes," Jake thought to himself.

"I have some ideas I'd like to run past you, with Jake's approval," Daniel finished with a smile.

----*----

Kola was in a world of her own as she worked the many aspects of assembling the space station. Mostly operational in its incomplete form, they had ships dropping in from FTL and resupplying at an almost constant rate.

As part of the overall strategy, the cruisers and destroyers used the space station as a transfer point with the Lanai Transports ferrying goods to and from Earth. The demand had become so great that several of the combat versions had been pressed into cargo duty to get the station saucers stocked up.

Besides all this, there were several groups in training, using her hangars as practice for deployment and recovery. She had fighters, transports, and combat patrol ships coming and going from all directions.

"Kola, can you verify the delivery date for the last sections of the space station?" Captain Connor asked as she was working through her schedules.

"ALICE-3 confirms the last two sections will be shipped in ten Earth days," Kola replied after a momentary exchange with her sister via the NeHaw network. A necessary evil considering the distances, the ALICEs had devised their own codes when utilizing the medium.

"I won't rest until this thing is complete," Isabella commented quietly as she stared out the bridge windows while watching the assembly of saucers.

"I share your concerns. Once completed, this station will equal anything ALICE-3, or I can provide an offensive capability. Until then, it's vulnerable to attack," Kola responded.

"And we are tied to its defense. I am sure you've been tracking the goings-on back home?" Captain Connor asked.

"Yes, they will be ready soon. We will need to vacate some hangar space to accommodate the entire attack force," Kola replied.

"Any Lanai ship not involved in the effort can be left with the station until we return. Major Jacobson will be bringing his own ships," the Captain responded.

"Full of Chinese combat troops and equipment," Kola added.

"That is a good point, are we appropriately provisioned to accommodate them. I don't believe we have operated with that high a concentration of Chinese to be concerned about their specific ethnic needs?" Isabella replied. While she was sure they would make do with whatever was available, it was only common courtesy that they attempt to meet their needs.

"I have Dallas and ALICE ensuring their ships are stocked with essentials before they leave Earth," Kola replied.

"Best that they do," the Captain replied.

----*----

Patti escorted Sara back to the quarters she shared with Jake while in London, as he, Daniel, Gemma, and a rejuvenated Jacob slipped off after dinner. Nigel and Helen made their own excuses for leaving the four to their own devices. Jake had decided to let the kids talk first to see where this was going.

"So, what's on your mind?" Jacob asked as the four sat in one of the private rooms in the facility. As in the American ALICE facilities, the London location had recreated spaces for the occupants to relax in their off-hours. The room they currently occupied was patterned after a proper gentleman's club, wood paneling, and overstuffed chairs included.

A self-service bar at the far end of the room catered to the needs of those who relaxed here. Bookshelves and art lined the walls in all directions. Jake smiled to himself as Jacob took the long way around the room, avoiding the bar entirely.

"I was wondering if you might have some open cycles in your production in Hawaii?" Daniel asked directly to Jacob and Gemma.

"Ships?" Gemma asked, sounding dubious.

"No, more along the lines of personal equipment," he replied.

"What are you thinking?" Jacob asked, the statement getting his interest.

"I was hoping you might be interested in manufacturing a line of SAS specific gear. Please don't take offense, but the Marine battle equipment is not tailored to the missions I foresee," Daniel replied, directing the last at Jake.

"No argument here, if you think you need something special, go for it," Jake replied casually. He was the last person to object to innovation.

"If you are free tomorrow, I have some sketches and specifications drawn up in my office?" he responded.

"You need me?" Jake asked the three.

"I think we can manage," Jacob replied for the group.

"Have fun," he replied as he rose and headed out, leaving the others to continue their discussion. A small part of him was dying to see what they dreamed up.

----*----

Jason got the burst transmission in the middle of the local night. As it wasn't his turn to be on watch, it woke him from a dead sleep.

"We are getting a resupply in just under 24 hours," he passed on to the other three in his team as some had been woken by the same event. The timeline meant the goods must already be on their way, as that was the travel time from the edge of the system.

Checking the details of the transmission, he could see there were five drones inbound, with enough supplies for twice the allotted duration. The drones would hit in a fairly well-spaced distribution, so should one become compromised, the others would not be lost as well.

Confirming the team's location and measuring the distance to the closest two drops, he made the decision to split his team and pre-position them nearby. A quick snatch of at least two of the drops would ensure his unit's survival should things go badly for the rest.

He and the corporal would each take a shooter, and if his calculations were right, they needed to leave about three hours before the drones touched down to be in the right spots. Shooting everyone their instructions, he set his internal timer and went back to sleep.

Chapter 15

Jake and Nigel were touring the area around Westminster Cathedral with a small detachment of SAS. With all the nearby buildings, he had a serious concern about the security of the participants for the wedding. The group was riding in two of the Jeep type vehicles Jake had relocated from America early on.

"You don't think we need to be concerned about these buildings?" Jake asked as he pointed to the glass and steel structures just across from the entrance to the church. They had stopped in an open area and exited both vehicles at this point.

"We will sweep the area for days before the event and have troopers stationed inside on the day of the wedding," the SAS officer replied as she pointed to the various structures. Mentally Jake tagged her as a second lieutenant. He couldn't remember if the Brits held the tradition in America of just calling her LT.

"I can give you Marines for the security detail as well?" He said with a quirked eyebrow.

Next to him, Nigel was spreading the map of the area out on the hood of the jeep. Nearby, they sat several overhead photos of the area, taken the day before. It was really tight on all sides of the square, and he wasn't comfortable with it.

"If you like, but I can say that the locals do consider this place to be quite sacred. Most days, you will find people wandering the area in peace," the woman replied.

"Besides, who doesn't like a wedding?" she added with a bright smile.

With that, the young woman turned to the troopers accompanying the party. She split her force into two groups, sending each off to sweep the outside of the Church, while Jake and Nigel followed her up to the large front doors.

Expecting them to be bolted, he was surprised to see them swing free, allowing the party easy access into the structure. As they entered, it struck Jake at how clean and organized the interior was. That mystery was soon solved, fortunately, as he watched three men approach the party.

"Father, how good to see you again," Nigel said as he took the offered hand in greeting.

"Back again for more confession?" the priest teased the man.

"Not today Father, and I fear my companion's confession would tie up most of your day. Father Joseph O'Reilly, may I introduce Colonel Jake Thomas, from America," Nigel replied.

"Colonel Thomas, I have heard a great many things about you. It is truly a pleasure," Father O'Reilly replied with enthusiasm.

"Jake, please, Father. I hesitate to ask what stories you've been told, but my curiosity overwhelms me. How did you come to be here?" he asked while waving at the building around them.

"Ah, yes, well, like most in London now, we are descendants of people relocated from the countryside. Catholic priests established a small seminary here upon their return, and like these seminarians, I heard the calling and came to serve here."

"So, you carry on the faith?" Jake asked as he realized he had no idea what the state of the Vatican was in Rome.

"As I said, we were fortunate to have Church leaders come in from the countryside to help restore order here," the priest said.

Jake noted the SAS officer had taken a position off away from the group, hand on her holstered sidearm while she scanned the area, alert and on guard.

"Father O'Reilly will be performing the ceremony," Nigel commented.

"Wonderful, I only hope the Bishop grants dispensations," Jake added lightly. While he wasn't positive, he was pretty sure Jacob wasn't Catholic. Jake also doubted they had a Bishop handy.

"Ah, yes. Well, we will just have to make do," Father O'Reilly replied with a knowing smile.

"Are you Catholic?" he asked, acknowledging Jake's understanding of Catholic doctrine.

"No, Father, but I almost married one a long time ago," Jake said with a laugh.

"Haven't we all," the priest replied dryly, adding to the humor.

From there, the priest led the group on a tour of the Cathedral, more for Jake's benefit, he was sure. He was fascinated at how well the structure had been preserved and was equally surprised at the number of individuals about inside.

He was quite surprised to see a number of women working beside the men there.

"Nuns?" Jake asked as he indicated a small group tending the greenery outside.

"As resources are scarce, we do have a convent of sorts on-premises as well. It provides a safe haven for those women who desire a life of servitude in the name of the Lord. The sisters here are very active in the local community," Father O'Reilly replied.

Jake was starting to understand why this part of London was so well behaved.

"Is there anything you require before the wedding?" Jake asked the man.

"Maybe one or two things to help the cause," the priest replied while indicating those working diligently around them.

"Whatever we can do," Jake responded, noting an approving nod from Nigel.

"Splendid," Father O'Reilly said as he produced several folded pages with handwritten contents from a pocket. As Jake scanned the pages, he had the distinct feeling he had just been played.

----*----

Robert and Bo knew Jake was in London dealing with family matters, and as such, agreed that their equipment testing should be their own responsibility. While both

142

intended to jump the very last transport for London to attend the ceremony, they saw no need to interrupt their very tight schedule before then.

Today, they had one entire tank platoon and two of the fighting vehicles in the Texas badlands, evaluating the firepower of each. As part of the exercise, they had been delivered by Lanai transport, where they simulated a landing. With them, they had pirated several of Dallas's target drones for use in the desert as adversaries.

The target drones they had selected mimicked both land craft and flying vehicles, challenging the combat targeting systems in the armor with multiple scenarios. The tanks had been fitted with the larger railgun/energy cannon combination while the fighting vehicles had a smaller caliber pair of each. In addition, the fighting vehicles were quite a bit faster than their heavy metal cousins.

"Let's try the wedge formation with breaching force," Bo suggested as the tanks sat in a line, their crews waiting for instructions. The pair of fighting vehicles were stopped just on the other side and had been test firing their guns against flying targets.

With the proper commands issued, the two men watched as the armor reformed with the fighting vehicles centered inside the tanks in a wedge formation. Bo was impressed at how quickly the individual vehicles could reposition, now able to move in all directions like a hovercraft, floating just above the ground.

Using some natural formations as the enemy perimeter, they had the target drones positioned as defenders. The two watched as the units pushed forward, firing as they maneuvered. In a short time, all the drones had been engaged and neutralized before a single tank had been flagged as destroyed by the simulation monitor.

"Again!" Bo ordered as he smiled. Robert nodded in agreement. Things were coming together nicely.

----*----

Jacob and Daniel sat in the latter's office, going over the design ideas for the SAS without Gemma. As was usually the case, or so he was told, the bride to be had far too much to do before the wedding to be distracted while he was left with nothing. Every time Jacob had asked to help, both Gemma and Helen had proposed he find other things to occupy his time.

As such, he embraced Daniel's request with vigor, and the two men walked through the pile of specification sheets Daniel had compiled for the various proposals. After a lengthy discussion, they selected a couple of simple projects and one more complex.

"How soon do you think we can have prototypes ready?" Daniel asked as he watched Jacob working at the terminal. They had long ago extended the ALICE network into the London facility. While they didn't have an on-site ALICE system, they had direct access to all eight earthbound locations.

"Give Lanai a week, maybe sooner, to work through the details and source the materials. These three will be no problem, it's the last one I'm guessing will take a bit longer," Jacob replied as he pointed down the list on his screen.

"Splendid," Daniel replied with a smile.

----*----

Since their return to Earth, Edwin had been doing his best to remain invisible. While he greatly sympathized with Jake's domestic problems, he had no desire to be drawn into them. With that in mind, he took the opportunity to mingle with the residence of Patti's Pit, the primary tactical group, in their effort to win the war.

His status as one of the three primary military leaders gave him a certain notoriety among the group, but he tried to do his best not to interfere with their duties. As he watched the room full of analysts, he was impressed by the sheer volume of information they were processing. Fully aware that in the background, there were ALICE systems, filtering

144

and directing specific bits of data to particular people, it was still amazing to see in action.

"Colonel, do you have a moment," he heard from one side of the room. Turning, he could see one of the women on the far side, motioning to get his attention.

"What might I do for you?" he inquired as he approached the young woman.

"Normally, I would run this past Colonel Thomas, or at least Patti, but as they are all in London at the moment, I really didn't want to bother them," she started out with.

"Admirable," Edwin replied as he waited for her to continue.

"We are detecting a pattern in the NeHaw ship movements. I think we might have located some form of supply planet," she explained.

"How are you following their ship's movements?" Edwin asked, curious as he was under the impression that one could not track a ship in FTL. The analyst paused for a moment before replying.

"First, I must tell you that this is highly compartmentalized in addition to being top secret. Every time we engage the NeHaw, some of the railguns are fitted with a special round that contains a tracker. So far, the NeHaw haven't detected them as they are made to embed in the hull without creating a breach. Every time they drop out of FTL, they call home with their position data. We made them function just like the NeHaw navigation systems, so they are almost undetectable," she replied with a devious smile.

"Devilishly clever, that," Edwin replied with a smile of his own.

"Exactly. So anyway, we have seen the recently engaged ships all returning to the same place. They hang around for a day or two, and then they are off to other places. We think they go here to resupply before heading off to their next assignment. It might also be some kind of command and control center, but we think it is a supply depot based on its location."

"Ok, sounds reasonable. What's the problem?' Edwin asked.

"I'd like permission to send a reconnaissance drone to check it out. I don't want to spook the NeHaw, so maybe just a quick in and out to prevent detection?" the woman explained.

"Absolutely, I think it's a splendid idea. You have my permission," Edwin replied as the smiling woman turned back to her station and began typing out what he presumed were the instructions to get the mission moving.

"Let's just keep this our little secret for now, shall we?" Edwin said as he stood thinking.

"No problem, but you do know the ALICEs know everything?" the analyst replied without turning from her work.

"Good enough," he said with a smile.

Turning to leave, Edwin now had a few calls of his own to make. If this really was a supply depot, he had just the team to go in and blow the place to pieces.

----*----

After returning to Earth, Ivan had taken the opportunity to go home to see his own clan. People in America and England continued to mistake the fact that he was not the Ataman of his clan, thinking him in charge, so he tried to make regular visits to update the real leaders. He found the circumstance of little concern to the Ataman and the Starshina as the recruitment for the Patrol ships had given them a significant amount of notoriety in the region as it was.

Russians, Cossack or not, had flocked to Avacha Bay in hopes of joining the war against the aliens. Even though this region was still woefully behind in the recovery, Ivan was amazed to learn that the volunteers had come from hundreds of kilometers away. He was aware that the number of Russians in training exceeded the number of available ships at this time.

146

Every time Ivan returned to the bay, he tried to bring something back for the good of the community. Sometimes it would just be food supplies or tools. Other visits had seen him deliver updated weapons that were an immediate hit. This visit had him offloading a pair of hovercycles for the clan to use in patrolling the area around the bay.

He had commandeered one of the V-27 Falcon transports from one of the ALICE hangars to bring them along. Slower and smaller than the Lanai Transports, they were in far lesser demand these days. Even so, the aircraft was more than spacious enough for the pair and unrelated additional supplies.

These particular hovercycles were a special order, configured with added instrumentation as the riders would not be wearing the usual combat suits and helmets. For this reason, Ivan had also requested a speed limiter, capping their top speed to 200 kilometers per hour, to prevent rider injury.

Most hovercycle riders took the protection of their combat suits for granted, as it's not the speed, but rather the impact of any objects they may encounter in the air that made it dangerous. A bird strike at high speed would be deadly otherwise.

"Ivan, you have been away far too long!" his sister replied as she greeted him. She had come in advance of the small party that always gathered at his arrival. Mostly consisting of the community elders, they were destined to live out their lives here by the bay, content to let the younger men and women run off to fight the great evil.

"I have a gift for you," Ivan replied after she released him from her hug.

"You should not! You spoil me!" she replied, but the look of eagerness in her eyes betrayed her excitement.

Ivan quickly went up the loading ramp and soon returned with a bundle that was long enough to require both arms. As he reached the base of the ramp, where his sister was waiting, he peeled back the material to expose rolls of finely colored silk.

147

"From China," was all he said as he passed them back to her. Ivan knew he could have had any of the ALICEs create a wondrous garment for her, but she preferred to create such things on her own. The material he had provided would permit her to design something that would make her the envy of all the others.

"It's beautiful!" she replied as she fingered through the bolts of material.

"So, you have come to steal more of our people?" one of the elders announced in jest as he greeted Ivan warmly.

"Only the useful ones's so you need not worry!" Ivan replied with a laugh before embracing the speaker.

"What trash have you come to dump on us now?" another asked as he indicated the two hovercycles now resting on the ground nearby.

With that, Ivan walked the party over to the pair and explained how they worked. He could see their eyes light up as he talked of the possibilities. Placing two of the oldest on one of the hovercycles, he put his sister behind him on the other. Climbing aboard, he set the pair in sync mode, ensuring the second mirrored everything his ride was instructed to do.

Assured everyone was ready, he lifted both off the ground and slowly piloted the pair into town, where he expected a very warm welcome.

Chapter 16

As the morning of the wedding broke under a clear English sky, Jake was not so sure he was ready for the ramifications of the event. Besides the implications of Nigel and Jake's families becoming one, something he hoped Bo and Ivan didn't take in a negative light, it was the marriage itself that was troubling.

He was extremely outspoken in his original opposition to the circumstances that he now found himself in. He was bound by parenthood to five women, none of whom he was actually obligated to by marriage. That fact alone made the pending ceremony very uncomfortable to him, particularly since Sara was to be seated right next to him.

He was grateful that she had not repeated her demands that he cut all ties with the others, but he doubted she had either forgotten or changed her mind. With the declaration of renewed interest from Linda and Kathy and an implied desire from Jessie, he was on the verge of returning to the days of the rotation. In typical male fashion, he chose not to question the current state of affairs, selecting to wait and see if it resolved itself.

Mentally dropping the subject, he turned his focus onto the security arrangements for the ceremony and surrounding area. After their visit to the Cathedral, Jake had passed on Father O'Reilly's wish list to others to see it filled and delivered quickly. The note thanking him provided all the evidence he needed for its completion.

He had been notified earlier that both Edwin, Robert, and Bo had arrived in the transport delivering the goods from America, but had yet to meet up with either. For someone with no actual function at this wedding, he found his schedule particularly full. He still regularly scanned the intel reports relating the continued NeHaw harassment, sending instructions, and proposing solutions.

Designated as a father to the groom, he was set upon to provide all that was required for the honor of the position. Besides hosting the rehearsal dinner, an event he had catered via ALICE-9 kitchens, stasis boxes, and a high-speed transport, he hit upon an idea for the Honeymoon gift.

After running it past Helen, Nigel, and Sara- all of whom approved it enthusiastically- he spent a considerable amount of time preparing the location to make sure it would be ready in time. In combination, he also drew upon the Marines in training to provide a platoon of infantry for boots on the ground here in London.

Placed under the command of the SAS officer who had accompanied Nigel and himself, they were to ensure there were no interruptions during the ceremony. If there were any objections to the duty, Jake heard nothing of it. He suspected the SAS hosts ensured the Americans enjoyed their time here.

With all this going on, he had little time to check up on Robert and Bo after approving their attack plan. He reviewed their status reports as part of his daily morning reading but had been unable to contact them directly. He presumed the subject would come up today at some point.

Satisfied that he was as ready as he would ever be, he headed off to see if Sara required anything.

----*----

Sara had spent the night with her sister Becky and Patti, as she expected to need their assistance in preparing for the wedding. Normally she would have wanted to be there for Gemma, but in her current condition, she knew she was more of a hindrance than a help.

Her dress for the wedding had been delivered the day before, a special gift from ALICE. In trying it on, Sara found it especially easy to put on while appearing quite elegant. She wondered if it was in some small part an apology for the games they had played in blocking and then allowing her pregnancy.

As the question went unasked, she simply remained thankful and dreamed of the day when this pregnancy would be over. It was during this introspection that a quiet knock came at the door.

"Bonnie!" Sara cried as she opened the door to find her middle sister on the other side.

"Oh my, look at you!" Bonnie replied as she hugged her older sister ever so gently.

"When are you due?" she followed up as she came inside, motioning Sara to sit.

"Not soon enough," Becky answered for her as she and Patti came into the room from the adjoining bathroom.

"My *know it all* sister tells me any day now, but I've been hearing that for a week!" Sara replied.

"Are we getting ready here?" Bonnie asked, changing the subject before Becky could respond.

"Yes, you are welcome to join us," Patti replied as she gave Bonnie a hug.

"Where is Robert?" Sara asked as she motioned to the closed door, indicating he had not come with her.

"Sulking somewhere. He and Colonel Bo have been building an invasion force to attack the NeHaw. They are ready to go now, but I told him they can wait one more day and come to the wedding."

"That went well, I am sure," Patti replied sarcastically.

----*----

Colonel Bo Chao and Major Robert Jacobson sat in one of the many lounge areas of the London facility, formally dressed and waiting. Bonnie had accompanied Robert for the wedding but was presently seeking out her sisters, leaving the two men to fend for themselves.

Both men were quite anxious for the day's activities to commence, as they had an invasion force preparing to board three Lanai transports headed to Kola at the edge of the solar system. As promised, they had eight tanks and six fighting vehicles modified and tested for the endeavor. In addition, they had two platoons of Chinese infantry in support.

Besides their forces, Robert had verified that Kola contained two additional Combat Patrol ships and two squadrons of fighters ready and willing to cover their assault.

In his communications with the ALICE ship, he swore Kola was chomping at the bit to see some action as well.

As a steward for the space station construction, she complained to him that she had been working in a support role while her sister was roaming the known universe, fighting battles to protect the Earth. Robert completely understood her frustrations.

Both men intended to gain Jake's approval once the wedding was finished, to sneak off, and begin loading their forces. The four-day trip to where Kola lay waiting was a necessary delay, but one they intended to make the best of by leaving Earth as soon as possible and training along the way.

----*----

Colonel Edwin Banks had his own need to talk privately with Jake after the ceremony. Once the mystery of the NeHaw supply depot had been verified, he had reached out to Leftanant Atkins to prepare a mission plan. The goal was to take a SAS team into hostile space, secret themselves onto the planet undetected, and destroy the enemy resources there while escaping unharmed.

Daniel had been quite enthusiastic about the idea and had promptly volunteered to lead the effort, which came as no surprise to Banks. While Edwin didn't envision leading the ground team himself, he had every intention of piloting the spacecraft.

The Phantom was an integral part of the mission plan as it was the only ship currently available that could get the teams into position undetected. Of all the equipment required, it was the one absolute. It was during the planning phase that Edwin learned of Daniel's request for specialized equipment. Although most of it wouldn't be ready in time, one particular piece of gear would be.

----*----

After ensuring that Sara had a proper means of transportation and escort to the wedding, Jake left the London Facility via the MI-6 secret exit and headed to

152

Westminster Cathedral. He was surprised to find Edwin, Bo, and Robert already on site and there to greet him.

Of the three, only Robert was in a suit. The other two military men were splendid in their dress uniforms. Jake had to assume they were correct for the rank and nation as they were created eighty years after he went into stasis.

"Fancy meeting you here!" Jake said as he exited the vehicle, his own Marine dress uniform an ALICE recreation. While the Mameluke Sword was a pain in the ass when sitting, he wouldn't be without it.

"We hoped to have a word before things got too hectic," Edwin replied with nods from the other two men nearby.

"Why am I suddenly worried?" Jake asked of the three men before him.

"We simply request an early release, to begin the long voyage to the edge of the solar system," Bo replied while motioning to include Robert in his statement.

"And you want to join them?" Jake asked Banks, the surprise evident in his voice.

Rather than replying, Banks presented Jake with a few sheets of folded paper from inside his dress uniform jacket. Reading through the sheets provided, he went back over each before speaking.

"Are we sure about this?" he asked Banks, unsure what the other men knew about the information.

"Straight out of Patti's Pit. I believe they were trying to confirm the information from the same sources that corroborated your last soiree," Banks replied, referring to the strike Jake had led on the alien base.

"And the reply?" Jake asked.

"Inconclusive, I am afraid. They could neither confirm nor deny the assumptions," he said flatly.

"Still, it's worth a shot," Jake said quietly more to himself.

"Indeed. A strike on a major supply depot would be a significant blow," Banks confirmed.

"And you need the Phantom," Jake suddenly blurted.

"Yes, we do," Banks confirmed with a smile.

"That's a lot of troops off-planet, all at once. With both Kola and ALICE-3 as well," Jake commented to all three this time.

The three men just nodded in agreement, all apparently waiting for Jake's reply. Turning his attention back to the papers in his hands, Jake wasn't reading a word. All this effort kept coming back to the same thing, Patti's earlier question, *how are we going to win this war*.

"Ok, let's do it," Jake announced.

"I have a SAS team ready to depart as soon as the nuptials are complete. Unfortunately, Leftanant Atkins is a member," Banks said.

"Then, you get to tell Patti!" Jake replied as he waved the men inside the Cathedral.

----*----

Sergeant Hillestad was busy recording the activity at their Target 2 vantage point. He was relieved that they had been able to recover three of the five drops without detection. In addition, he had no indications that the other two had been discovered, so he presumed they sat undisturbed, available at a later date should they need it.

Resupplied now for the duration, they began the methodical survey of all three target locations. After several days of observations, it was his opinion that site 3 was only a supply depot, in support of 1 and 2. Since arriving, they had seen five NeHaw cruisers land for what he assumed was some kind of repair or upgrade.

So far, only one of the five had left the planet's surface, with the remaining four still undergoing whatever the process was they came here for. As he watched, he attempted to document his observations, but frankly, he was a grunt, and the technical aspects of what he was seeing escaped him.

His main hope was, once the attack ships appeared at the edge of this system, the data he would transmit would be of some value to the tech geeks on board.

----*----

Jake was standing off to one side, just inside the doors, as he watched the Cathedral filled with guests. He was mildly surprised at the number of people streaming in through the large double doors. He was even more surprised when Ivan showed up, leading a delegation of Cossacks in full regalia.

"Colonel, may I present my Ataman and the Starshina of the regions around Avacha Bay," he announced while motioning to the group around him.

"It is my pleasure," Jake replied as the group filed in.

At that point, Ivan went through a series of introductions, leaving Jake's head spinning with names he would never remember.

"We should talk later. There is a lot going on," Jake whispered to Ivan as he led the party further inside. The Cossack gave him a nod of understanding before disappearing in the crowd.

A short time later, the group escorting Sara appeared, with the bride not far behind. Sara was quickly escorted to her place of honor, the advanced state of her pregnancy overriding any ceremonial duties.

From that point on, it was something of a blur for Jake. He was sure what he witnessed was as close to a proper Catholic wedding ceremony as any he had ever seen in his previous life. Gemma was radiant in her gown, and Jacob had selected the traditional English style tails, waistcoat, white bow tie, top hat, and all.

Nigel and Helen sat across the way in the church, Helen awash in tears. Jake caught a wink from Nigel, the father of the bride beaming with pride. As the ceremony continued, he caught several of the women on his side of the aisle, reaching for tissues as they dabbed at moist eyes.

No sooner had they said their *I DO's* than Sara grabbed Jake's arm

"It's time," she said suddenly.

"Yes, I agree, it is about time this thing ended," he replied, referring to the pair at the altar and the length of the ceremony.

"No, Jake, it's TIME!" Sara repeated, indicating her protruding belly.

"Oh," he responded as he reached past Sara to attract Becky's attention.

No sooner had Jacob and Gemma retreated down the aisle than the group ushered Sara, at a brisk pace, out a side door to a waiting vehicle. At this point, Jake handed off the family duties to an anxious Patti while he accompanied Sara and Becky.

"Let Jacob know what's happening," he said quickly before the door closed in his face, and the jeep sped away.

Thankful for Becky's care of Sara, he directed the driver to get them to the MI-6 building where they could catch the underground train car to the facility. Sara required the waiting stretcher once they reached the garage at MI-6, and the stretcher bearers did a double-time getting her to the train car.

The short train ride seemed to take forever, and once at the facility station, a waiting gurney whisked Sara into the medical wing where they had a long wait before Jake and Sara's twin girls arrived. Their beaming Aunt Becky proudly introduced them to their mom and dad, one at a time.

Eventually, Jake left an exhausted Sara, and the twin's in Becky's good care while he went to spread the good news at the reception. The party was in full bloom by now, and he arrived just in time to help present the Iceland trip to Gemma and Jacob as their honeymoon gift. He gave a toast explaining that a tropical vacation for someone who lived in Hawaii seemed somewhat redundant.

Privately, he knew that a great effort had been made to locate and secure a place for the loving couple. He had been quite surprised to learn that a great number of Icelanders had survived the initial NeHaw attack. Fortunately for the remaining population, their previous self-sufficiency had enabled them to endure and flourish, even as isolated as they were.

In the end, Jake and Nigel agreed on two locations for the young couple to relax and enjoy one another.

Fortunately, both spots were quite remote, and with ALICE on guard, their safety was assured. Besides, the locals they encountered in exploring other parts of the island were overjoyed to learn about the recovery, offering to assist in any way possible. Jake's proposed gift had accidentally ignited another recruitment drive.

As for the honeymoon locations, Grjotagja in the north was selected for its wonderful cave setting. Once too hot to bathe in, it had since cooled to more desirable water temperature. Only about thirty miles south was Viti, a volcanic crater that was open to the world, unlike Grjotagja. Each location provided a vastly differing experience, but both magnificent in their own way.

To facilitate travel between the two, one of the residence containers, identical to the ones placed in California and Australia, had been fitted with replusers. A simple request to ALICE and the unit was relocated to prepared sites next to each attraction. A small transport helicopter and jeep had also been provided should the couple wish to explore. Apparently overjoyed by the gift, both Gemma and Jacob appeared anxious to go.

Quietly slipping out after the announcement, Jake was able to return to Sara's room without incident. He had feared being sidelined by one of the many well-wishers in the room, but with the drinks flowing, he wasn't sure how many people could even recognize him.

"I was wondering when you would be back," Sara commented as he entered the room.

"I'm sorry, I thought you'd be sleeping. Jacob and Gemma say congrats by the way, and they are happy you are doing ok," Jake replied as he crossed the room and gave her a gentle kiss.

The room they had placed Sara in was quite homey, in Jake's opinion, not like the more sterile rooms of the ALICE MED bay. He noted the empty bassinets near her bed.

"Where are the girls?" Jake asked, referring to the nearest bassinet.

"You know the nurses, they were whisked out of here the moment they started to fuss. I am supposed to be sleeping," she replied.

"We do need to give them names," Jake stated as he moved a chair next to Sara's bed.

"I had thought, twins and all, we should do something associative?" Jake suggested.

"What, like hand and glove or sock and shoe?" Sara asked sarcastically.

"No, like Amber and Jade. They are both precious and beautiful," he replied earnestly. The reply brought a tear to her eye as Sara reached out for Jake to hug her.

"I think that would be amazing," she whispered in his ear.

Chapter 17

With Jacob and Gemma married and off to Iceland, Sara settled in Nevada with the twins, and the Chinese and SAS on their way to the edge of the Solar System, Jake thought it might be a good time to take a look at the New York situation. He arranged to get Abby and a small contingent of the 10th and had them rendezvous in Maine, as it was the closest ALICE facility to New York.

ALICE-5 was initially established as a medical facility before the attack, a role that was now considered less essential when compared to weapons manufacturing. While they did continue to make medicines and other medical supplies, the majority of the staff were there to learn. Designated as a recruitment training center, a large percentage of those in residence were new recruits getting a basic education before being sent to specialty training.

"Welcome Jake," Five announced as he set his fighter down in the main hangar area. Nearby, he could see the hovercycles of the 10th lined up neatly in a row. Five in all, it confirmed Abby, and one troop had arrived as requested.

"Thanks, where are the kids?" Jake replied with a tinge of humor.

"Abby and Troop B of the 10th Cavalry are in the level 3 dining hall. They asked to be informed when you arrived," the ALICE system replied.

"Please have the five of them wait for me there, and I will join them shortly," Jake replied as he dropped his helmet on the seat and descended the ladder. Around him, the hangar was far less crowded than most, with only small transports and helicopters nearby.

Passing into the facility from the main entrance off the hanger, he was able to locate the office that had his research packet waiting. Before leaving Nevada, Jake had asked for a work-up on the areas of New York, specifically around large concentrations of people.

The ALICEs tended to track the world population by default, a function they had perfected after the fall. More of busy work activity, Jake had called upon it several times since his awakening to help decipher situations in the cities.

"Good to see you, Colonel," Abby announced as she and the other four troopers of the 10th rose from their table.

"Sit," Jake replied as he waved them back into their seats while taking one himself.

Dropping the packet he had picked up on the way in, he pointed to the collection of photos and papers.

"I asked ALICE to get us everything they had in the Central Park area of New York. It looks like you stepped into a bit of a mess there?" Jake explained as the five began to sort through the contents.

"How so, sir?" one of the new troopers asked.

"It appears that one of the old gangs in New York has taken control of the area around Central Park. As you can see in some of the photos, the gang colors and markings are distinct. ALICE believes this particular group was once related to MS-13. What they call themselves now, we have no idea, but they have similar tattoos," Jake finished while pulling particular images out for the group to see.

"Why would they care if we removed the stuff from the museum?" Abby asked.

"They probably don't. I suspect it's more like a turf thing. I haven't decided how to handle this yet, but what I do want is more Intel. That's why you are here," Jake said with a smile.

"From the observations ALICE provided, we suspect that they are holed up in the buildings along Museum Mile. That entire area was once a High Rent district, with fine accommodations for only the best," Jake commented sarcastically.

"Ok, boss, what do you need?" Abby said with a broad smile, her red hair pulled back in a ponytail, so her face full of freckles lit up at the prospect of action.

"Here is how I want to play this," Jake replied as he leaned in on the group and outlined his plan.

----*----

160

Edwin Banks was sitting in the pilot's seat of the Phantom as they headed out to the edge of the solar system. Although not visible to the naked eye, the screens on his console indicated there were three Lanai transport ships ahead of them, holding the Chinese strike force. He was well aware they were headed to a rendezvous with Kola.

With him in the navigator's seat was Leftanant Atkins, more for the company than anything else as the man was not flight trained. Everyone else on the SAS strike team was either in the galley or below in the main hangar. The ship was still configured in the same layout as it had been from the last mission, something that Edwin found fortunate.

"Everyone settled in?" Edwin asked Daniel as he continued to scan the console before him.

"Yes, Sir. It was most fortunate that the ship was ready to transport an assault force. The delay in reconfiguring the ship would have been maddening," Daniel replied to Banks query.

"We can thank Colonel Thomas for that. I understand some members of that action are still aboard Kola?" Banks asked as he turned to face the younger man.

"Yes, Sergeant Carson is training with a small contingent," Daniel replied.

"Perhaps they might like to join us?" Banks said with a smile as he did the math on the number of SAS troopers below decks.

"I shall inquire," Daniel responded as he turned to open a communications channel with the space station ahead.

----*----

Robert and Colonel Bo had decided to travel separately, each in one of the three transports headed to meet Kola at the edge of the solar system. It was Robert's understanding that they had already transferred a number of ships and personnel from Kola's hangars to the space station's control in order to make room for his ships.

As big as Kola was, almost three miles in total length, the Lanai transports, and combat patrol ships tended to require a

161

significant amount of floor space, even within her two massive hangars. In addition, the need to place them in stasis bubbles while in FTL required them to offload any equipment needed in transit, as well as all the onboard crew.

While there was no risk to the people should they be placed in stasis while traveling in FTL, most found the option, not to their liking. Besides, the last-minute preparations for an attack usually required a final briefing before dropping out of FTL, and that meant they needed to be available.

As it was, they would need to drop out of FTL just before arriving at the jump-off point to restock the transports beforehand. The goal was to arrive at the edge of the desired system and launch the attack force immediately, reducing the time the NeHaw had to prepare.

So, with that in mind, both Robert and Bo had their people training the entire four days to the rim. The end goal was a force honed to perfection. So why was Robert so worried?

----*----

It was very dark as Jake wandered the streets of New York. Riding behind Abby on the way in, he had been dropped in Central Park just after midnight, not terribly far from the MET. Once Jake was on the ground, Abby had her troopers spread out as per the plan, all hovering just above the building tops and with their night vision and infrared enabled.

Besides the visual equipment in the helmet of each rider, each of the hovercycles had Jake on a tracker. As he made his way into the buildings east of the Museum, they could follow in hover mode. Spread out in all four compass directions, their main function was not to track Jake, which was Abby's job. Their function was to alert everyone of any possible hostiles as he moved through the buildings below.

In support of the 10th, ALICE had both satellite and drone coverage of the area. At this time, Jake suspected there was not another area on Earth with more scrutiny. Carrying a suppressed submachine gun and sidearm, he was not really interested in killing anyone. He just wanted to verify the threat and possibly gather a little Intel around who ran things here.

Moving up to East 81st Street, the tall buildings on either side assisted him as they blocked what little light was making its way to the ground. Sticking to the shadows, with his combat suit doing its best to camouflage him from prying eyes, he caught the occasional flicker of light from above. No more than candlelight in strength, he had little fear of it exposing his movements.

"Jake, that building to your left has quite a few heat blooms inside," Abby whispered in his ear. While he was positive no one could hear what was being said into his helmet, everyone had a tendency to whisper at times like this.

"That building faces the park. I bet the apartments here were pretty pricey in their day," Jake replied as he studied the recess where the entrance was. He imagined a doorman standing outside, both assisting the residence and shooing away unwanted visitors.

A movement inside the windows confirmed the entrance was likely guarded still, now with guns. Scanning the outside of the building, Jake could see a decorative ledge, running crosswise to the structure and looked into the fifth-floor windows. Moving further east on 81st, he passed the entrance undetected and then crossed the street until he stood at the southeast corner of the building.

With one leap, he managed to catch the edge of the ledge and slowly pulled himself up until he was standing on about 2 feet of stone fascia extending out from the building. He stood there quietly for several minutes, waiting to see if he had been detected before he started moving west along the ledge, back towards the park.

"Jake, just so you know, we have sentries moving on top of the building," Abby confirmed.

"Searching or just moving?" he replied as he froze in place.

"Looks to be just moving, wait, he stopped at the edge over you," Abby replied.

As Jake stood motionless, he suddenly detected a stream of liquid from above, passing him by thankfully.

"Jake, you are not going to believe…" Abby started before Jake cut her off.

"He's pissing, yeah, I know," Jake responded.

Jake held his place, for fear the sentry might be looking over the edge as he relieved himself. Luckily, it stopped soon enough, and he got the all-clear to move once more. Using both night vision and infrared, Jake located a window where there were no indications of life on the other side.

Slipping the pane up was easy as it wasn't locked, being the fifth floor and all, he slid inside the room and closed the window. Doing a quick sensor sweep, he found no indications that the rooms in this particular apartment were occupied. Silently, he moved to the door to the hall and again, tested for any bodies beyond. Once he had the all-clear, it allowed him to open the door and check the empty hallway.

One particularly handy setting Jake had picked up in his helmet was a small display window inside his facemask heads up or HUD. While he was seeing the world in an enhanced Night Vision/Infrared mode, he had a small pane showing what the actual conditions were. In this case, enhanced, he could clearly make out both ends of the hall, while an unenhanced occupant would see total darkness.

Slipping into the hallway, he made his way past several doors before he found the stairwell. Again, he found the stairwell in complete darkness and empty of any occupants. Entering on the fifth floor, Jake had counted a total of twelve floors from outside the building.

On his approach from the park, he had seen several dimly lit windows on the top floor of the structure. Unsure if it was nothing more than squatters, the high concentration of occupants in the building gave him the sense of a place of importance.

As he ascended the stairs as quietly as possible, he heard noises from above, indicating someone was coming down. He thought he heard two voices in hushed conversation as they continued to come closer. Telltale candlelight indicated someone was holding a candle, lighting their way down the stairs. Quickly checking the door on the eighth floor, he slipped inside a darkened, empty hall as he waited for the two to pass.

Pushing the larger weapon to one side as it hung from its strap, he drew his suppressed sidearm. At this close range, should they enter the same hall, he could press the muzzle against the two in quick succession, ensuring additional suppression and quick kills.

The candlelight under the door was as bright as day to his night vision as the two men reached the landing for the stairs on eight.

"I tell you I saw something in the sky. It was floating above 83rd, north of here," one of the men said to the other as they paused on the landing.

"Dude, there is no moon, how did you see shit?" the other replied as he stopped. Jake's helmet sensors told him someone had just lit a tobacco product nearby.

"Hey, you got one more," the first man replied. Jake presumed he was asking for a cigarette. As he waited, he heard noises of movement beyond the door.

"The stars, man, they flickered," the first replied after making the distinct inhaling sound of one drawing on a cigarette.

"Stars flicker, you asshole, that's what they do," the second man replied as they continued their trek down.

"Not like this," the first replied. From that point, the two men had descended past the point of Jake's concern.

"Abby, you copy that?" Jake asked, wondering if she had heard his audio pickup.

"Everyone, add five hundred feet to your hover," Jake heard in response on the tactical net.

"Copy," came the uniform response.

165

With that, Jake continued up the stairs uninterrupted until he reached the 12th floor. He did a quick recon to verify that the last level opened up onto the roof. Slipping back down one level, he found the door to 12 locked. In addition to the door handle, there was a deadbolt for extra security on the steel fire door.

"Abby, can you scan the roof and the top floor. I'm looking for an empty room," Jake asked as he considered his options.

By now, he was fairly certain they had happened upon a gang house. That made sense, considering the significant amount of fire they had taken once discovered working the Museum across the street. His only quandary was, did he go in shooting or ghost in and out as originally planned.

"Jake, I still have two warm bodies on the roof. Every room I can scan on 12 has occupants, but from the vitals, I think most are sleeping. Either that or they are almost dead," Abby replied.

The response gave Jake an idea. Slipping back up to the top of the stairs, he checked the roof door, and finding it still unlocked, he slipped onto the roof undetected. With his night vision, he could see both sentries at the opposite ends of the roof, each looking out and away from him as they scanned for threats.

Long ago, Jake had enhanced the combat suit he used for such excursions. Slipping silently around the edge of the structure where the stairs exited onto the roof, he quietly approached the first sentry. Grabbing the man by both shoulders from behind, he sent the equivalent of a Taser shot through the man. It was only Jake's grasp that prevented him from dropping to the ground.

Placing him silently to one side, out of view of the other, Jake repeated the process on the second man.

"Ok, Abby, come down here," Jake instructed.

Once she had set down in an open area on the rooftop, Jake proceeded around to the rear of the hovercycle and rifled through the storage box until he found what he was looking for.

"When I say go, drop these down those ventilation shafts," Jake commented, handing her three of the grenades he was holding. Walking over to the center of the structure, Jake looked down to see the open central section of the building, where the interior was open all the way to the first floor.

"Now," Jake said as he pulled the pins on two of the grenades he held and dropped them into the open void. Turning, he was in time to see Abby finish the last of her three.

"Follow me," Jake said while motioning for Abby to follow. Pausing just long enough for her to grab a suppressed weapon identical to the one he carried, the two descended to the 12th-floor landing and waited.

"That should be good enough," Jake commented after several minutes. His suit sensors had alerted that they detected the gas he had just deployed seeping up from below.

Placing the muzzle of his weapon near the door lock, he proceeded to demolish the deadbolt with two shots. A swift kick did the rest, leaving the door wide open. Wandering from apartment to apartment, they found the entire floor unconscious.

"What are we looking for?" Abby finally asked after following Jake through several rooms.

"The leader," Jake replied. After a knowing grunt from Abby, the two split up and continued the search. After an hour of searching, they had selected three likely candidates. One by one, he called in one of the remaining four troopers. The subjects were restrained and confined unconscious to the rear seat of the hovercycle, where they would be held in place until released.

After the last of the three possible gang leaders were secured, Jake left a communicator and a note in one of the rooms. Then he returned to the roof and took his seat behind Abby as they shot northward to ALICE-5.

Chapter 18

The morning following their snatch and grab of the suspected gang leaders, Jake was awakened by the ALICE-5 command center communications tech with an urgent message.

"Colonel, there is someone screaming obscenities at us from the communicator you left in New York?" the young woman explained as the reason for waking him.

"I am sure there is," he replied with a chuckle before asking her about the prisoners.

"Anything from our guests?" He asked sleepily.

"If you mean the three detainees' pounding on the cell doors, more of the same language as the New York source," she replied flatly.

"Let's let them all stew a bit then. I'll reach out to you later with instructions," he replied before going back to bed.

----*----

Jason knew the most dangerous part of this type of mission was the time when you knew the end was near, but you just had to wait. People became complacent and anxious for the mission to be over. Then they got sloppy, and that's when bad things happened.

It was for that reason that he had his team constantly on the move, repeating the duties required from different hides every night. This was very fortunate as they discovered a disturbing fact, as they crossed over a place they had previously used.

One of the miraculous abilities of their combat suits was its ability to recycle water from both urine as well as external sources. However, it was a well-known fact that defecation was not a product the suit handled well. In fact, the suits Jason's team was using had been specially modified for long term use. They were set up in a way that allowed the wearer to go cleanly, jettisoning the waste product rather than retaining it.

All one had to do was dig a little hole, activate the waste cycle function, squat, do your business, and then cover the hole. On the whole, it was the fastest, easiest way he had ever gone in his life. There was, however, an apparent downside.

"Sarge, you gotta look at this," one of his shooters said as they entered an old hide from several days before.

Jason immediately knew what the woman was referring to as he looked around the spot. Being well trained, there was nothing left behind that would have ever betrayed their use of the space. However, over to one side, at the spot they had used as the latrine, every bit of plant life was dead and shriveled.

It was very apparent that human excrement was toxic to the plant life of this world. At the moment, all Jason could think of was how many spots they had used as a latrine that would be visible from above.

----*----

Daniel was sitting in his quarters near the bridge, going over the latest Intel on the target planet K-82734. Unlike the Chinese objective G-43578, they didn't have eyes on the ground, scouting the area for them. As such, the analysts had set up irregular drone runs that would pop in, scout the planet for detailed data on the target areas, and then FTL off before the locals got wind of their presence.

Frequently, the drones caught various NeHaw ships in orbit and on the ground, taking on supplies. There was two particular image captures that Daniel suspected depicted resupply vessels there to replace depleted inventories. Their massive size and extended presence implied a significant amount of material to move.

It was hardly surprising as that was the intent of this particular location, close enough to the action and centrally located. The appeal to Daniel was the opportunity to not only destroy the depot but also cripple the movement of additional supplies in the future.

The unfortunate thing was without further data, they had no real way to coordinate their strike with delivery from one of these ships.

----*----

"You got no right to lock me up!' the man behind the clear partition screamed as Jake and Abby sat calmly on the other side. It had been two days since the snatch and grab, and the three prisoners were just now starting to wind down.

Jake had ensured they were all well fed, the thrown food from the first temper tantrum an anomaly after they didn't eat until the next meal cycle. In addition, he made sure that none of the detainees knew of their compatriot's plight. All thought that they were alone in their incarceration.

"You attacked my people," Jake replied calmly as he waited for the man to stop pacing. It was very obvious to him that none of these men had been challenged in a long while. Their attitude of self-entitlement was pervasive.

"You stuck your nose where it didn't belong. If you don't let me go, my people are going to gut you," the man replied as he stopped pacing to face the two.

"And the things they will do to you," he said while pointing to Abby and making a clicking sound with his tongue. Jake was proud that the young woman didn't take the bait.

"Why would they care, you think you are someone important?" Jake asked, taunting the man.

"You just wait and see how important I am," the man said sarcastically.

"Good idea," Jake replied as he dropped the transparency setting on the wall.

With that, Jake and Abby repeated the process with the remaining two prisoners, challenging each to try and get them to reveal who might be in charge. At the end of the day, the two convened a meeting in a small office to compare notes with the ALICEs.

"I think it's number one," Abby started as they settled back in padded chairs while drinking what Jake liked to call low cal. lite beer. While neither he nor Abby was big drinkers, the stresses of the day had taken their toll. The low alcohol content of this particular brew was a good compromise.

"Abby may be correct in her estimation," ALICE-5 replied.

"Thanks, Five," Abby replied with a smile.

"He seemed the most outraged at the snatch, blustering at us as if attempting to intimidate without specifics on how that would be accomplished. The other two displayed more deference in their manner," Jake said thoughtfully.

"Is there a point to this exercise beyond entertaining ourselves until the attack ships reach Kola?' Abby asked aloud.

"I believe we are trying to ascertain if these people can be reasoned with," ALICE replied.

"Bingo," Jake replied with a smile while holding up his glass in a toast.

"It's clear we are not going to adopt these guys and bring them in as recruits. We might, however, be able to strike a bargain, a treaty of sorts," Jake added.

"Jake, are you considering arming these people with better weapons?" Five asked with a tone of surprise.

"Not on your life. We can, however, give them non-lethal aid. So far, I haven't killed anyone. We simply slipped in and snatched their top guys. That has to rattle them some. If we make a point of respecting their turf, we might get cooperation," he answered.

"Are you serious? I can never tell when humans are joking," Five replied.

"At this point, I have no interest in trying to civilize New York. We are barely making headway in Los Angeles, with Chris bearing the brunt of it. Oh, and in case anyone has forgotten, we are fighting an all-out war in space at the moment," he replied while referring to Chris Wade in Los Angeles.

"What do you suggest?" ALICE asked Jake.

"Let's let them see each other now. Can you make the walls between the cells transparent?"

"It would be best to relocate them, but yes, it can be done," Five replied.

"Knock 'em out first and then move them while they are asleep. I don't want any incidents where they get an idea they can run. It would be a setback if we had to kill someone, though, at this point, I am not completely opposed to it. Then let's let them talk and see what we can learn," Jake replied, knowing his frustration was showing.

"You are the boss," Five replied with a less than convincing tone.

----*----

Robert had his crew running drills the entire run to the edge of the system. For this mission, he had doubled up on the regular complement, both for a proper crew rotation on a 24-hour clock, but also to man the new weapons he had installed in Nevada.

Besides delivering the Chinese to their drop points, he had every intention to engage any misguided NeHaw vessel that was foolish enough to challenge them. His ships had shields equal to any Earth combat vessel and almost as many guns now that the upgrades were complete.

They had to deal with a few glitches as they traveled to the edge of the system where a waiting Kola would take them aboard. His technical staff was working around the clock to ensure there were no issues by the time they were required to place these ships in stasis for the trip in FTL.

"Major, Colonel Bo would like a word," his communications officer said.

"Thanks, I'll take it here," Robert replied as he sat in an open weapons station. Activating the display, he found Bo's face staring back at him.

"What can I do for you, Bo?" Robert asked. He had developed an informal relationship with the Colonel, in great part because of the extended number of hours they had spent getting ready for this mission.

"Robert, my people report that some of the systems on Transport 2 are malfunctioning. Will this be a problem?"

"The doors on the starboard pod are not indicating operational. The only way I can test them is to open them, something that is not conducive to the health of the troops in that space. Once we get aboard Kola, I can verify if they are working properly."

"And if they are not?" He asked calmly.

"We will fix them if we can before we go to FTL. If not, those troops can exit behind the armor out of the main doors. It's really a minor thing and one that we can work around if necessary. They got messed up when we installed the gun turret right above the opening. The guns do work in case you are curious."

"I hesitate to mention, but the food on this Transport?' Bo said hesitantly.

"Yes, look, I am really sorry about that. That's my fault. I should have made sure that the food was loaded as a cultural mix. I had no idea that you had only the supplies intended for the American and British members on board. Please feel free to take anything with my name on it as compensation," Robert replied.

In a rush to get airborne, they had hurriedly loaded all the supplies without consideration of cultural needs. In this case, they left the entire US food supply on Transport 3 while 1 and 2 had mostly Chinese.

"I do appreciate that; however, can you please explain, what is Tex-Mex?" Bo asked.

----*----

As the three transport ships closed in on Kola, nearby, the Phantom had preparations of their own to complete. Every so often at irregular intervals, a drone would transmit the raw Intel dump from the last flyby, providing Daniel with the latest images of their target areas. He was beginning to see the value of all the time he had spent with Patti and her analysts as he updated their attack plans.

173

The thought of Patti sent a shot of guilt through him. She had been less than pleased at his decision to lead this mission, although he noted that she didn't appear all that surprised when he announced his plans to take the SAS off-world.

The discussion was fairly one sided as Patti completely understood the need for the mission. What was lacking was a good reason for Daniel being the one to lead it. In the end, she had just accepted the fact that he was going, and she made sure he experienced the depth of her emotions regarding him that night.

Patti accompanied the mission team to Texas, where they boarded the Phantom and was, at this very moment, in Patti's Pit in Nevada, scrubbing data for him. It gave him great comfort to know that she had his back on this mission.

Clearing his mind, he went back to assessing the targets, looking for any indications that the aliens had increased security.

----*----

Jake was running out of time. Both the Phantom and the Chinese invasion force were almost to the edge of the solar system. Once they all went to FTL, he wanted to be in Nevada, where he could be accessed easily should something go awry. With Banks on the Phantom and Chao with one of Robert's transports, he was the only ranking officer on Earth.

He needed to resolve this New York situation soon, or it would become a lingering problem, and he hated lingering problems. The desire to send in the Marines and just have them clear the area out was tempting, but he knew it wasn't the right thing to do,

Like it or not, the gangs there had set up a stable environment, and even if it wasn't to his liking, it wasn't at all like LA. There weren't the same destructive activities where groups were constantly shooting it out with one another.

Here, they had established boundaries, each marked off their territory, and protected their turf without seeking out violent confrontations with others. His reports indicated life inside the gang zones was actually pretty calm, with small families and clusters of communal living.

There was something here that gave Jake cause to consider the situation with the NeHaw. The idea wasn't quite formed yet, as it had started in the workshop before, but he filed it away for further consideration.

"Five, any updates on our guests?" he asked as he sat in the small office he had commandeered.

"Abby's guess was right. Number one is our leader. The other two are his closest lieutenants, and they were all quite concerned that no one was left in charge," she replied.

"Have we seen any activity in New York to indicate that there are problems now?" Jake asked, concerned that he may have upset the apple cart.

"Not at this time. I believe the term is, they are all laying low," Five replied.

Jake wasn't sure if his encouragement was the reason the ALICEs attempted these sayings or if they did so naturally, and he encouraged it, but he had to laugh with each one.

"Well, that won't last," he said more to himself.

With that, Jake made his way to the detention area and divested himself of any weapons, pocket knife included before heading to the access panel. Letting himself into the room with the gang leader, he surprised both the man and the guard standing just outside, who rushed to notify the shift commander.

"You a brave man to come in here unarmed," the leader of the New York gang said to Jake as he entered the holding cell.

Pulling up the single metal chair, Jake took the seat as the man stood staring at him from across the room. The two men just stared at one another before Jake finally spoke.

"Are you done posturing, or did you have more to say?" he said without emotion.

"What do you want?" the man finally said as he sat on the edge of his bunk.

"Uninterrupted access to the museums of New York City," Jake replied, taking the man by surprise.

"Why?" the man finally asked after regaining his composure.

"To save what we can of the world's art before it's destroyed by vandalism and neglect," Jake answered.

"What's it to me?" the man snapped back.

"Do you like the way you live? Are you happy scrounging in the city?" Jake asked, changing the subject.

"We do, alright. I got the biggest gang in the city," he answered with pride.

"That's good. If you work with me, you still will. All I want is for you to convince the other gangs to leave my people alone, and we won't interfere with your life there. In fact, we can make your world a whole lot better," Jake replied, dangling the carrot.

"Ha, you ain't nothing. We chased you off…" the man started to say before Jake cut him off.

In a move of amazing speed, he leaped from his chair, closing the distance between himself and the gang leader. Grasping the man's throat with one hand, he lifted the struggling form off the floor, holding him high, as his feet dangled freely.

"Listen, you little turd, I pulled my people away before they made the streets run red with your blood. The only reason any of you are still alive is you are no threat to me or any of my people. If you play ball, not only will you survive this little indiscretion, you might actually come out ahead," Jake snapped.

"You should listen to him, man," Jake heard from one side. As he looked around, he could see the walls had been made transparent, and the other two prisoners were watching the incident with keen interest.

"I'm listening," the man replied hoarsely after Jake set him down.

As Jake outlined his proposal, he could see all three men nodding in agreement. The basic proposal was as he indicated, they would leave them alone to do as they had

176

been for the last 80 years, and the gangs would steer clear of any art recovery activities. For this, Jake would provide food and medical services, even setting up a regular mobile clinic visit and emergency medical services should something unexpected come up.

"What about guns?" the man asked cautiously.

"No weapons. I am not going to destabilize your current environment by arming you or any other group with superior firepower. You should be glad for that because it means I won't supply your rivals either."

In the end, they agreed to accept Jake's terms, at least for now, and he saw to it, they were returned with sufficient supplies to convince any doubters of their intent. As the three were escorted into the hangar for the flight home, Jake also made sure an excessive number of troops were visible, all armed to the teeth.

----*----

As he worked in his office in the High Command, General KaLob was not satisfied with their current state of combat operations. The events of the attack on the Wawobash shipyard had shown promise, but the cruiser from that engagement was still unavailable for combat duties.

With that cruiser currently tied up in phase two of the upgrades they had created, KaLob had assigned two more warships for the same weapons evaluation. Unenhanced with the hull upgrade the cruiser received, they would next travel to G-43578 once the cruisers there were complete.

Until then, he had to satisfy himself with the constant harassment they were inflicting on the human ally's interplanetary shipping. Absently, he wondered what the humans were plotting at that moment.

Chapter 19

Kola dropped out of FTL at the very edge of the gravity well created by the target planet's sun. At that very moment, she stopped, the stasis bubbles encasing all the ferrous metaled ships in her holds disappeared as well. She knew that Robert and Colonel Bo had prepared their crews and passengers for immediate loading once their ships were made available.

After leaving Earth, they had made one stop prior to arriving here. In that stop, all the heavy equipment and supplies that could be safely moved in FTL had been loaded back into the transports. This allowed any training or gear prep to occur during the voyage to the system, avoiding any last-minute emergencies. She only needed to wait for them to load up, and she could release them to space.

It was, with some surprise on her part, a fairly short wait as the two combat patrols, three transport ships, and two fighter squadrons were ready to depart and requesting permission to launch within minutes. Captain Isabella Connor granted the request, and the flight operations officer gave them the sequence with which they were to depart.

It wasn't terribly important in what order they left the hangar as far as the attack was concerned. They would have 23 plus hours to reform before they encountered the defenses on the planet. It was more an issue of control, trying to ensure no one ran over or otherwise trampled the smaller craft.

All too quickly, Kola could see the entire attack force headed away from her hangars and on toward the target world. It was now time for her to take up a defensive position, guarding against inbound NeHaw ships that may be dispatched to counter the human aggression.

----*----

Jason was alerted the moment the Earth ship appeared at the edge of the system. Seconds later, he triggered the burst transmission containing all the information they had been gathering since being informed of the pending attack. Once he received the acknowledgment, it was then quickly followed by instructions to retreat to an extraction point, where one of the transports would collect them once they had offloaded their troops.

He wasn't sure he was happy with those orders. His team had invested a serious part of their life in setting up this op, and now they were being pulled out just when the fun was starting. Pulling out his map, he surveyed the notes on the various locations they had occupied until he found what he was looking for.

"Let's go here for now," Jason said to his corporal as he indicated the spot on the map.

"Didn't they say pull back?" she asked as she noted the move placed them closer to the primary target.

"Depends on how close they land the Chinese," Jason said.

"Besides, how can we shoot anything from back here?" he said as he pointed to a place far in the rear.

The corporal looked confused for a second, and then the light turned on.

"Good point," she said with a smile as she started to gather the others and move out.

----*----

Leftanant Daniel Atkins led the small unit through the winding maze of gullies and eroded the earth as they closed in on their objective. While currently devoid of any liquid, it was easy to tell that these were once water passages and recently used. The plant life overhead grew so thick that were one to look straight down from above, you would not likely see any of the team as they stealthily moved along.

He was aware that his teams were slightly ahead of the Chinese attack force on G-43578, but their intent was to be in and out undetected before the Chinese landed their attack. Using the Phantom to slip on the planet unnoticed, his team was one of four units deployed. All four units had specific instructions for search and destroy missions on K-82734.

This was to be a coordinated attack, a hit and run sort of thing.

The NeHaw had been using this planet as a staging area for resupplying their fleet. Deep in NeHaw held space, the planet was at the edge of a small solar system and had an earth-like atmosphere and environment. The slight difference in the atmospheric makeup had them all in full-face masks, but helmeted combat suits were not required.

The planet was the only orbiting body around a small, dying sun. The lack of a strong gravity field made the location ideal for ships dropping from FTL to travel the short distance and resupply. The travel time from the edge of the gravity well, caused by the star, to the planet's surface was a bit over 8 hours, making it an ideal location.

The weak sun did, however, provide only the minimal amount of life-giving warmth, making for temperatures in the daytime just above freezing. At night the thermometer dropped to -50 C, which made things quite uncomfortable for anyone without suits. The plant life seemed to have some form of antifreeze in its makeup, and the heater function in their undergarments provided enough warmth to keep Atkins and his people from freezing.

The new combat suits Jacob and Gemma had dreamed up for them were amazing. Besides the expected visual camouflage capabilities, the bloody things made his people almost invisible to the naked eye. Adapting some of the science learned in creating the Phantom, they incorporated the technology in the weave of the uniform materials.

There had been just enough time to get a limited number produced for this mission. They were unable to field test them beyond the time spent on the way to the edge of the system. So far, Daniel had no complaints.

In addition to those properties, they reflected both the heat and electrical signatures, preventing detection in other spectrums. To avoid giving themselves away by other means, Atkins used hand signals to direct his team as they neared their objective.

Arriving at the jump-off point for entry into the compound beyond, Daniel waited until his entire team was clustered nearby. Popping his head up just enough to get a look at what lay ahead, he couldn't help but react to what he saw.

"Oh, bugger!" he whispered to himself.

----*----

Jake was in the command center with Linda and Sara as he tried to track all the ground operations they had in play. Between the SAS and the Chinese, he had more troops off-world now than ever before. With the SAS on the ground and the Chinese soon to be, he was anxious for information on their progress.

At the moment, they were going over the data provided by the Scout/Sniper team on G-43578, code named Rest Stop. The data was surprisingly complete, and the team there had done a great job of assessing the threat.

He noted that the commander of the people on site had ordered the team to retreat for extraction. He privately wondered how well that went over. His curiosity was soon satisfied as the team had requested permission to act as sniper cover for the invading force.

Caving to his internal emotions, Jake quickly approved the request, a clear violation of his non-interference rule. His inner Marine just couldn't let that team miss out on a chance to actually perform the function they had trained for. He was sure he would hear about it later in one form or another.

"Jake, we have word from New York," one of the communications personnel announced.

Moving over to the console, he scanned the message Five had forwarded.

"All gangs have agreed to stand down. Medical treatment is requested immediately for several individuals. Central Park designated a Neutral Zone for all gangs to allow centralized access to services and supply drops equally."

Jake laughed at the Neutral Zone reference but stopped laughing as he considered the concept.

181

Daniel had his team pull back slightly as he considered the new information he had just received. His short peek at the perimeter fence had revealed a new security force distributed at regular intervals along the energy barrier. The aliens were all in full combat suits and carrying energy weapons familiar to the Leftanant and his team.

Their original plan had been to reach the barrier fence, a partition of energy that incinerated anything that touched it and breach the barrier, undetected. One of the new toys Jacob had invented for the mission would create a void in the fence without disturbing its function and alerting the occupants. Daniel had expected to pass his people through the void, where they could then plant the charges they carried.

Rethinking their strategy, Daniel did a quick transmission to the Phantom, warning them of his discovery, and then receiving the data he requested. Reviewing the images they had taken just before landing on a small display attached to his forearm, he could now see the guards they had missed earlier. Their suits disrupted the visual spectrum, so in the image, they appeared as nothing more than objects along the fence line, indistinguishable as individuals.

Scanning the rest of the sizeable compound, he could see nothing indicating roving guards or any more posted on the interior. Satisfied on the viability of his new strategy, he relayed the information for Phantom to pass on and informed his team of the change in plans.

Once everyone was briefed, he led the group back to a spot near the fence, but out of view of the sentries. Removing the tool he had intended to use on the fence, he gently but firmly pressed it into the side of the bank. Triggering the device, he watched as the dirt all around the rod vaporized, leaving an opening about four feet in diameter in the bank.

Jacob had cautioned Daniel, when demonstrating the device, that it was intended to temporarily disrupt the energy field of the perimeter fence, leaving about a six to eight-foot void in the barrier. However, any solid matter within the area of influence vaporized into thin air as the wand disrupted the atomic bonds that bound them together, just as the fence did.

The energy fences were actually a weave of energy streams that interwove into a blanket of disruptive force. Any solid matter that came in contact would have its molecular bonds disrupted until it became free molecules, destroying the physical form. The energy the rod projected had the same properties, but operated in a reverse fashion, destroying the energy weave of the fence, leaving a void until the fence fabric reassembled.

In a demonstration, Jacob placed the rod on a tabletop, the end only reaching the center of the table. Holding the handle, he activated the device, and instantly the middle section of the table disappeared, leaving the far half as the only solid matter holding the two ends together.

Careful to ensure he was always behind the handle, its bell guard protecting his hand, he made sure he did not let it slip past the safe zone. In that fashion, he continued to extend the rod before him as he created a tunnel toward the fence line. One by one, the troopers behind him followed in the darkness as Daniel tunneled his way under the fence and into the depot above them.

----*----

Robert Jacobson was on the bridge of one of his transport ships as he checked on the formation. In the lead and only minutes ahead of them were the two combat patrol ships surrounded by the eight fighters of the VMFA-232 Red Devils and VMFA-323 Death Rattlers.

Besides all that firepower, the three transport ships had undergone a partial refit adding guns positioned to cover the landings. All three were now sporting additional energy and railguns to supplement the basic firepower each was provided during construction. Robert liked to call the upgraded ships his assault transport model.

Inside each ship was a combination of Chinese tanks and assault vehicles that were updated to reflect the new type of fighting they expected. Spread among them were two platoons of Colonel Bo's best infantry.

Each transport had been loaded with a mix of troops, tanks, and fighting vehicles that was specific to their mission and target. The transports were supposed to cover their area unless called upon to assist in a more critical situation. While they were still a good 20 hours from the planet, he was anxious to get the ball rolling.

----*----

General KaLob was traveling to inspect the cruiser recently repaired on G-43578 and enhanced with a new weapons system. He had seen the images of the battle with the humans off Wawobash and wanted to see for himself how the repairs had gone. The cruiser was recently returned to the NeHaw homeworld on KaLob's request after the weapons upgrade.

"General, Sir. We have an urgent message from G-43578 that I think you want to see," an orderly advised.

Taking the display from the orderly, KaLob started scanning the contents. He then flipped to the images, one showing a significant number of inbound ships and another depicting the massive ship, stationary just outside the system.

"When did this come in?" KaLob asked as he scanned the additional information in the report.

"Just a few subcycles ago. I verified the contents before coming to you with it. The closest ships capable of responding are cycles away," was the reply.

"What of the four cruisers on the planet?" KaLob asked while referring to the data in the report. It was stated they had four ships currently under the upgrade process on the planet.

"Due to the upgrade process, none are space worthy at this time," the orderly replied cautiously.

"Get me back to my office," KaLob ordered the pilot on the other side of the ship.

----*----

According to Daniel's display, he was about 100 feet inside the perimeter fence and just below an open space between stacks of storage containers. The problem was the instrumentation was not so precise underground, and if they came up under one of the stacks of containers, they might flood the tunnel with who knows what as they breached the object.

Laying on his back, he pressed the rod into the ceiling and began the effort of tunneling up into the depot itself. While the troopers behind him, were silent as the grave, the body heat, and lack of airflow did make for a less than comfortable experience. Thankfully, the facemasks helped greatly in providing breathable air.

As Daniel worked, he tracked his progress until his proximity display alerted him to distance from the surface above. Set to notify him once he was within three feet of the ground, Daniel passed the word for his team to get ready. Once they breached the surface, they were the most vulnerable as they exited the tunnel.

As he eased the rod forward, removing the last obstacles above him, he suddenly stopped as the bottom edge of one of the containers appeared in the dim light. Shifting the rod out slightly, he continued until they had an opening sufficient for the troopers to exit their underground passage.

By now, the sunlight was fading, the temperature was dropping, and Daniel had returned his faceplate display back from Night Vision mode needed in the tunnel to normal mode. The cold air rushing in the opening was startling against his exposed skin. The undetected opening in the tunnel itself was a relief, a hole allowing him to scan both directions in the alley created by the stacks of storage containers.

Similar in size to the containers he had seen in earth history books, these containers were rectangular in size only significantly larger than the ones humans had used. A dull gray in color, each had unintelligible markings that Daniel assumed to reference the contents. Stacked a good twenty feet high, it allowed the entire team to exit the tunnel unobserved.

While darkness was descending on the group, no one took for granted that they would be completely invisible to the alien guards. With that in mind, the team split up, each member tasked with depositing their charges unobserved, and then back through the tunnel to rendezvous on the other side of the fence line.

Prior to beginning the tunneling, Daniel had been able to adjust their equipment to alert the wearer should an alien in combat gear come into view. Blooming like a red halo in their display, it would help the wearer quickly identify threats as they neared.

Taking the farthest objectives as his own, it took Daniel some time to safely traverse the significant distance from one side of the depot to the other and back without detection. Several times he had to hold in place as an alien worker performed some task nearby.

He was almost to the tunnel when he saw the area suddenly light up in extra lights. His RF meter also started bouncing in what he assumed were pulsed broadcasts.

"Leftanant, target two just went up early," came the message in his ear from Colonel Banks back on the Phantom.

"Bloody hell," Daniel replied as he ducked into a small opening. As he watched, the alien sentries were scrambling around in all directions making his exit impossible.

Chapter 20

Jake was watching the holographic image relayed from Kola, depicting the attack force closing in on G-43578. He could see the ships forming as planned, with the Combat Patrol ships and fighters leading the way. Separately, the Scout/Sniper team had relayed in a video stream of the flurry of activity at the primary target location.

The aliens were doing everything they could to prepare their defenses, including directing the guns of the four cruisers skyward. It was a move one expected for an assault from above. It was for that reason that the Chinese assault would be coming on the ground from the sides.

Early on, the analysts had determined that the defensive ring each of the alien locations had constructed consisted of gun towers that covered from the horizon to the sky. Only in the sky could all the towers be brought to bear on an assaulting force.

By bringing in the tanks and the troops at ground level, they removed a significant number of the towers from being able to target them. The combination of assault troops on the ground and low-level strafing runs from above. The objective was to neutralize as much of the defensive capability as possible without destroying the facility itself.

Once the area was secure, a team of technical analysts would sweep the facility, gathering as much information on what the NeHaw were doing as possible, to either counter the technology or mimic it for Earth's own use.

Checking the display, Jake verified the ship with the specialists was preparing to depart, if not somewhat reluctantly.

----*----

"Yes, sir, I do see your point. However, we are paying a substantial sum for this service," Brian repeated for the third time as he tried to get the Wawobash to depart for G-43578.

"You must understand kind sir, that our people are not prepared to engage in hostile activities. We were assured that we would not be required to perform our work in a battlefield," the Wawobash Captain replied in the display.

Brian had become used to seeing the canine face speaking, their facial abilities more capable than their terrestrial look-alikes. While they were incredible builders and technically brilliant, their bravery was not what one would call heroic.

They would risk life and limb, all six limbs, that is, to work in space as they constructed ships for other racers. But heading into a combat zone, so they could determine what the NeHaw were up to, was something entirely outside of their comfort zone.

"It will be a day before you are able to land on G-43578. By then, my people will have the planet secured, and you will be quite safe," Brian replied.

"How can you be sure?" the Wawobash Captain asked pointedly.

"I was in the Battle of Klinan," ALICE-3 voiced into the conversation.

The Captain paused, turning to look off-screen before responding.

"We will depart immediately," the alien replied before cutting the connection.

"Thanks," Brian said to ALICE-3 as he sighed in frustration.

"My pleasure," she replied with what sounded like a laugh.

----*----

"What happened?" Daniel asked as he did his best to look invisible to all the alien troops around him.

"A charge must have been accidentally detonated by one of the alien workers. Fortunately, the team had completed its work and was not present when the chain went off. No casualties."

Daniel understood that Colonel Banks's reference to the chain was the link the charges had with one another. The charges could be linked to go off all at once or in any sequence one chose, to provide the most amount of destructive experience. The downside to that was, you were always conscious of the fact that an accidental discharge would take out all of the team members carrying one piece of the chain.

"Situation?" Daniel heard Banks ask.

"Currently, I am wedged between two piles of containers, waiting for the blasted aliens to quiet," he whispered as a pair of armed aliens hurried past.

"Remain where you are, and we shall see what we can do to remedy your predicament," Banks replied before dropping the connection.

----*----

General KaLob was in the situation room of the Military High Command building, watching the feed from G-43578 of the incoming attack force. They had additional information transmitting in from a reconnaissance ship sitting well out in space, beyond the reach of the human's enormous blockade ship.

While they didn't expect to be able to assemble a force sufficient to counter the human attack in time to prevent it, they were still trying to form a response. Due to the size of the ship sitting just outside the planet's solar system, they had estimated they would need at least eight to ten cruisers and twice the number of destroyers to counter the firepower the ship represented.

How the humans managed to operate these vessels with such small crews was a mystery to the NeHaw, while stuffing ferrous hulled monstrosities inside. In addition, how they were still capable of FTL travel was a double mystery to all the empire. KaLob had promised a reward of a tribute free existence to any planet that solved the mystery. So far, all attempts to replicate the feat had failed.

"General KaLob, we have another report of an attack in progress. This one is a bit confusing as no one can verify who the attackers are?" the officer stated as he handed his superior the report.

189

Scanning the information, KaLob could see the images confirming the destruction at one of their supply stops, planet K-82734. Scanning through the information, he paused.

"It's just this one site? The other depots on the planet remain undamaged?" he asked, confused at why the humans would stop there.

"Yes, sir. Nothing more," the officer replied.

"I want two security detachments sent there immediately. There is more to this, I think," the General ordered.

"Yes, Sir," the officer replied as the General turned back to the pending battle.

----*----

The command center in Nevada was a beehive of activity as the various groups managed the continuous flow of data. Jake was aware that something had happened to the SAS mission that had exposed the operation there before they were ready. The initial desire had been to trigger the charges at the depots after the Chinese had landed in an effort to get the NeHaw to split their attention and resources in haste.

The turn of events wasn't a total disaster, as it could still be used to influence the enemy. He just needed to weigh his options. That bad part of things was Patti's obsession with gathering details on the incident. Jake was well aware that her Daniel was hip-deep in that operation.

The fact that no one had been hurt or killed did little to dissuade her pursuing more details on the status of the troopers. When she finally learned that Daniel was alive but trapped inside one of the depots, she was not relieved one bit.

"Jake, we need to do something about Daniel," she said as she rushed over with a printout of the situation.

Reviewing the information, Jake did a quick check on the status of the Phantom and the remainder of the SAS force. Walking over to one side of the room, he found the analyst he was looking for and made a request.

"Can you get me Colonel Banks without causing him any problems?"

"Yes sir, we are streaming data to and from the Phantom now," she replied before initiating the communication.

"Banks," came the curt reply.

"Edwin, this is Jake, you need anything?" Jake asked as Patti stood nearby.

"At present, not a thing. However, I could use a diversion in a bit. We seem to have lost one of our lads, trapped actually. Once I have the rest of the team on board, I was considering plucking him out of the yard before it all became rubbish," Banks replied.

Looking at the analyst expectantly, she flipped through a few displays before replying.

"We still have one drone in orbit. Presently it's being used to monitor the supply yard that Lieutenant Atkins is hiding in," she said hopefully.

"Edwin, are you going in cloaked?" Jake asked.

"That was the idea. Unfortunately, once we drop the ramp and ladder, we will be quite visible to those below us," the Colonel replied.

"Here is my idea," Jake replied as he began explaining his thought.

----*----

Daniel was starting to worry as the short cycle of night and day on this world was about to expose him to the occupants. While the suit provided extremely good camouflage at night, the harsh light of day made it less effective. He had made several attempts to ghost his way to the tunnel only to be thwarted by a roving patrol or some of the yard workers.

The longer they left the charges undetonated, the more likely it was that someone would stumble on one. Even more worrying was the thought of one accidentally being detonated, which would not do his health a bit of good.

As he was preparing for another attempt at relocating to the tunnel entrance, he got a ping from the Phantom.

"Confirming your location," he heard from a voice that was not Colonel Banks.

Checking the display strapped to his forearm, he could see the little map of the supply yard and his blinking location finder.

"Confirmed," he replied.

"Prepare for vertical extraction in one minute," the voice replied.

"Vertical?" Daniel repeated to himself. He suddenly got an image of himself dangling at the end of a cable as he was lifted free of the area. He was not delighted with the thought that he was about to become target practice for the alien sentries nearby.

Just then, there was a huge explosion at the other end of the yard, and he could see several of the nearby guards rushing off in that direction. No sooner did the disturbance occur than the Phantom loading ramp appeared overhead, and a line was dropped.

Attaching the clip to his integrated harness, part of the kit he wore, he then felt a terrific jolt as he was rocketed skyward. His head snapped forward, and as he recovered, he noted several of the aliens bringing their weapons to bear.

That was interrupted by a blinding flash as the charges he had helped set went off all at once. His last vision before being drug into the Phantom was flying debris, smoke, and flame below.

"Leftanant, so glad you could join us," the Colonel said with a smile as he offered his hand in helping the man up.

----*----

The drone impact had provided the effect that Jake was hoping for, drawing the alien security away for just long enough to get Daniel hooked up. Once clear of the danger area, the explosive charges had put on quite a show as they lit the area up under the Phantom.

Jake had ordered all the other supply yards destroyed at the same time, not only covering the Phantoms exit but sending a message to the NeHaw that nothing was safe. Once he was sure the SAS had safely recovered Daniel and was swiftly headed for space, he turned his attention back to the Chinese operation exclusively.

By now, the fighters and combat patrol ships had begun to engage the defensive systems floating in orbit around the planet. As they closed on the planet, these gun platforms opened fire with energy cannons, doing their best to converge on the rapidly moving fighters.

Unable to withstand even the smaller railgun fire from the fighters, it wasn't long before the combination of fighter and patrol craft fire had cleared a swath across the surface of the planet. At this point, the transports had been hanging back, firing at targets of opportunity, but doing nothing to risk their precious cargo.

The attack force had reached the point in the plan where the transports were to split away from the combat ships. This move was to allow them the ability to close on the surface of the planet in places not covered by the planetary defenses. As they did so, the two fighter squadrons and the Combat Patrol ships strafed each of the three target locations, removing as many of the gun towers and other defenses as possible before moving to the next site.

Working methodically, they started with the two support sites that didn't contain the cruisers providing additional firepower. The fighters came in first, low and fast, railguns ripping through the towers raised high above the compounds they protected. Firing the entire time, they scored multiple hits, disabling what they could. Right behind them, the Patrol ships heavier guns destroyed position after position, leaving piles of smoking debris behind them.

Near the first target, no more than a few miles away, the first of the transports set down. Two of the Chinese tanks and two fighting vehicles burst out of the ship's hold, firing at the remaining defensive positions as they came into range. Behind them and shielded by the vehicles, squads of troops filed down the transport ramps, preparing to overrun the positions inside the compounds once the fences were down.

Of concern to Jake was the enemy was rolling out additional weaponry from of structures around the compounds. Apparently stored away and out of view, he could see mobile gun platforms, similar to 90 or 100-millimeter anti-tank guns of old Earth. These, however, were a mix of single-barreled energy cannons and smaller multi-barreled charged particle weapons.

In groups of two or three, he could see the alien gun crews position the weapons along the fence line, facing the incoming Chinese forces.

"Patti, make sure to raise the threat condition for Robert and Bo. We are seeing additional firepower coming into play," Jake commented, wanting to ensure the two commanders on the ground was aware of this new development.

----*----

Colonel Bo watched the progress of his forces from the command deck of the first transport to land. Wanting to be in a position to make changes should the first effort go badly, he stood watching the action supplied by Kola's overhead feed.

Twice he stopped breathing, as first one, and then another of the tanks took direct hits from the energy cannons still in play. Both vehicles paused for a moment as if confused and then returned fire, the railguns in the turrets ripping the enemy positions to shreds. While not stasis shielded, the heavy iron armor took the hits well.

Seconds seemed like hours as the small force worked its way forward to reach the perimeter, where a once highly charged energy fence vaporized anything that touched it. Chao watched as first his fighting vehicles, and then tanks floated right into the facility grounds while taking small arms fire from all directions.

He could see the troops as they fanned out after passing through the breach, engaging the few security personnel brave enough to confront his troops after the pounding the armor gave them.

"Bo, check Target 2," he heard from Robert, who was in another transport supporting that drop.

He looked to the technician working the display, who acknowledged him by shifting the image to the second target, also the one without the cruisers. Here, the tanks had not quite reached the fence. He could see the aliens had scrounged up some portable weaponry, locating it along the approach boundary inside the compound.

As with Target 1, this force only had two tanks and two fighting vehicles in the attack. He could see one of the fighting vehicles was inoperable, its hatches open, and crew scrambling for cover. It was then that both tanks fired, converging on the point in the center of the cobbled up defense force.

In a blinding flash of light, an explosion leveled the cluster of defenders, leaving a gaping hole in the ground and the fence. From there, it was short work for his people to sweep into the compound ahead of the armor. He could see his troops swarming into the structures there as the aliens retreated.

The tanks quickly moved in behind the ground forces, engaging defensive positions on the far side of the compound, not visible to them on their approach. While the fighting was still fierce, Bo was satisfied his people had things well in hand.

----*----

After the shooting started at the other locations, Jason and his team watched as the primary Target started to buzz with activity. Prior to the landings, they had surveyed their target area and mapped out the locations, and identifying the priority of their targets.

Now the target landscape was changing by the moment. As the four watched, new weapons were being revealed and brought to bear in the compound. Alien troops were positioning themselves all along the fence line in defensive positions created on the fly.

Marking up his map once more, Jason reassessed the target values before turning to the other members of the team.

"Once the shooting starts, feel free to engage," he commented to the loose members of the team.

His spotter would be busy keeping him on track, but the other two members of the team would be able to engage targets of their own. While not capable of the same accuracy and damage as the sniper railgun Jason was using, their personal weapons had the legs to take out personnel at this distance.

Noticing the transport that had just landed was now belching out troops with the armor maneuvering into position, Jason gave his team the green light.

"Ok, let's burn some ammo," he said with a smile.

Chapter 21

Leaving that massive amount of activity at Target 2 for his field commander to manage, Bo had the technician move to Target 3, the big prize.

"Colonel, we are being informed the compound is secure, should we move in?" the transport Captain asked, referring to Target 1.

"One moment please," Bo replied while pointing to the display.

Both men watched as the tech widened the image to take in more action. With the four cruisers in the compound, the Patrol ships and fighters were still engaging the defensive forces there.

Again, this transport carried two of the fighting vehicles, but in this case, there were four tanks. Approaching from two directions, the tanks had split into pairs with one fighting vehicle attached to each pair. Here, an entire platoon was spread between the two approaches, intent on not only securing the compound but taking possession of the four NeHaw cruisers as well.

As he watched, something caught Bo's eye. Every so often, one of the alien defenders would just fall, and not rise. With his troops still so far out of range, and not yet engaging the defenders with small arms, it was like the hand of God was reaching out and swatting the aliens, one at a time.

Not an overly religious man, he said a little prayer thanking whatever power it was that was helping them his day.

----*----

Jason was in the zone as his spotter called out target after target. After weeks of sitting and watching, everyone on the team was itching for some action. Having been set up for quite a while before the attack forces hit the ground, he and the corporal spent their time before the assault mapping out their targets with precision.

Once the shooting started, they quickly walked through the preassigned targets, using the various rounds the railgun rifle had available to neutralize the opposition. Once those were ticked off the list, they next moved to targets of opportunity.

"Right two and up three," the corporal announced, giving him a new target in reference to his last shot. Moving right and up, he found an alien in a combat suit, directing a small group of others. A gentle squeeze, and it was down.

"Sarge, there is a group of those gomers trying to get the gun working on T5," the corporal said, referring to a preassigned target that they had already neutralized.

Swapping the railgun round out for an HE option, he mentally pictured the map they had drawn earlier and shifted back to the location designated T5. Another gentle squeeze and the group of three aliens erupted in flame and body parts.

He had to admit this railgun rifle was the bomb, literally.

"Left four and down three," the corporal said again, not pausing to celebrate.

----*----

Jake watched the holograph as the Chinese forces spread out before moving in on their last objective. He felt a tinge of pride as the analysts called out the sniper team's work, removing threat indicators as they neutralized dangers. He was a bit envious of the shooter, whoever it was.

Focusing on the armor, he could see the tanks leading the advance, with the more maneuverable fighting vehicle sprinting toward targets of opportunity as the battlefield data was being fed to the vehicle commanders.

Unsure of the origins of the defenders, Jake found it hard to believe the NeHaw themselves were actually fighting on the ground. It was a mystery that would be solved soon enough. Whomever it was, Jake had to give them credit. They were putting up a good fight considering their limitations.

By now, they had redirected the fighters to support other activities while the two patrol ships continued to slug it out with the cruisers and the remaining gun towers. That interaction prevented the defenders from concentrating their fire on the armor as it advanced.

That thought was premature, unfortunately, as one of the advancing tanks exploded in a bright ball of fire and light. The concentrated fire from two gun towers plus the closest cruiser completely engulfed the vehicle.

As if in retaliation, both gun towers toppled right afterward as railgun fire ripped their supports out from under the gun turrets. With that, the remaining tank and fighting vehicle surged forward, carrying a wave of soldiers in their wake.

Before long, Jake could see the Chinese troops pressing into the compound as vast sections of the barrier fence was powered down.

"Looks like Bo and Robert delivered as promised," he said to the open room filled with people as a loud cheer broke out.

----*----

HeBak was a bit surprised by the meeting request he received first thing in the morning. The message simply asked if he was available to speak to Colonel Thomas later that day. He was aware that was the name of the human resistance leader and that the two had met several times before. However, HeBak treated the question as if it were a request for an audience.

So far, the humans had been more than accommodating to his prolonged stay. In part, that was because they originally captured him trying to escape after stealing precious metals. However, the fact that he had never actually asked to leave held a certain sway in the circumstances.

He eventually accepted the request and then spent the remainder of his day doing nothing particularly special to prepare for the visit. He was sure the humans wanted something from him, or they would have simply arrived at the door to his ship and requested entrance.

That particular point did strike him as strange, as the humans had never actually demanded anything from him once he declared himself a refugee from his homeworld. Though he doubted they actually believed the story he had provided, thin as it was, they had simply accepted it and moved on.

So far, HeBak had profited greatly from the current relationship, and he firmly believed that the humans had done so as well. The last time the humans had reached out to him, it was to assist in the eventual location of the space armada that was destined to attack them here. The reward for that mission had been particularly large.

Since then, HeBak had been left to his own devices, patiently awaiting the day he could return to civilization and begin spending the massive wealth accumulated in his ship's hold. He has still not decided on whether to return to the homeworld or if he wanted his own moon as a massive display of wealth.

It was as he was considering his options that the ship's systems notified him of his visitor. Moving from his sleeping quarters, where he had been resting, to his lounge space on the ship, he was in no particular hurry. He finally settled into a comfortable chair before releasing the lock on the airlock hatch and allowing the human access to the airlock.

HeBak maintained his native atmosphere inside his vessel to provide for his comfort. He was keenly aware that the humans couldn't breathe inside his ship, so they would be at a disadvantage, something he had experienced many times when dealing with them on the outside.

A noise at the entry to his lounge drew his attention as he watched the human they called Jake standing at the opening.

"May I come in?" he asked as he motioned.

"Please, do have a seat," HeBak replied as he indicated one of the least comfortable seats in the room.

The human wasn't wearing one of their uniforms, as HeBak had expected. Rather this one wore only a face mask that covered its eyes, nose, and mouth. He could also see the headpiece that only this particular human seemed to be able to use to communicate. He had never seen it used by any other.

While it still required its simplistic audio speech to be translated, it could natively hear HeBak, something that frankly disturbed him. It was like having a pet that could suddenly write.

"How may I help you?" HeBak finally asked after the two sat quietly for several microcycles.

"Actually, that is exactly why I am here. I need your help in arranging a face to face meeting with the new NeHaw leadership," the human replied.

At the statement, HeBak did something he could not recall ever experiencing. He laughed aloud.

"Not to be rude, but why would they agree to such a meeting?" he finally managed to get out after calming himself.

"There have been certain events recently that you may not be aware of. The Empire has suffered certain losses that might be the incentive for such," the human replied.

HeBak stopped mid retort. He was about to tell this upstart that nothing they could do would inspire NeHaw leadership to meet with beings so far beneath them. Then he remembered that those leaders were gone, and those now in power might want an opportunity to see these creatures as he had. Once that set in, another thought came in its place.

"You may recall, I am not in favor on the homeworld right now. My sympathies for your people have made me an outcast, a refugee of sorts," he replied, sticking to the cover story he had created when captured. Frankly, the thought of returning home under the current circumstances terrified HeBak. It was possible they would execute him on sight.

HeBak watched the human for a reaction. He felt he was getting to the point where he could tell what they were thinking by their body language and facial expressions. So, it was with great surprise that he listened to the response.

"Let's cut the crap, shall we? You are no more a refugee than I am a NeHaw. I don't know what you did back home to get exiled, nor do I really care. Frankly, considering we caught you stealing, I suspect you are some form of criminal, and hiding here is your best bet at staying alive. Putting all that aside, you are far more likely to survive a trip home than any of us would just trying to find it," the human finished.

"Perhaps you are correct, however, why would I choose to take such a risk," HeBak responded in a candid moment.

"Two reasons. The first is at some point you want to leave here so you can spend all that treasure you have in your hold. I doubt seriously that just sitting down there and staring at it all day is all you want to do? This might give you an opportunity to make amends for whatever you did to get exiled in the first place by bringing them a very valuable opportunity. We will give you something to present to the new leadership there that will ensure your safe arrival."

"And the second?" HeBak asked after considering the first and accepting the statement as valid.

"Besides paying you a vast sum for your effort, if you don't do this, you may be here for a very, very long time."

----*----

General KaLob was not in a particularly good mood. He had just witnessed the capture of four NeHaw cruisers and the facility they were relying on to give their ships a fighting chance. In addition, the total destruction of supply depots on K-82734, a supposedly safe place.

He was still weighing the options between retaliating against the humans elsewhere or directing those same forces to retake the planet and destroy the ship in orbit there. The latter was much more desirable, but he knew it would come at a great cost.

At one time, his people might have brought to bear one of the now forbidden weapons to deal with the situation. They had learned at a terrible cost; some things were not worth the price you had to pay. That lesson had almost cost them their very existence.

Pushing the thought from his mind, he continued to work through his resourcing reports. He was trying to find the right combination of ships and crews to push the decision one way or another without gutting their harassment of the Earth aligned planets.

----*----

Robert and Bo were wandering the compound identified as Target 3 in their attack plan. The NeHaw had not gone down without a fight, and Robert had the broken wreckage of two fighters, one tank and one fighting vehicle to prove it. Stuffed into one of the transports, they had sent it, and one of the Combat Patrol ships back to Kola with one squadron.

Since both squadrons had lost a fighter, the pilots surviving the crashes as they safely ejected, it seemed irrelevant, which went back to Kola and which stayed behind to cover the ground forces, should something unexpected come up.

The big concern presently was that a NeHaw force would be sent to retake the planet before the humans had retrieved the Intel they came for. Almost laughably, the Wawobash had appeared right after Target 3 had fallen. Even now, Robert could see them scurrying around as they bounced between the cruisers under modification and the building surrounding the landing pads.

"Major, may I have a word?" Robert heard from behind him. As he turned, he found the Marine Sergeant he had met the day before approaching them.

It had been quite a sight that day, as he and Bo had been organizing the security forces within the compound, to watch the four man team come strolling in from outside the fence. Bo seemed to have some eureka moment as he realized the Scout/Sniper team had been assisting in the assault on the compound.

"What can I do for you?" Robert replied, not overly concerned about the rank thing. In his eyes, this man and his team had earned the respect of everyone here.

"If you don't mind, my people and I would like to hitch a ride back to the ship. We have been in the boonies for weeks, so a hot shower and cold beer would be very welcome right now."

Looking at Bo for a response, he received a nod of agreement.

"I can't see a good reason for you to stay unless you want to go out and look for escaped NeHaw," Robert replied. There had been a small number of NeHaw security force members that had slipped out after the fall of the compound, but most had been quickly rounded up.

"Thanks, sir, but no," Jason replied with a smile.

"Check and see when the next run to Kola is scheduled and get on it. If anyone questions you, tell them to see Colonel Bo or me.

----*----

While the Earth was battling aliens in space, Joe and Abby were on duty, watching the art recovery teams back at work in Central Park. They had complained to Jake that they would be of far greater use on the battlefield than here babysitting. He had replied that while others were securing their future, they were ensuring the past would not be lost or forgotten.

So now, besides working as security for the teams scrubbing the museums throughout New York, they were doing double duty as a team of medics worked an ever-increasing line of civilians. The ragtag group of men, women, and children had come from all over the city to seek medical attention.

Arriving before the ships, the 10th had established an ironclad rule that once the ships had landed in the park, no weapons would be allowed within the boundaries of the park, no exceptions. There were a few incidents in the beginning, and examples had to be made of some nonbelievers.

After one of the troopers took a shotgun blast to the chest with no effect, in front of a large crowd, the point was made.

The unconscious form of the offender was drug off by his gang, and no other challenges of the restrictions were made. Joe was happy to see the gangs policing themselves at the very next visit.

He was concerned, however, that Jessie had made mention of crossing the Atlantic soon in search of more museums to plunder. With the troubles here, he wondered how many other cities they were going to have to subdue.

Chapter 22

The tracker they had placed on the NeHaw HeBak's ship was designed to report back to Earth every time the ship dropped out of FTL and then go to sleep to avoid detection. Attached to the ship's navigation system, it would use the same link the pilot used to verify their location in NeHaw space by attaching to the nearest link point.

Linda had a 24-hour monitor on the feed, creating a track and following the NeHaw as he bounced around the star systems of the NeHaw Empire. Apparently, it was a standard practice for a NeHaw to never return home in a straight run, thus protecting the location.

Linda wasn't sure what Jake's plan was, but it all hinged on learning the exact location of their home planet.

"He has dropped out of FTL again," one of the analysts commented as the display lit up with the latest data. The red dot in the 3D holograph showed a haphazard pattern leapfrogging all across the map, from sector to sector. If Linda didn't know better, she would swear HeBak was procrastinating.

----*----

Colonel Banks and Leftanant Atkins were sitting on the bridge of the Phantom, evaluating a fresh piece of Intel. After their successful raid on the supply planet, K-82734, they had paused to do a damage assessment when the information came in.

During the assault on G-43578, the analysts on Earth were alerted to a large-scale movement of vessels away from their stationary locations but not to a mustering point. That movement left other targets of opportunity unprotected.

The current object of interest was an asteroid floating free in space. As a celestial body unattached to a solar system, the NeHaw had been using it as a base of operations for several sectors. Unlike the supply depot they had just destroyed, this was a command center of some kind.

Both men envisioned it as a wonderful chance to grab intelligence as well as an opportunity to disrupt the NeHaw command and control for the region.

"I'm submitting the request now," Banks said as he hit the transmit key.

"Let's hope they see the brilliance of our proposal," Daniel replied with a broad smile.

----*----

General KaLob had decided on a course of action regarding the humans' latest activities. It made little sense to try and drive them off G-43578 as they were now the entrenched defender, and it would require a significant force to overcome them and the massive ship protecting them.

It was the opinions of his planning division that the facilities there would not survive the encounter intact. Therefore, they would be fighting over nothing. With that decided, they turned their attention to other opportunities throughout the rebellious region.

The Earth's capital ships were usually clustered near their homeworld, making any attempts at striking at the heart of their civilization risky at best. Now, however, they found the human resources scattered throughout the universe, providing a rare opportunity.

So it was, with rare NeHaw urgency, that KaLob issued an emergency recall command for a significant number of ships to converge on a new target.

----*----

HeBak was not as sure as he had once been that this was going to turn out the way he had hoped. The human they called Jake had made a good argument that should this mission be successful, his safe return to NeHaw space would be not only possible but likely.

In preparation for the voyage, as he would need his ship for the return flight to the NeHaw homeworld, his vessel had been emptied of its precious metals. He had not been so eager to see his wealth removed from his hold for

207

safekeeping. As they would certainly search the vessel once he returned home, that much wealth would not only raise suspicions but would likely be confiscated, taken for the good of the empire.

His only hope of retaining his hard-earned retirement was to leave it behind for safekeeping with the humans. It also ensured his completing the mission and not just skipping off, as the human had candidly explained.

So, HeBak had left the Earth and began the long and monotonous voyage to the edge of their solar system. Once there, he got a good look at the monstrosity they had constructed there. While it was not a NeHaw trait to build such free floating orphaned structures, as they tended to utilize planets, moons, and asteroids for such fortifications, he understood the need.

Finally, he engaged the navigation system autopilot to perform a sequenced set of FTL jumps designed to confuse anyone attempting to track his movements. There would be several jumps to irrelevant locations before finally arriving at the desired destination. This was a standard NeHaw practice drilled into anyone who went off the planet.

Once engaged, HeBak retreated to his lounge, where he planned on becoming one with a meal.

----*----

"Can you repeat that please?" Jake asked incredulously as he conferred with the lead Wawobash scientist responsible for reviewing the facility on G-43578.

"We have determined that the NeHaw are utilizing an older process for creating hull plating. We once used the same process but abandoned it long ago as it is quite a time consuming and expensive. The materials required for the manufacturing process are only found in certain parts of the Empire. This planet is the most well-known source of that material, which is why they came here."

"So, you are telling me we took this planet to learn about something you already knew how to do?" Jake asked, doing his best to remain calm.

"It is unfortunate you did not discuss this with us prior to your attack. You might have been able to avoid the encounter entirely. However, I should point out that you now control a significant source of materials that resist your railgun weapons. That alone is of some value to you," the Wawobash scientist finished with what Jake took to be a smile. Unfortunately, with the canine features, it translated to a snarl in the human experience.

"We will be providing a detailed report on the facility and how the plating materials work against your weapons. I hope you find that information equal to the payment provided, as we do not find fault in our work here. Our contract was to analyze your conquest for military applications and provide recommendations for use and countermeasures. That work was made simpler for us as it is a known technology."

"Yes, thank you," Jake replied as he waved Patti over to handle the logistics of the situation.

"This is unbelievable," Jake mumbled as he left the conference room.

----*----

With the minor damage to ALICE-3 created by the NeHaw attack repaired, Brian and ALICE-3 had moved to the edge of the Wawobash system. The events on both G-43578 and K- 82734 had them on edge, so the move put them in a position to jump to FTL for either location, at a moment's notice. In a reversal of roles, they had the four Combat Patrol ships placed in a picket line between them and the shipyards.

In an effort to prepare for the worst, they had all four ships resupply from the battleship's stores to ensure they could survive for an extended period, should ALICE-3 need to vacate the area. Noting their tolerance for a broad range of foodstuffs, the Russian crews joked that they could always hit the Wawobash up for food. Brian explained that it was likely a private joke neither ALICE-3 nor Brian chose to explore.

Once everyone was up to 100% operational capability, and in place, they all went back to their earlier waiting game.

----*----

Jake was taking a much-needed break, having left the conference room after the brief on G-43578 in less than an up mood. He had left Sara and the twins earlier that morning, the girls doing great with Sara still exhausted and recovering. Becky was spending all of her free time helping her sister while playing the doting aunt to her nieces.

For that, Jake was incredibly grateful, as he had enough on his plate and was feeling extremely guilty that he wasn't there with them. So, satisfied the world could survive for an hour without him, Jake suited up and jumped on his hovercycle. Popping up through the hangar doors, when they had barely parted, he streaked south.

Within minutes, he was above Las Vegas, with the sun overhead on a clear sunny day in the desert. Checking his scanners, he looked to see if there were any concentrations of people below.

"Jake, do I need to remind you that we can't detect people deep inside the buildings," ALICE warned.

"Don't worry, I am just doing a little sightseeing."

"The last time you went sightseeing, you brought home two children," ALICE reminded him.

"How are Jon and Padma doing anyway?" Jake asked absently as he circled the area looking for something to catch his eye.

"I will not be so easily distracted. The kids and Sandy are doing just fine, as you well know since you check on them at every opportunity," ALICE chided.

Swinging south to the far end of what was once called "the Strip," referring to the area lined with casinos, Jake passed over part of the airport. Nearby were clusters of retail and industrial centers, before giving way to residential areas.

Having passed the area of interest, Jake turned and did a sweeping one-eighty degree turn when a movement below caught his eye. Dropping lower, he was just in time to see something slip into an abandoned grocery store. Setting the hovercycle down in the parking lot, he could see the faded Whole Foods sign on the side of the structure.

Grabbing the suppressed submachine gun out of the back, he cautiously moved toward the entrance. He had little concern of anyone messing with the hovercycle as it automatically locked down once he stepped away from it.

Jake did a quick scan of the interior of the building as he looked through the open doors, finding nothing of concern. Even so, he entered cautiously, repeating his scan and using infrared and night vision inside the darkened structure.

The bright Vegas sun did provide quite a bit of light, but the windows on the front of the building hadn't been cleaned in decades. A shuffling noise to his right drew Jake's attention. As he quietly slipped forward and to the right, he scanned aisle after aisle of the trashed interior.

Stopping, he caught a movement and froze as he slowly turned to face the open aisle. There, standing in the center of an open area with trash all around, was a dog. Jake realized it wasn't just any dog. From the looks of it, the dog was as close to a purebred German Shepard as one could expect from eighty-plus years of neglect.

Pulling a candy bar from his pocket, he slowly approached the animal, careful not to move quickly and spook it. Timid at first, hunger won out as it stepped forward and snatched the offering from his gloved hand. A quick check revealed it was a she and probably several years old.

While a bit thin and dirty, she looked to be surprisingly healthy. A second offering was accepted more slowly this time, and Jake was eventually able to reach out and stroke her head gently. Slowly and without spooking her, Jake sat in the aisle and provided a third treat as he quietly and gently stroked her coat.

Knocking what was likely years of dirt and grime off her, Jake had to assume that she had human contact at some point in her past to allow him such familiarity. Looking around for the first time, he realized the two of them were in what was once the coffee aisle of the store.

"What am I going to do with you?" he asked as he offered her a drink from a water bottle he carried for just such occasions.

----*----

"You brought home a what?" Sara asked as she talked to Jake from the display in her room. He had apparently gone off on one of his solo trips and brought home another stray, literally.

"It's a dog. ALICE agrees she's mostly Shepherd and in really good health. I'm here in the med bay while they check her out and clean her up."

"What are we going to do with a dog? Jake, you have no idea where it's been. I hope you don't think you are bringing it near the girls?" Sara asked defiantly.

"Honey, you need to trust me on this. Once she's cleaned up, you are going to love her. And besides ALICE, no one is a better protector of children than a German Shepherd."

"You have gone insane!" Sara replied before cutting the connection.

----*----

Robert was sitting with Bo in a small room off the bridge on one of his transports. While they controlled all three facilities on G-43578, none of the buildings were configured for human occupancy. To accommodate the troops living needs, one transport each had been parked inside the compound of that location.

There, they acted as a home for the duration. When not on duty, it permitted the troops a place to rest and relax, all within the safety of the ship. Those on duty were split between patrolling the compounds and guarding the prisoners.

The aliens protecting the three target locations turned out to be a combination of NeHaw and another race that the

212

humans had yet to encounter. As both were roughly humanoid in appearance, the ability to distinguish them in environmental combat suits was impossible.

There was a third race that was indigenous to the planet and required no special accommodations. These were the double tetrahedrons they had seen in the Scout/Sniper reports. A nonviolent race, they were the scientists and engineers that performed the ship upgrades, very similar to the Wawobash.

In fact, it had been the Wawobash that vouched for the race, called the Aseristic. A kindred spirit to the Wawobash, they had negotiated for the humans and established a nonaggression pact. As long as the Earthlings let them continue to operate and repair the damaged locations, they would do nothing to assist the NeHaw prisoners, nor would they resist in any way.

Both Robert and Bo were surprised at the offer. It was only after the Wawobash guaranteed the deal, did they take it seriously. The final decision point in allowing the work was the place was no good to Earth unless it was operating properly. In the end, they agreed to the pact.

The real surprise was the confusion around all three races' status as prisoners of war. None of the races understood at the beginning that they were not to be executed. It had taken a considerable amount of time, with Kola and the Wawobash doing more of the translations, before they understood their status.

That created a new problem as there was nothing on this planet that even resembled a detention center. This was made even more complicated as both nonresident species required different environments to survive. Apparently, the captured NeHaw had been members of the cruiser crews and had been using their ships for accommodations while in refit.

As that was no longer an option, the Wawobash on-site, with the help of the Aseristic, had been contracted to convert one of the maintenance buildings into a NeHaw dormitory. Members of the other race- the Holsec- who were the normal security force, were confined to a building that conveniently functioned as their living quarters before the attack.

By relieving them of their environmental suits and removing any communications equipment from the structure, they were effectively confined to the building. Unlike the NeHaw, they were actually quite cooperative once they learned they would survive the experience. Again, the Wawobash went a long way to helping them believe what they were being told.

"Jake seemed quite upset to learn about what they did here?" Bo asked as the two men shared a meal. Robert laughed as Bo shared his delight at finally gaining access to his own menu.

"Yeah, I think he feels we lost people needlessly," Robert replied, referring to the losses they experienced in the attack.

Both Bo and Robert had previously agreed that the 17 killed and 23 injured in the assault were incredibly fortunate. While everyone agreed that a single loss of life was regrettable, this was war, and people died.

Here, they had attacked an established defender with superior numbers and prevailed. Not only had they defeated the NeHaw, but had captured the objective intact, which was a big win in anybody's book.

Chapter 23

"You are sure you can do this safely?" Patti asked her image a transparent portrait of concern on the communications display. Daniel studied her face, again debating his choice to come with Colonel Banks, but internally confirming it was the right thing to do. Even so, the worry in her eyes was evident to anyone who cared to look.

"As safely as we can, Luv," he replied softly.

"I've had the team here go over all the information. Everyone agrees that the target value is high. Jake is really pissed about what happened on G-43578 and made us triple check the sources for this," she replied with a nervous laugh.

"Tell him not to fret. We will pop in and out again before they even know we were there," Daniel replied, trying to reduce her concerns.

"You had better," Patti replied, before mouthing a kiss and cutting the connection.

----*----

As Jake headed to the command center, he felt the newly familiar bump of Kona as she followed him through the hallway. Whenever asked, Jake explained the Shepherd's name as something derived from where he found her. Discovered on the coffee aisle in a Whole Foods store, he would reply that he chose Kona because Breakfast Blend was just too awkward to say.

While they say that rank does have its privileges, Jake soon discovered that it was Kona who had developed celebrity status everywhere he went with her. A case in point, once he entered the command center, it was her that all the analysts and technicians greeted, some providing treats they had set aside just for her.

Jake waited at the door of his office as she finished accepting her rewards, then he motioned her inside ahead of him as he entered. Inside, Patti was already there, a pile of paperwork spread across the small conference table.

"Good morning, Granddaughter," Jake announced as Kona first checked the woman before finding her place in the corner. Someone had placed a folded blanket and water bowl there, as it had just appeared one day without anyone asking.

"Daniel is going to lead the team," Patti declared, assuming Jake knew what she was referring to, which he did. He had seen and approved the request earlier.

"He will be fine. They are the best at this," Jake replied reassuringly as he walked over to the table and stood sorting through the documents and photos she had laid out there.

He was aware that the target was a free-floating asteroid that the NeHaw had stabilized in open space. Besides his interest in how they had pulled that off with a celestial body, the intelligence contained in the computers there was a treasure trove.

If nothing else, just the information around the ship movements they had been tracking and what the NeHaw command had up their sleeve was worth the try.

----*----

HeBak had paused the flight plan he had been executing, to float just off some obscure, irrelevant system at the edge of NeHaw space. He was having second thoughts about returning to the homeworld. Even if the High Command accepted his story, the likelihood that they wouldn't execute him on the spot was not very high.

Several times during the voyage, he had attempted to access the data cube he carried from the humans. How they had managed to encrypt access in such a fashion that an experienced communications operator such as himself could not gain access was mind numbing.

Without assurances that the humans had insisted on his safe return, HeBak reluctantly declared to himself that he was playing a very dangerous game. For now, he would take some time and think about his future before making any decisions that could lead to his demise.

----*----

"Jake, HeBak has stopped again. Systems analysis reports he has tried to access the cube, several times now," Linda supplied over the communication's link as Jake sat working at his desk. Patti had left earlier to return to her team. He was sure she wanted to go over Daniel's attack plan one more time.

"Did he get in?" Jake asked after a moment.

"No, ALICE locked it up good. Only after his ship's navigation systems report he's home will it unlock the cube," Linda replied with a laugh.

"So, we get what we want regardless," Jake replied with a laugh of his own.

"Precisely," ALICE replied for Linda.

----*----

Colonel Banks brought the Phantom in at a particular vector as they approached the asteroid. The analysts back home had theorized that approaching from this angle enhanced the ship's cloaking capabilities as it helped mask the energy spike created as they dropped from FTL.

The specific spot they dropped from FTL was calculated to be a blind spot for the sensors at the facility, created by an unintentional void. The sensors had been installed in natural depressions on the surface to protect them. By appearing very close to the body of the asteroid, their energy burst was invisible. If they stayed in the sensor shadow, it was proposed that they could approach and land without alerting the NeHaw to their presence.

He piloted the ship in very cautiously, wary of any indication they had been detected as there were no other ships in the area to blend their drive signatures with. As he did so, Banks did a quick check to see if Atkins was ready below.

Originally proposed as a smash and grab, the analysts on Earth had contrived an alternative mission. If they could slip in undetected, they might be able to plant a tap on the secure computer network there. Once enabled, it would give them unfettered access to all the NeHaw military information, including communications and pending operations planning.

"Right-o boyo, are you ready?" Banks asked as he queried Atkins in the airlock.

For this mission, they were only going to land a four-person team, with Leftanant Atkins in command. Without an atmosphere of any kind, they were all in full American combat suits fitted with the EVA equipment necessary for extended use.

Besides not having a breathable atmosphere, the hollowed-out interior of the asteroid was NeHaw standard. That meant there wasn't breathable air anywhere to be found on this rock in space.

"Walk in the park," Daniel replied as they waited for the green light to exit the airlock.

Setting the Phantom down precisely where instructed, Colonel Banks waited the requisite amount of time to ensure they had not been detected before granting permission to open the airlock. Next on the list of things to do was carefully scanning the signal spectrum for the automated equipment management.

Banks had been instructed that a significant amount of the work required to dock a NeHaw spaceship was managed by automated systems. All a Captain had to do was put his ship in close proximity to the desired location, and the systems negotiated with the necessary components to attach and dock the craft.

The goal here was to locate the discrete system used to open and close the airlocks without alerting the rest of the facility to the activity. The ALICE systems on Earth had even located a maintenance routine that cycled the airlocks every so often to prevent them from seizing up from lack of use.

Utilizing the programs he had been provided, he was soon able to locate and isolate the nearest service airlock and transmit the location to the waiting SAS troopers. Estimating the time required for them to reach their objective, he prepared the service program to allow them to gain access undetected once they had arrived.

Unfortunately, once inside, it was up to them to complete the mission and return safely.

----*----

HeBak hadn't bothered engaging the cloaking device until the final jump, as his appearance in any other location was a nonevent to most systems. Once at the homeworld, he cautiously approached, taking great care not to be crushed by the heavy space traffic around him, those ships being unaware of his presence.

When he finally arrived at a safe location, he took one last moment to review his story, and then with a shudder of resignation, triggered the automated communication systems. His detection was almost instantaneous.

The increased security since his last trip home had been alerted to his presence, and within microcycles, he was completely surrounded by security ships. Transmitting the proper identity codes, his ship was quickly escorted to a secure landing zone, and a gravity clamp was placed on his vessel, preventing its escape.

"What is your business?" he heard on his ship's communicator as the spaceport security officer finally challenged his arrival.

"I was a prisoner of the human rebels. I bring information for the High Council," HeBak replied.

"There is no High Council. General KaLob is now in command of the NeHaw Empire," the security officer replied.

HeBak paused as he considered the information. He had feared that the remnants of the High Council might remember him. This changed things, as he only needed to convince this General of his value to the Empire.

"Excellent. Announce my arrival right away," HeBak commanded.

"I will see if the General has any interest in you," the officer replied disinterestedly.

"You might want to consider I have a message from the Human leader," HeBak snapped back at the incompetent. That seemed to do the trick.

"Arrangements are being made," the security officer replied in a more conciliatory tone.

"Indeed," was his only reply.

----*----

"Jake, sorry to wake you, but we just got confirmation. HeBak has arrived at the NeHaw homeworld," Linda offered on audio. Even without the visual, she was speaking in very hushed tones, trying not to wake those nearby.

"Thanks, that's great news. I will see you in the morning," Jake replied, ending the conversation. Turning, he could see Sara in the dim light, still sound asleep next to him. Beyond her was the oversized bassinet, holding the twins, both thankfully silent.

Finally, he looked down to see Kona lying on the end of the bed, awake and watching him without raising her head. Facing the only doorway into the room, he knew she was silently on guard.

----*----

General KaLob had been notified of the recent arrival. At the moment, he had much larger issues to address. Besides, nothing the humans had to say at the moment held any interest to him. KaLob had his own communication he was preparing for the humans, and it was one they could not mistake.

Routing the assembly communications through the fleet communications hub, a converted asteroid in the middle of space, he sent the go codes to all the ships awaiting his orders. In a very short time, the NeHaw would get retaliation for the damage done on G-43578.

----*----

Daniel and the three troopers with him were hiding just outside the service airlock when they received the go order from Colonel Banks. Within seconds the doors slid open, allowing them access to the airlock itself. The four hurried inside as they had been instructed that the maintenance cycle for these doors was very short.

The last trooper had just slipped inside when the door quickly slid shut behind her. Daniel checked the indicator panel next to the airtight door that would allow them access to the inside of the facility. Unlike humans, the NeHaw did not use indicator lights for the status of the airlock.

There was a display pad next to the hatch that held a symbol. When it was safe to open the door, a large O was shown on the monitor. An unsafe situation, as when the outer door was open, displayed a large X, indicating no access.

With the O clearly showing on the panel, Daniel had the team spread out to either side of the airlock. Weapons at the ready, this was the moment where they would have a successful infiltration mission or a search and destroy. It had been decided from the beginning that if they couldn't pull this off, then they were to grab what they could before blowing the place to pieces.

Triggering the hatch, Daniel held his breath as he got the all-clear from the pair opposite him. Glancing down the passage in his direction, he was relieved to see there wasn't a soul in sight. Slipping quickly inside and closing the airlock before it was noticed, the four quickly slipped deeper inside the asteroid.

Daniel had been amazed to learn that the NeHaw had the floorplans for his facility easily available in their archives. With little effort at all, the analysts on Earth had been able to map out a route that would take them through the least occupied portions of the facility.

The interior was supposed to be a NeHaw normal environment, and to Daniel, that meant dark, smoky air with a tinge of red to everything they saw. He wasn't sure what the air was made of, but he imagined it was the same thing you found in hell.

The sound of voices had Daniel pull the team into a maintenance room, right off the main corridor they had been following. As the NeHaw didn't actually speak, their suits had all been configured to receive the radio waves the aliens emitted.

While he had no idea what the two were discussing as they passed, as NeHaw military, he assumed someone was complaining. In his experience in the military, someone was always complaining. A positive to the experience was it demonstrated that the radio the NeHaw emitted was detectable much sooner than an audio stream would have been. So long as the NeHaw were talking, they would hear them in plenty of time to hide.

Back on the move, the four descended two levels before reaching the area marked as restricted on the floorplans they had seen. Sure enough, there were large X's on several passages display panels, warning those aboard the station. Daniel was relieved to see there wasn't a guard in sight, and nothing was actually locked. He had to assume no NeHaw would risk the punishment of unauthorized access.

Slipping down the passage, they reached the door indicated on the map he had been following. Pausing to see if they could hear anyone on the other side, Daniel finally took a breath and triggered the door mechanism. After a quick glance inside, the team slipped in behind him. Daniel indicated that the last one in stand by the door while he led the others deeper into the room.

He recalled he had been invited once into the rooms that held the ALICE systems in Nevada. Patti had warned him not to touch anything and then walked him through the room while pointing out what was human and what was NeHaw. The experience had left an impression on him that was unique until now.

With no sense of familiarity with what he was looking at, he quietly passed groups of equipment, looking for the systems he had been shown in the briefing. Unlike the human computer rooms that were organized in rows, the NeHaw apparently liked to group things in islands. Although he had no idea how that helped or why they did it, it was apparent that there was a method to their madness.

Soon enough, he found the cabinet he was looking for. While it wasn't actually a cabinet in the human sense, he pressed the place where the access panel he needed opened was triggered and slipped in the tap. Placed precisely as instructed, he closed the panel and waited for confirmation.

"Tap in place," he transmitted.

"Checking," came the reply.

"Proceed to station two," came the success code.

Repeating the process several more times, they placed over a dozen taps in the equipment before they had finished.

It was as they finished the last check that a sound came from the door.

"Incoming," came the alert from the door guard as she scrambled to find cover.

With that, the rest of the team dived for anything that would conceal their presence.

Chapter 24

Linda was working with the team that was tied to the SAS operation. A more accurate statement was Linda was working with Patti as she dominated the SAS operation. Considering Linda's relationship with Jake, she was more than understanding about the young woman's concern over her love interest's wellbeing. While not the same intensity, Linda was always concerned when Jake put himself in harm's way.

It had been a scramble to get the SAS team the materials they needed for this mission, particularly the taps they wanted to use on the NeHaw equipment in their computer room. Fortunately, there had been a Kortisht vessel inbound that stopped at the space station for a handoff. Not only did they have the taps Earth needed, but they also had the results of the analysis on the cube Jake had sent to them.

The good news was, it did cause the FTL failures experienced by Jake and the others before him. The bad news was it couldn't be blocked. The only way to prevent it from disrupting the field required for FTL was to turn it off. She remembers Jake's reply that destroying the offender's ship was one way of turning it off.

"Ma'am, we are getting strong feeds from all sources," one of the analysts announced.

Linda noted it was Private Grace Middleton, a lost child returned to the fold. Jake had pulled Linda aside at one point and indicated to her that he would like Grace to be kept challenged in her work. She didn't take the comment negatively, rather like someone assessing a gifted student.

Slipping up next to the young woman, Linda could see the massive amounts of information coming in. Concerned about the NeHaw detecting the leakage, ALICE explained that the taps they were using were the same devices the NeHaw military used.

The taps linked to the same network as everyone used. They just rode a different frequency, so to speak. The traffic generated by these taps would be nothing more than a trickle when compared to the massive data flow this station was managing. The reason the Kortisht had extras was that they manufactured them for the NeHaw.

"Oh dear, someone, please find Jake," ALICE urgently announced.

"What's wrong, ALICE?" Linda asked, concerned at the statement.

"The NeHaw are coming," she replied.

----*----

GeSec had his cruiser in FTL, destined once more to lead the charge against the humans. Earlier, he had been scheduled to meet with General KaLob and demonstrate the new weapons system they had been fitted with. That meeting, however, had been canceled due to the assault on G-43578.

Now his was one of three ships equipped with the new weapon, and all three were to converge on the target from different directions. Unlike missions he had been assigned in the past, there was to be no mustering of forces this time. This order was transmitted as a timed event, where ships from all across the Empire were provided the go order in independent transmissions.

It was GeSec's understanding that all warships would arrive on the target simultaneously, due to the time they got their orders and the travel time calculated by the operations division of the High Command.

Considering this target, he only hoped they got it right, or his time on target would be very short indeed.

----*----

Daniel and the other three troopers were cautiously moving about in crouched positions, constantly trying to keep one of the islands of hardware between themselves and the NeHaw wandering through the room. Several times he caught a glimpse of the tech as he or she paused in front of one or another display, checking the readings and making notes on a pad it carried. Unsure if it was male or female,

225

Daniel questioned if that really mattered as he considered his options, were they to be discovered.

Killing the NeHaw would be no problem, as more than once, one of the troopers had almost been forced to do that exact thing to avoid detection. It wouldn't even be hard to dispose of the body as they could space it on their way out. The challenge was how to do so in a way that wouldn't raise suspicion with the rest of the station crew.

His dilemma was set aside as he suddenly caught the NeHaw staring across the room. Following its gaze, he could see someone's shoulder extending no more than half an inch past the equipment they were hiding behind.

"We are discovered," Daniel announced as he stepped up behind the NeHaw. As it turned to run from the trooper it saw across the room, it hit him squarely in the chest and bounced off. It started to rise but stopped as it received a solid blow to the forehead from another trooper's rifle butt.

The NeHaw dropped to the floor, apparently out cold. Without delay, they bound the alien's arms and legs to keep it from escaping while Daniel searched the body for anything resembling a communicator.

"Colonel, we have an issue," Daniel transmitted as he considered the unconscious form at his feet.

----*----

The war room in Nevada was packed, as everyone gathered to hear the urgent news. Jake was standing off to one side, going through the brief that they were about to present, while mentally debating their options. He was delighted to learn that the taps the SAS had placed were already proving worth the effort.

Having read the presentation earlier, he wanted to hear what others thought of the information before making a decision.

"Everyone here?" Patti asked as the various remote locations checked in.

Satisfied she had all the relevant parties, she looked to Jake, who gave her a nod.

"We have recently received information that a NeHaw force is headed this way. While we haven't established the exact size or makeup of ship types, it was an Empire-wide call to arms. We are expecting a significant number of military vessels from all sectors within a few hours of travel."

At this point, Patti had a visual projected in a 3D holograph for all to see. In the holograph, a vast star map was displayed first, followed by a 3-dimensional grid that outlined the sectors the NeHaw used as reference locations. Highlighting a small group of boxes representing the sectors in question, the image zoomed in.

"This is us," Patti commented as a lone box off to one side started blinking to emphasize its location.

From the display, you could see how the box only touched the rest of the grid on one corner, leaving everything else bounded by uncharted space. In this view, it became quite obvious why the NeHaw considered Earth a backwater planet, so far off the beaten path as to be almost irrelevant.

She then brought the view in closer, so only our sector, Nu Tao Beta, was centered in the room. Located at the far end of the sector point closest to the rest of the Empire, the Earth's solar system was even remote in their own sector.

"As you can see, from where these ships will be traveling from, their approach vectors converge here," Patti said as, first, representative lines indicating the travel vectors from NeHaw space into Nu Tau Beta appeared. Next, the display zoomed once more, leaving only Earth's solar system.

At the point of convergence sat a small, stationary object as the rest of the planets rotated around the sun.

"This is our new space station," Patti explained.

The demonstration was more to place relevance on the station's location in space, not related to Earth, but rather its relevance to anyone entering the sector Earth's solar system occupied. By maintaining its place in the sector of space, it ensured any ship approaching Earth from outside the sector would need to pass under its guns in the solar systems orbital plane.

"Any ship attacking Earth will have to drop out of FTL here," Patti said, indicating the convergence point.

"What if they just bypass the station and try to come in from the far side?" someone asked, pointing out the open spaces on the top, bottom, and the far side of the system.

"Faster than Light travel is linear. To make that move, they would have to drop out of FTL and then jump again. We would detect that as we have placed monitoring systems in all the probable locations. The station is FTL capable and could jump in time to intercept," referring to sensor packages Jake had asked the ALICEs to place a year before. He called it, locking the back door.

"Here is the point of all this," Patti said as she focused on the image.

"Currently, Kola and ALICE-3 are both out of the solar system. Almost all our destroyers and cruisers are as well, working convoy duties or protecting treaty planets. Between Earth and that space station, all we can muster is 2 destroyers, 6 combat patrol ships, and 2 fighter squadrons."

"We have ordered the 4 Lanai transport ships on the planet to be fitted with guns, but that will take some time. With the 4 day trip from the edge of the system, we hope they will be ready in time. That's all we have, people."

Jake noted that the room was decidedly quiet as everyone did the math. Should the NeHaw show up with another armada, the small force would be overwhelmed quickly. He was doing his own calculations on pulling a weapon from ALICE-9 and getting in place.

"This is an all hands on deck event. If anyone has an idea about how to better prepare or fight, don't be shy," Patti added, making it very clear that everyone should be thinking about this fight. Jake could see several nods, but no one spoke up.

"Ok, everyone, let's get back to work and stay focused," Jake announced as he headed to his office.

----*----

Patti had no sooner returned to Patti's Pit when she was awash in analysts. Everyone here had continued to work while the briefing was being conducted for the larger audience. With the SAS team the immediate priority, they needed to ensure their safe extraction while others worked on the battle plans.

"Patti, you need to see this," Sam said as she led the other woman aside.

Promoted to Lance Corporal, Samantha Watts had moved back into the analyst's role due to the current crisis. As an experienced Marine and trained analyst, she was a valuable addition to the team.

Taking her to her station, Patti began reading the transcript from the Phantom.

"Oh crap, what else can go wrong," she mumbled.

----*----

With Sara still recovering from giving birth and Patti managing the SAS mission still in progress, Jake and Linda were alone in his office as they discussed the situation.

"We have a recall order out for all ships within a four hour or so return window. Beyond that, they would just be here in time to watch," Linda said glumly.

"It's not as bad as you think. Not to say we aren't in trouble, but we still have a few cards to play," he replied without expanding on the statement.

"You know, I really hate that shit you do with hidden plans and secret weapons," Linda snapped, clearly frustrated at his comment.

"Yeah, me too. Trust me, though you don't want to know the shit I know," he replied as he hoisted the coffee cup, he was sipping from in a toasting fashion.

"So, do you have some magic left in your hat?" Linda asked, hopefully.

"Only the things of nightmares. But yes, I will soon be busy making sure the Earth will live to fight another day.

----*----

Daniel and his team cautiously moved through the corridors of the NeHaw asteroid, making their way back to the Phantom. Two of the troopers were hauling the unconscious NeHaw between them. As they moved from place to place, Daniel worked through their list of options for the captive.

Without a NeHaw space suit, taking the tech with them was not an option. Even if they could get it on the Phantom, they didn't have an environment to place it in to survive the trip to Earth. As it was, in this condition, it wouldn't survive the trip from the airlock to the ship.

That brought up the option of just spacing the captive. Dead anyway, if they attempted to keep it, they could just kill it and let the body float away in space, covering up their deed. Daniel was concerned, though, about what the disappearance might mean to the others on the station. A detailed search might reveal the taps they had gone to so much trouble to place and keep hidden.

The third and most complicated option was to make the death appear as some kind of accident. If they could stage the death to appear natural, like crushed under a stack of crates or cut in half in an airlock door, it might be passed off as uninteresting.

It was as he was considering the last that he suddenly was brought back to now with a voice in his ear.

"Daniel, can you hear me?" Patti's voice sounded.

"Yes, Luv. I am kind of busy at the moment," he replied, somewhat impatiently.

"Yes, I know, idiot. I have an idea for you, but it's risky," she answered sarcastically.

"I'm all ears, Luv," he replied.

"Is the NeHaw still alive?" she asked.

"Yes, slumbering nicely," he replied as he had the team pull back into some kind of storage room so they could talk.

"I think we can make him forget what has happened. Do you have any Aspirin?" Patti asked a confused Daniel.

----*----

GeSec was preparing his crew for what was to come. A mere few microcycles away from leaving FTL, he wanted them to be ready to engage at once. Privately he feared they would arrive before the rest of the ships assigned to this mission, but that was not a thought he shared.

Checking the roster once more of warships assigned to this attack, he mentally calculated how many should be with him provided they performed their duty as ordered. It did little to ease his concerns as most were not upgraded as his cruiser had been.

Regardless of that fact, there would be additional firepower with their presence and a distraction for the humans once they began the attack. Checking the countdown clock once more, he heaved a sigh and braced himself for what the next few microcycles might present.

----*----

Popping four aspirin down the NeHaw's throat, he managed to get the thing to swallow without choking. The reaction was swift as the tech suddenly went limp and slumped over.

"Did we kill it?" Daniel asked, surprised at the reaction.

"No, aspirin makes them pass out and then forget. Just get out of there now," Patti replied urgently.

Daniel wanted to know how in the blazes they learned that but took the advice to heart. Placing the NeHaw's pad next to the body, he backed away. Next, he led the troopers quickly out of the storeroom after making sure it was clear of traffic, and then they made their way back to the airlock without incident.

"We are a go," he transmitted to the phantom after all four had entered the airlock, sealing the door behind them.

Almost immediately, the outer door opened, surprising the trooper next to it. With a shove, the next man pushed her out, and the remaining two followed, Daniel being the last to leave. With that, the four made their way to the still cloaked Phantom, ensuring they left no trace of their passing behind them.

Once inside the ship, Colonel Banks lifted off and gently maneuvered the ship back into the sensor shadow before engaging the FTL drives and sprinting away.

----*----

KaJep woke to find himself lying on the floor of a storage room, alone. Slowly sitting upright, he checked his head to see why it hurt so badly. Finding nothing wrong, just a swelling on his forehead, he assumed that had come from impact with the floor, he looked around.

He recognized the room as he had retrieved supplies from here many times. At this point, though, he couldn't remember why he was here at all. Finding his datapad nearby, he checked the log and found he had been in the computer room microcycles earlier.

From his notes, everything had been normal, and he must have departed after completing his inspection rounds. He had no idea how he had found his way here and decided the best course was to keep the incident to himself and head back to his quarters to rest the bump on his head. Who knows, maybe the rest would help him remember at some point.

----*----

Jake reached out to ALICE and ALICE-9 to arrange the movement of a doomsday device, should things go badly. Not quite ready to head to Georgia himself, he just ordered a ship to be ready, and the area evacuated before his arrival.

Rather than assign a badly needed destroyer, as he had before, he simply had his fighter transferred to the hangar there. Once it was clear that the NeHaw was headed inbound, he had plenty of time to send the bomb once more on a one-way intercept mission.

Chapter 25

HeBak was sitting in the detention area of the military High Command building, waiting to be called before General KaLob. He was well aware that he could be here for a short period or for a very long time, depending on the mood of the General and what they found on his ship.

He had no delusions that they were not scouring every part of his ship at this moment, looking for clues as to what he had been doing and why he was now here. Fortunately, the humans had also been quite thorough in helping HeBak sanitize the ship before leaving Earth. It had been in their best interest to ensure there was nothing there to incriminate HeBak as a human conspirator.

With that in mind, he simply made himself comfortable and requested a meal consisting of favorites he had been missing since leaving.

----*----

General KaLob was anxiously awaiting the convergence of his ships on target. To his knowledge, this was the first time the NeHaw Military had ever attempted a maneuver of this type, and so the outcome was unsure. As he scanned the situation room, he could see that there were others that understood the significance of the attempt.

Well known by most space travelers was the concept of mustering ships that intended to travel together. Once positioned, they coordinated travel, ensuring that they maintained the same separation while in FTL and upon arrival at their destination.

What most did not understand was, if you did not perform this synchronization, the possibility of dropping out of FTL on top of one another was not only possible but highly likely as captains tended to share their flight programs. In addition, the military had their regular routes mapped out for rotation of assignments.

If successful, the events that were about to unfold should take the humans completely by surprise and give NeHaw a long-deserved victory in this war of attrition.

----*----

The sudden appearance of three NeHaw warships just off the space station was not really a surprise, as everyone was prepared for the attack. The startling thing was they appeared from three different angles and opened fire on the station all at once.

Typically, they would see the massed fleet appear as one and then concentrate fire accordingly. This had them redirecting fire as various parts of the station came under attack at once. In addition, the close proximity to the station itself magnified the effects of the energy cannon and particle beams, giving them a greater damaging effect.

As the station's stasis shields had been up already, the initial onslaught was absorbed or deflected with little effect. However, there was a third weapon in play that was causing considerable damage to one section of the station's saucer.

"What the hell is that?" Jake asked as they watched the portion of the space station saucer explode into space.

"Unknown, analyzing," ALICE replied, her reverting to monotone replies, a sign of stress.

As they watched, the cruiser closest to the damaged section came under a withering counter fire, causing it to divert its approach. Within seconds more ships appeared, popping up all over the open space around the station.

"Jake, I think they are targeting the station itself, not us. Several had an opportunity to bypass the station guns and turned into its path instead," Patti said as she appeared in the command center. Several more of her analysts stood near the doorway, watching the hologram that consumed more of the command center. In the mix, Jake picked out both Sam and Grace as they watched the hologram in the center of the room.

"Patti is correct, the NeHaw are concentrating fire on the station from all sides," ALICE confirmed.

"And that explosion?" Jake asked.

"Still analyzing," came the reply.

----*----

General KaLob was overjoyed at the first images they received in the attack. As theorized, the NeHaw ships had appeared well inside the effective range of their weapons and struck a solid blow to the structure the humans had created there. The newly developed micro missile system had performed exceptionally well at that distance.

Unable to discern how the humans transported the ferrous components in their railgun weapons in FTL, a race loyal to the NeHaw had developed a weapon of similar abilities. Rather than accelerating the projectile using the magnetic rail accelerators, they made the rounds self-propelled, like miniature missiles.

Each projectile was additionally infused with an explosive element that detonated on contact. While the human shields could absorb the impact of the missile, they could not withstand the additional explosion created by the explosive charge.

As he continued to watch the feed provided by a surveillance ship that had arrived with the first wave, he could see more destroyers and cruisers joining the fight. Unfortunately, he did witness two destroyers impact one another as a second appeared from FTL, leaving the first with no time to maneuver.

That incident was offset by the appearance of the other two ships fitted with the micro missile guns. Dropping from FTL almost on top of the station, both opened fire before being driven off. One delayed just a little too long and erupted in light and debris as it exploded in place.

KaLob sighed at a loss but was content to watch the other two equipped ships wreak havoc on the station.

----*----

"These things are dropping in on each other!" Jake commented as he watched two NeHaw destroyers collide.

The observation did nothing to diminish the effectiveness of the tactic they were watching.

With energy cannons and railguns firing in all directions, the station was ablaze in streams of fire, both outgoing and incoming. Operating as designed with overlapping fields of fire, Jake was both impressed and panicked at the same time. While he expected the NeHaw to challenge its effectiveness, this was hell in space.

He could see several small eruptions on various saucers, as the new NeHaw mystery weapon scored hits with the appearance of two more ships. It looked to fire like a railgun but seemed to be effective only within a minimum distance. In addition, it was not coming from every vessel, only from a select number of ships.

One of the newcomers got raked by the station's railguns, leaving it a flashing field of debris as it exploded, showering the station as it did so.

"Jake, that's the cruiser that attacked ALICE-3 at Wawobash," Patti pointed out as they worked to identify every ship attacking the station.

As if to emphasize the statement, they saw it turn to close on the station once more, and the mystery weapon sent a stream of fire at the central hub of the station. Everyone watched as an energy cannon beam caused part of the stream to explode in space while the initial fire struck the station. The resulting impact breached a part of the saucer, belching flame and chunks of the station into space.

"That's some kind of explosive projectile!" Jake announced as the NeHaw cruiser peeled away once more to avoid the concentrated return fire. As it did so, Jake could see where two of its four repulser drives were almost gone on the back of the ship.

Pausing to consider the situation, Jake went to one of the open display panels in the room and taped in a query. Reading the results, he turned to the hologram once more. The station was absorbing so much energy in its shields, Jake could actually see the grid pattern light up as it dissipated the energy blasts coming in from all directions.

"ALICE, what's the station damage report?" he asked.

"3 of 6 modules are damaged, but all are operable. Shields are at 70%, and weapons capability is at 68%. Casualties unknown," she reported.

"Hang on just a little longer, baby," he whispered as he watched several more NeHaw ships appear.

----*----

GeSec was both elated and concerned. As the only remaining NeHaw vessel with the micro missile gun still in operation, his place in history was guaranteed. The effectiveness of the weapon against the human shields was proven, provided one could close on the enemy within the effective range.

The unfortunate aspect of that caveat was his ship had taken a beating and was almost inoperable. With two of his four drives shot to pieces, he was unsure if his FTL systems even operated. There were hull breaches everywhere, and he had ordered his engineering staff to don environmental suits to address the breaches from the outside of the ship if necessary.

The chief engineer had thought him joking at first, and then crazy when he realized he was serious. The appearance of several more ships had given him the relief he needed to take a moment and repair before he engaged with the enemy once more. Moving away from the fighting, they had paused to deal with the worst of their damage.

"Sir, we have two more ships dropping from FTL on my scope directly astern."

Those were the last words GeSec heard before the side of his ship peeled away, and he was sucked into space.

----*----

Brian was not a particularly religious man. Some might even say that after the loss of his wife so long ago, he had even forsaken the concept. However, the scene in front of him was as close to a depiction of hell as any he had ever envisioned. The space station was actually glowing red from all the energy its shields were absorbing.

Dropping from FTL, they had appeared right behind a NeHaw cruiser that had retreated from the fighting, apparently making repairs, as they could make out suited figures crawling over the hull. Without waiting for orders, ALICE-3 had sliced the ship in two with a battery of forward-facing railguns.

Beyond that, the station itself was a blaze of energy cannon and railgun streams as they targeted ships in all directions. Nearby, Brian got a tinge of nostalgia as *Revenge* appeared and began firing on the unsuspecting ships in its path toward the station.

"All guns commence firing," Brian announced unnecessarily as the initial railgun burst was taken as tacit approval.

----*----

Jake finally exhaled as ALICE-3 and *Revenge* appeared behind the NeHaw ships harassing the station. With the removal of the three specially armed warships, the remainder of the attacking force found little opportunity to inflict damage beyond rubbing salt in the existing wounds.

With the destruction of several more NeHaw ships, the remaining attackers apparently took the hint and vacated the area. As the command center erupted in celebration, Jake quietly sent the stand-down message to ALICE and ALICE-9, happy he would be skipping the Georgia trip after all.

----*----

General KaLob was not in the mood to entertain remnants of the old regime, much less someone he considered corrupt and a bureaucrat. The upheaval of recent events and the setbacks they caused had him reassessing plans for future offensives against the humans.

The fact that the incompetent possessed a communique from the Human leader was the deciding factor in receiving him at all. Normally when a ship appeared out of nowhere with criminal technology on-board, like this one had, the General would have had it vaporized.

This ship, however, had first begun transmitting secure military codes, known only to those in the High Command offices and the ship's commanders. They were outdated, but quite valid none the less.

Once it appeared, it was escorted to a secure landing pad next to the High Command building where it was screened and then searched before its single occupant was allowed to disembark. KaLob had the security team escort the pilot to a holding area where he had him wait for an appropriate period of time to establish who was in command here.

Once he was satisfied, KaLob ordered the pilot brought before him. As he sat at his desk, he watched security escort a sorry excuse for a NeHaw before him.

"You are?" KaLob asked the disgusting blob of NeHaw flesh standing before him.

"I am HeBak, former Supervisor of High Command Secure Communications," the blob declared.

"And you have a message from the humans?" KaLob asked suspiciously.

"Yes, Sir," was the reply. As HeBak started to step forward, both security members latched on to his arms, preventing him from moving further. KaLob gave a subtle signal, and HeBak was permitted to step forward. As he did so, he produced a small data cube, one the General recognized as a NeHaw standard device.

"How did the humans get this?" he asked sternly as he stared at the cube, hesitant to touch it at first.

"I suggested that they use a data cube to aid in transporting the information required. They are a primitive species and use audio waves as a means of interaction. Their first proposal was to send you written material in their native language. They are really quite a backward race," HeBak stated.

"Yet they continue to win battles," KaLob replied. He doubted much of what was being said. However, he needed to know what was on the cube.

"You have seen what is on the cube?" KaLob asked.

"Ah, no, sir. They have coded the cube's security so that anyone but me can see the message," the NeHaw admitted, looking embarrassed by the admission.

"But really quite a backward race, you say? How did you end up with the humans anyway?" KaLob asked, still looking at the cube as it sat untouched at the end of his desk.

"I was captured on a secret reconnaissance mission for MeHak, Head of the High Council. She required someone above suspicion and loyal to the Empire to seek out and report on the threat," HeBak replied confidently.

"Certainly, as no one would suspect that you were capable of such a thing. Why is there no record of it in the archives?" KaLob replied, adding emphasis to the first part of his statement.

"Perhaps she feared other council members would betray me to the enemy?" HeBak replied speculatively.

"Perhaps. You are dismissed for now but will remain under guard until the Intelligence Service has had an opportunity to extract everything you know about the humans. Once that is finished, we will see if your life is of any more value," KaLob replied as he finally picked up the cube and examined it.

"General, I was told that these humans will only accept a reply from me, and I must be in their presence. The cube should say that!" HeBak replied with a bit of a panic.

"Possibly, we shall see about that. I wonder if they are specific as to what condition you must be in?" KaLob added as he waved the group away while still examining the cube in his hand.

Once he was alone, KaLob gently placed the cube on the reader, and immediately his display lit up with documents in NeHaw, as well as a hologram on his desk. In the hologram, a human was sitting behind a desk quite similar to his own. The image sat frozen as it waited for him to activate the recording.

KaLob studied the human, as this was his first opportunity to see the species in great detail. As he suspected that this was the leader of the enemy that had turned an Empire upside down, he was cautious to not let the arrogance of the past cloud his impression. This human had proven resourceful, cunning, and, worst of all, successful in his efforts.

Triggering the recording, he listened to the perfectly spoken NeHaw, referencing the provided documentation several times during the presentation. Finally stopping the recording as it began to replay, he sat back from his desk, absorbing all that had been proposed. At first, he rejected the inferences, but as he considered the consequences, he slowly began to see the possibilities.

Finally, he sat forward, snatching the cube from the reader and locking it up in his private safe. Apparently, HeBak was going to return to the humans unharmed after all. With the item safely locked away, KaLob cleared his calendar for the next few cycles.

Next, he placed a request with his research department, asking for any data they had on the humans, including their history, customs, and social structure. If he was to meet with their leader, he wanted to be as prepared as possible for the event.

Chapter 26

With the amount of damage the space station had sustained in the attack, the decision to post ALICE-3 nearby was an easy one. Overall, 3 of the 6 modules were damaged, and there had been a measurable loss of life. On the positive side, it was still operable and had more than held its own in the fighting.

Personally, Jake was becoming a bit concerned at his less than concerned attitude about the casualties. As he scanned the reports, he realized he didn't recognize a single name, and that bothered him.

In the Battle of Klinan, he had personally known most of those that had died in the fight, and that had tempered his decisions since. Now, these faceless names had him wondering how many more battles he was willing to plan and execute, without major concern for the lives lost in that cause.

He remembered Patti's question once more about what did success look like in this war. The question had haunted him and prompted his actions with the NeHaw HeBak. As he waited for the reply, he only hoped his counterpart had the wisdom and foresight to embrace the opportunity he was presenting.

----*----

Colonel Bo Chao was delighted with the outcome of the battle at the edge of the solar system. The timely return of the battleship ALICE-3 had been a fortunate turn of events accelerating what Bo perceived to be the inevitable success of the struggle.

What confused him, though, were his instructions to remain on G-43578, even though they had determined the strategic value here to be minimal. When queried as to the reason for their delay, Jake had simply explained that he did not want to release the bargaining chip just yet.

Bo wasn't sure what plans Jake had set in motion. He simply respected the man's wishes and continued to beat Robert at Xiangqi while Robert humiliated him at poker.

----*----

It was two days after the fight over the space station that the Phantom appeared at the edge of the system. Considered a noncombatant as far as the fight in space went, the SAS team, under Colonel Banks, had found one more opportunity before returning home.

A simple smash and grab operation, they had located an outpost at the edge of a larger system. Breaching its defenses, they overcame the small defense force there and stripped the facility of any usable information before the reaction force could arrive.

Going stealth, they had slipped past the ships coming in to rescue the captives and taken the Phantom FTL as they landed. Jake laughed when Banks explained how they had taken the outpost without firing a shot and then locked up the staff in a supply room. In the short time they had available, they had emptied out the computer room, loading the entire space into the Phantom's hold.

----*----

"Jake, I think we need to talk about some things," Patti opened at the meeting she had called in his office.

"When a woman says we need to talk, it's never good for the man," Jake replied snidely.

Besides Patti, Jake had Sara, Linda, and Ivan in his office as well. Online, and conferenced in, were Nigel, Bonnie, and both Bo and Edwin linked from their positions in deep space.

"The events of the last few weeks have seen you, Edwin, and Bo all leading combat missions off-planet and all considered very high risk," ALICE offered as a way of broaching a subject Jake had been dodging for quite some time.

"All successful, I should point out," Jake replied, concerned at where this was going.

243

"Regardless, you three are the leaders of the military for this planet. To have you constantly placing yourselves at risk is irresponsible," Patti added.

"Someone must always be seen as a central leader. While there are many Starshina, there is only one Ataman," Ivan offered.

Jake could see heads nodding, acknowledging the Russian's comment.

"And you are proposing?" Jake asked, dreading the reply.

"Congratulations, old son, you are now a General," Nigel announced as if it was a good thing.

"It was decided that, with both Colonel's Banks and Chao off-planet, that you should be promoted as the head of all the armed forces," ALICE explained.

"Look, you all know how I feel..." Jake started before Banks cut him off.

"No point in arguing, old boy. It's been decided. Neither Bo nor I am in a position to provide the leadership you can. You are an innovative leader that inspires the best in everyone you touch," Edwin continued.

Acknowledging the inevitable, Jake caved to the unanimous decision with a shrug and a sigh.

"Thanks a lot," he replied, with an almost genuine smile.

----*----

HeBak's return had Jake on edge, as the alien traveled the four days needed to reach Earth after dropping from FTL. Since the NeHaw leader had replied using the same technology as provided him, there was nothing that could be accomplished until the ship landed in Texas.

Arriving in Texas the day before he expected the alien to land, Jake settled into a waiting mode that had him back in his workshop there. Wrenching on the 1966 Cobra, he was happy to find a stack of parts recently fabricated by Dallas and Seven, created to replace the decayed rubber he had already removed.

Although the car was far from ready to drive, working on it allowed Jake a moment to think and focus on more important issues. The contents of the data cube currently in route represented the future of the human race.

Should the NeHaw agree to his proposal, Jake was optimistic that they stood a very good chance of living a war-free existence for the foreseeable future.

----*----

Patti and Daniel were in the process of celebrating his return when Gemma and Jacob dropped in. Having enjoyed their honeymoon in Iceland, the couple had returned first to Lanai, where they got caught up on all that they had missed. Satisfied that everything was running smoothly there, they had taken a few days to get settled in before traveling to the London facility.

"I must say, your new combat suits are a lifesaver," Daniel said as he praised the two engineers.

Rather than shuffling off to one of their private rooms, Patti had suggested the four meet in one of the many restaurants the Brits had recreated in their subterranean home. While not actually a restaurant, as no one was charged for their meal, the atmosphere was one of a quaint bistro rather than the more sterile cafeteria-style of the ALICE dining halls.

"He means that for real," Patti added.

With that comment, Daniel went in to the story of his adventures on K-82734 and his almost certain discovery at the hands of the security forces there. Patti could see her brother beaming with pride as Daniel explained his use of the disrupter rod in tunneling beneath the perimeter fencing.

Expanding on all that had occurred in the following missions, both Gemma and Jacob sat mesmerized, drawn in by Daniel's descriptions of their technology in use.

"So, how is married life?" Patti finally asked as they moved off of work talk.

"Other than the wondrous time we had in Iceland, it's not terribly different than before. My mum, however, has completely transformed. The prospect of grandchildren has her happy as Larry," Gemma offered after a bite of dessert.

"I, however, am still on probation," Jacob added with a laugh.

"Not so, Luv. She fancies you for a son in law. She is just slow to warm up to people," Gemma replied while patting his arm.

"Well, I know for a fact Nigel thinks you are the best," Patti added.

Glancing at Daniel, Patti sensed there was something troubling him about the conversation. As they discussed the in-laws, she could see his mind was not on the conversation directly.

"Patricia, I have something to ask you," Daniel suddenly blurted as they were chatting after the table was cleared. Slipping off his chair so he could take a knee at her side, Daniel took Patti's hand in his.

"Would you do me the honor of being my wife?" he asked as he looked up into her eyes.

Taken completely off guard, Patti could hear her answer before she spoke it.

"YES," she replied before bursting into tears.

----*----

Jake was present as he watched the NeHaw HeBak lower his ship into the Texas hangar. He watched breathing gear in hand and wireless helmet already on his head. Once it settled on its landing gear, he had Dallas transmit the access request as he approached the airlock.

Apparently, expecting the request, the outer door opened as soon as Jake arrived, allowing him access to the ship. With his mask on and helmet in place, he entered the small space, triggering the outer hatch to close and then waiting for the NeHaw to give him access to the interior of the ship.

The NeHaw must have been in some hurry of his own as Jake found the inner door open almost as soon as he had turned from closing the outer. Stepping inside the ship, he found his host standing just inside, his arm extended.

"This is your reply. I am told you will have no issues accessing the contents, nor any trouble understanding it," HeBak added as Jake took a cube exactly like the one they had sent.

"This now completes my obligations. Would you please inform your people that they may begin returning my property immediately," the NeHaw added.

"Absolutely. Will you be leaving afterward?" Jake asked, curious what deals the NeHaw might have struck back home.

The question seemed to strike a nerve with HeBak as he stood frozen for several seconds before replying.

"It was suggested that I consider staying with you for a cycle or two longer until your business with General KaLob is completed. Is this acceptable?" He asked.

"I will inform Dallas that your hangar space is not available for other uses," Jake replied with a smile. He had no idea what had transpired on the NeHaw homeworld, but whatever it was, HeBak was not yet free to roam the empire.

----*----

Jake wasted no time in taking the data cube and retreating to his office here in Texas. With Dallas prepared to translate any information provided, he set the data cube on the reader and was instantly rewarded with the hologram and display filled with data that he had expected as a reply to what he provided.

The General introduced himself in a very human-like manner and then proceeded to walk through his response to Jake's proposal. It unnerved Jake slightly that the NeHaw was so businesslike in his approach, working in a very methodical fashion. They had so demonized the NeHaw leadership that it was with some difficulty that he had to imagine him as an empathetic being.

Clearing his mind of any preconceived notions, Jake set about evaluating the NeHaw response. It was several hours later when he had finally worked through the information provided and, with Dallas's help, formulated a plan.

It was clear that the General was hedging his bets on working anything out with Earth. At several points in the response, he had alluded to a war of attrition that Earth could never win. In the same sentence, he also acknowledged the damage the effort was doing to the Empire itself.

To make this work, Jake needed to provide a place where the two could meet, face to face, that didn't expose their efforts to the Empire or Earth's treaty partners. While Jake had no intent in selling anyone down the river, he knew that the more races involved, the less likely they would see a successful outcome.

To that end, he set the ALICEs on the task of locating a remote part of space that permitted the two to meet secretly while providing certain necessary components. Jake was very much afraid that he would have to convince General KaLob just how serious Earth was, and that meant demonstrations of power.

With that delegated, he proceeded to locate the other items he required for the meeting while creating one more message for General KaLob, outlining their next steps. While neither side had ceased their hostilities, his hope was there would be no further offensives until this meeting was convened.

----*----

Production Supervisor Valstorke personally addressed the latest human order, presumably requested from their leader himself. As he reviewed the request, he began to question the sanity of arguably the most powerful beings in several sectors. The two items outlined were a combination of mundane and bizarre.

While not a particularly difficult order for the Wawobash, the request came with a delivery date that required Valstorke to drop just about everything else he had in the process, just to complete it on time. However, the price to be paid for such a delivery ensured he would complete the job early and exactly as requested. No questions were asked.

Chapter 27

Robert was beginning to chafe at the delays in returning home. He and Bonnie had regular calls, but that just wasn't the same as being there. Colonel Bo Chao seemed less concerned at the delays in returning, responding that Jake had a good reason he was sure.

By this point, all three locations had been completely restored to full working order, with the defenses back in place. The prisoners were all behaving, with Robert even honoring a request of sending death notifications to their homeworlds, for those lost in the conflict.

Bo had Kola review all transmissions prior to any release, verifying there were no hidden messages or nefarious intent in the effort. Beyond all of that, the Aseristic had resumed their work on the four cruisers. Robert had assumed the humans would be taking them along as war prizes, and as such, the upgrades would be of value.

Positive he was not alone in his desire to be gone from this planet, Robert did his best to boost morale for the troops and crews on the ground and in space. He just hoped Jake didn't drag this out much longer.

----*----

As the two ships closed in on the designated meeting spot, Jake could see his ship's sensors dancing from the scans the NeHaw ship was performing on him. Both he and the small NeHaw vessel were given a very specific set of instructions to follow, for which any deviations would constitute an immediate cancelation of the meeting.

The place chosen for the negotiation was as remote a location in space as Jake had ever encountered in his travels to date. In this void, there were three floating celestial bodies, unattached to any star system, and were, in fact, intentionally chosen because they were far from any star system. On Earth, they would be considered a navigation hazard, which was why they were chosen. All of them were about half the size of Earth's moon.

A respectable distance away from the three barren rocks, sat a special module Jake had ordered constructed by the Wawobash. Delivered to the space station, it had been programmed by ALICE to FTL unmanned to an agreed upon locale where NeHaw security could scan and inspect it for treachery. Next, it was delivered to a final location known only to General KaLob and ALICE.

Docking at the port specifically intended for his ship, one he had ordered at the same time as the module, Jake exited the small craft and entered the half of the module designed to support human life. As he entered for the first time, he confirmed that the entire module was one large room with a clear partition separating his half from the NeHaw designed space.

Both halves contained a desk, each facing the other, as well as several chairs should either participant choose a more comfortable seat. No food or drink had been provided, should such a thing cause undue concerns to either participant.

Jake had no more entered his half of the module when the General entered opposite him. Both Man and NeHaw acknowledged the other with respect before taking their seats at the desks facing the divider.

"Colonel Thomas, my sensors confirm you came alone, as agreed," KaLob opened the conversation.

"As do mine, General KaLob. By the way, it is General Thomas now. Things have changed somewhat back home," Jake replied with a nod. As with HeBak, who was happily reunited with his gold in Nevada, the lack of lip movement when KaLob spoke was a bit disconcerting to Jake.

"My congratulations. You went to great efforts to arrange this meeting General Thomas. To what end?" the General asked, getting right to the point.

"What we are about to discuss is known only to myself and a very select few on Earth. It is my suggestion you consider the same security," Jake replied before placing a data cube on the reader and hitting a key on his desktop display.

Jake watched as KaLob began scanning the images that came up on his system. He wasn't sure, but it appeared the General was becoming agitated as he read.

"This information is accurate?" the General finally asked as he went back to flipping through the information.

"Unfortunately, yes," Jake replied truthfully.

"Are you insane? There was a reason these items were forbidden. How did you even come across the references for building this, this Pandora's Box of Death? This data is classified at the highest levels."

The reference to Pandora's Box caught Jake off guard. Apparently, the good General had been studying Earth, as Jake suspected. It was something atypical for the NeHaw and not to be underestimated.

"All the required information was obtained from a crashed NeHaw exploration vessel. You say it's classified, and yet your ships carry access to it?" Jake asked in reply.

"As you say, that was unfortunate. Unlike combat vessels, research ships have greater access to sensitive materials should they run across weapons or other such items in their role as first contact explorers. The ability to construct such things are still highly protected, with Captain's only access, how did you manage that?" KaLob asked suspiciously.

"Perhaps the crash removed such safeguards, I do not know as it occurred well before my time," Jake lied. Apparently, the ALICEs had inadvertently been able to access NeHaw encrypted data natively, which would explain why they never saw protected content in the NeHaw communications net until recently when things were dramatically changed. It was all open to them previously.

"So, the intent of this meeting is for you to threaten me with the use of these weapons on my homeworld?" KaLob asked pointedly.

"No, the intent of this meeting is to ensure that the use of these weapons never occurs on either side. On my world, in its history, we experienced something called Mutually Assured Destruction. Several countries had the ability to vaporize their enemies, should they get pushed in a corner. Thanks to your predecessors, that never happened as we were collectively almost obliterated."

"If they were aware you have these weapons, I would have done the same," KaLob replied firmly.

"Only you can confirm that. I am led to believe it was other factors that drove the attack on Earth. Regardless, we are now in a position where another attempt on my planet would force us to retaliate in a fashion detrimental to both species. Please note the navigation data on your screen," Jake finished.

"That is the NeHaw homeworld," the General acknowledged.

"So, we are even. You know where I live, and I know where you live."

"What are you proposing?" KaLob asked after a moment's consideration.

"An armistice. No one claims victory, or both do; I do not care. We just stop fighting. We need to agree to a buffer zone, a demilitarized area in space, composed of these sectors." Jake said as he manipulated the display once more, showing NeHaw 3D space navigation charts.

"You stay on your side, and we stick to ours," Jake finished as the sectors he proposed for Earth outlined clearly.

"You claim space you do not occupy?" KaLob noted absently as he manipulated the 3D charts to better analyze the proposal.

"Some of those sectors contain species aligned with our efforts and sympathetic to our cause. In addition, we chose natural voids where distances between sectors provided clear boundaries. A complicated web would be impossible to monitor and enforce, creating a high probability of conflict due to errors on either side. Besides, we occupy territory well on the other side of that boundary," Jake replied, referring to Robert and Bo sitting on G-43578.

Jake watched as the General moved through all the data provided, stopping and reviewing several pieces. Jake knew the NeHaw were an arrogant species, so he suspected that the

General had more than just this to consider. He had to sell this back home.

"And I am to take you at your word you have these weapons?" the General finally asked.

"I was afraid you would want a demonstration," Jake replied before hitting some keys.

With one motion, he activated systems that made the walls of their module transparent. Both could see the ships they arrived in as well as the open space around them. Jake motioned to the General to watch the three rocks floating a good distance away.

"I believe you are familiar with this," Jake said before activating the weapon.

As both watched, one of the three bodies displayed a bright white flash as the weapon Jake had secretly placed there earlier was triggered. The two watched in fascination and horror as the first of the three bodies began to fold in on itself, the explosion consuming matter until it was nothing but a bright flash of white.

Next, it reached for the closest of its neighbors, consuming it while reaching out for the third. Within minutes all three spheres were gone, leaving only black empty space.

"Good enough?" Jake asked as he returned the walls to their previous settings and focused on his counterpart.

"You really are insane," the General replied sadly.

"No, just desperate. We cannot beat you without escalating things, and that is something I will not voluntarily do. Please do not put me in a position where I have to choose between your survival or mine. I have no doubt that you can create these weapons, or that you may already have some stored away," Jake explained.

"It is meaningless as you have a vast Empire to draw from and would eventually exhaust our ability to fight. Only a truce will provide the means for us both to move forward. Who knows, maybe someday we can even be friends," Jake added.

Jake watched as the General sat staring at him as if studying a specimen in a lab. After several minutes, he finally replied.

"You will withdraw your troops from those areas on our side of these boundaries and cease all combat activities on a date and time to be agreed by both parties, D Day, H Hour, M Minute, NeHaw standard time. In return, I will order my ships to withdraw to our side of this DMZ and cease all harassment of shipping as well as other hostilities. Know that we have the technology to detect FTL traffic and will deploy such along the established sector boundaries," KaLob stated.

"As do we," Jake lied. He had no idea how one would detect ships in FTL but was sure that was now their top priority.

"Then I agree to the terms as stated. I believe this is a step in the right direction General," Jake added.

"And I believe we no longer need to battle with you. Your species is going to destroy itself," the General replied sternly.

----*----

The two Generals spent several hours hammering out an agreement that both promised to enforce back home. While Jake had no concerns about keeping his side of the deal, he wondered if KaLob would have trouble with the hard sell back home. Both agreed to keep it simple and not complicate matters with complex requirements.

The NeHaw assured him that while this was a one-of-a-kind event in NeHaw history, the relief this offered his people would be obvious to all. His bigger concern was in unraveling the mess the war left behind. Even now, the upheaval caused by the overthrow of the corrupt political class had him rebuilding a civil service organization intended to take over the non-military management of things.

With the exact date and time set for the agreement to begin enforcement as tomorrow, at the NeHaw version of noon, Jake had begun the peace process as soon as he departed the meeting with General KaLob. He transmitted the agreement home before going to FTL, in part, to postpone the inevitable questions. As part of their agreement, both parties sent the cease and desist orders out before departing the module. It required all warships to retreat to their side of the boundary within a fixed timeframe, and for Jake to ensure that Robert and Bo were to come home with Kola immediately.

Once they were back in their ships and preparing to leave, Jake destroyed the module, leaving no trace they had ever been there. General KaLob was quite happy to agree that the meeting and its contents, beyond the agreement, would remain undisclosed. Besides the revelation of the weapons locked away on Earth, it might be considered a sign of weakness should anyone learn about his collaboration with a human.

It took several weeks for Jake to get the word out that the war was over, and the NeHaw had agreed to a truce. As the ALICEs were integral parts of the initial proposal, they were prepared to explain the Neutral Zone to all the allied planets. While the concept of a DMZ was foreign to them, they understood the part about no more NeHaw warships in their space.

During the entire trip home, Jake was flooded with questions of who, why, and how. Most he could answer, but the one as to why the NeHaw had agreed to come to the table was one he skirted.

----*----

Grace Middleton was awash in work as she concentrated on the display in front of her. General Thomas had been good to his word, as she was now home in Georgia and working from the ALICE-9 facility there. While not officially doing anything for ALICE-9 herself just yet, the pair of them actively analyzed the southern states to locate possible communities to recruit.

After the announcement of the truce with the NeHaw, the need for combat analysts had dropped to a point where she was just in the way. With others intent on making that their career, she was more than happy to opt-out.

Once she was free, Jake had agreed to approve her transfer, on the condition that all her activities in Georgia be supervised by ALICE or Dallas. Considering ALICE-9 was still a newborn, the pair of them were on probation.

The restrictions were hardly an issue as the two were already conspiring to prove to everyone they had what it takes to make ALICE-9 a full-fledged facility.

"ALICE-9, look at this one," Grace said as she brought up the file and what she thought was a promising find.

Chapter 28

The weather in Lanai was a balmy, sunny, 75 degrees as the beach party was getting into full swing. Jacob and Gemma had been more than happy to host the party celebrating the Truce with the NeHaw. The beach they had chosen for the event was wide and long, providing more than enough space for the 100 plus people that had traveled to be there.

Jake and Sara had brought the twins from Nevada, with both Linda and Kathy, along for the ride. Sandy had come separately with Becky, as they had swung north to pick up Jessie, taking a long way around. Robert and Bonnie had come as well, completing the parenting count as all the kids were there.

Tracy, Julie, Timothy, and Ryan were all old enough now to be mobile and attracted to the sand and water. Amber and Jade were safely tucked away under a shade, preventing any overexposure. Finally, both Jon and Padma were in heaven as they raced up and down the beach, chasing any sea birds foolish enough to land nearby.

Adding to the mayhem, Jake had brought Kona along for the trip. The Shepherd was having a blast as she chased the kids up and down the beach. She was also mixing in among the adults as she begged treats from those eating. Twice, Jake saw her herding one of the little ones away from the water's edge, before even the mothers could intervene. He was positive the dog was having the time of her life.

Besides the kids directly related to Jake in some fashion, there were other families enjoying the freedom that Lanai provided in its natural safety and security. Jake was delighted to see so many people out having a good time. In his opinion, it was about time.

That thought brought him back around to others, mostly those regarding Earth. Now that the NeHaw were a concern rather than a threat, as he was not foolish enough to believe they would go away permanently, it was time to look inward.

New York was just the tip of the iceberg when it came to issues they would encounter with every city they visited. Europe, Asia, and everywhere else they went, people had reestablished themselves in non-traditional ways. Who was he to say that the gangs now running New York should be displaced, any more than a Warlord in Nepal or an Archduke in Germany?

And then there were places like Iceland, where they had never really stopped being…. Icelanders. Those places in the world where the people had just continued being themselves, ignoring the fact that the government didn't exist anymore.

"Why are you frowning?" Jessie asked Jake as she strolled up the beach in front of him. He couldn't help noticing the bikini she had chosen for the event was incredibly sexy. Who says moms can't be sexy, he thought to himself.

"You are just the right person at the right time," he replied as he recalled her interest in world history.

"There's a dune over there where no one would see us?" she replied as she gave him a wink.

"I was referring to your mind, not your body," Jake replied while wrapping his arm around her shoulders in a hug,

"Both are yours to do with as you please," she replied in a sultry voice as she pressed against him.

"Let's talk first, shall we?" He replied.

As they stood there, Jake shared all he had been thinking. Jessie would ask the occasional question as they exchanged ideas on his concerns and possible solutions for future interactions with the world's populations. While he spoke, he could see Jessie staring at the shore, where he assumed his words were giving her cause for thought. At one point, he paused, asking for her thoughts, and she replied.

"I think you are right in worrying about those things, but I fear we have another issue right under our noses," she said.

"What?' Jake asked, confused at her reply.

"Why aren't those two actually speaking to each other?" Jessie said as she pointed to the water.

From where they stood, no more than a few feet from the water, they could see Julie and Timothy at the water's edge. As they watched, they saw Timothy point to a stick floating near Julie, who was not looking at him but turned to where he was pointing.

The adults watched as the two children gestured to one another, and Julie squatted to pick up the floating stick and handed it to him. During the entire exchange, not a word was spoken, and as Jake and Jessie watched, the two began to wander away toward the other kids.

"Did you see that," Jessie asked, looking for validation.

"Not only did I see it, but I also heard it," Jake replied while pointing to his head.

Made in the USA
Las Vegas, NV
09 December 2021